JOE

MW00883726

by Richard Luce

The story of a young man caught between a criminal element of his family on one side and law enforcement on the other.

Based on actual events

Joe had vowed to resist the ongoing temptation of easy money offered to him by his criminal brother-in-law, and he has remained true to his vow until now. His impulsive decision to store some merchandise for just a few days would lead him and his family to near ruin. Added to that was the fear that his police captain father-in-law would find out, compounding his troubles. As he flees to hide the stolen goods, he reminisces about the good and bad experiences he's had during his years-long association with the Buccelli family.

Richard Luce

1

4801 N. Camden Lane

Crestwood, KY 40014

(502) 241-7046

email: richardluce@twc.com

JOE SHOES

A story based on actual events

by Richard Luce

TABLE OF CONTENTS

PROLOGUE

The meeting wasn't going well. Deep down inside, he knew this would happen, this whole effort would be a waste of time. You just couldn't reason with this guy. He knew it, his brothers knew it, but they still had to try. It was his idea to attempt to work out some solution to this mess, but now he was finally convinced it was hopeless. They would have to go through with the plan after all.

They had never considered anything like this before. They never had to. This was a huge step into the unknown, and they all knew that even if they got away with it, their lives would be changed forever. They were being forced into it by this hard-headed bastard. He was leaving them no choice, and so there was no other way. He glanced around the diner at the handful of other patrons, thinking how the poor fools had no idea what was about to happen.

Suddenly, the side of his face exploded as the big guy slapped him hard, knocking him to the floor. He sat there for a moment, dazed, then shaking his head, slowly got to his feet. This was his hangout, his place. The waitresses and cooks all knew him and maybe even feared him a little. He was a big man himself and now they all just saw him slapped to the floor like some *mezzo fanook*.He tasted blood in his mouth, not sure if it was from the slap or the rage building inside him. The other patrons in the dining room lowered their eyes and remained silent, fearing a major fight was about to begin. But this was not the place for that, and besides, he knew he could never beat this giant in a fight. Any reservation he might have felt about what was soon going to happen instantly evaporated.

"Alright, Max, you win. We'll settle up with you tomorrow," he said as he grabbed his coat and walked to the door. Stepping outside into the cold, clear night, he walked over to the curb and without any hesitation, lit a cigarette.

He sent the signal. There was no turning back now.

Max came out, and while looming over him, poked a fat finger in his face, warning him to be sure to show up tomorrow and fork over every cent he had demanded. If not, he would pay them all a special visit, including their families. He knew all too well what Max meant by a "special visit," and there was no way he would ever let this maniac crack the heads of any member of his family. That was not going to happen.

Two blocks away, unnoticed among the shadows of an abandoned factory complex, sat a dark blue Ford sedan. The car had been parked there for some time quietly idling, surrounded by a cloud of exhaust vapor. The three occupants sat nervously awaiting the outcome of the meeting, preparing themselves for whatever that might be. When they saw the signal, they knew the talking was over; it was truly going to happen. The headlights came on and the car began to drive slowly down the deserted street toward the diner.

Upon noticing the car approaching, he began to tremble and felt a sudden emptiness in his stomach. The realization that their hasty plan was about to become reality made him sick. Not wanting to draw attention to the car, he glanced up at the dark, blank windows of the surrounding buildings. Time seemed to stand still.

Max's eyes went black with fury at this perceived second show of disrespect. He was poised to begin a beating when the car pulled up alongside the two men. The back window rolled down and a voice from inside called out, "Hey, Max!"

Max turned to face the car, then walked over while bending down to look inside and began to say, "What the fu—"

The fiery blast caught him square in the face, lifting him completely off the ground before his body slammed onto the street. The other man quickly turned and ducked as he ran back inside the diner. The people inside stared at him in shock as he ran to the rear of the dining room and pressed his back against the wall. Two of the waitresses quickly went to the front window and watched as the car began to pull away, then stopped and backed up alongside the fallen figure. A shotgun appeared out of the rear window, and with the end of the barrel inches away from Max's shattered face, blasted again. The waitresses screamed in horror as they ran to the back of the room and began to cry.

Outside, satisfied the job was done, the dark blue Ford sedan quickly disappeared into the darkness.

CHAPTER ONE—VALENTINE'S DAY

The bullet whizzed past Joe's head, smacking into the dirt a few feet away. A second later he heard the report from the rifle, followed by the howls of distant laughter from across the sand pit. Joe instinctively ducked down low as he heard Big Al's voice yell out, "What's the matter, hump, you forget to duck?"

More laughter, then Big Al added, "Hurry up and set up those targets, we ain't got all day."

That was the first outing Joe had with his brother-in-law, Rizzo, and his family. It was nearly five years ago, but Joe still smiled when he thought about that day. He came to realize that he was never in any real danger of being shot. It was just Al's weird sense of humor, something he witnessed again many times over the years. All five of Rizzo's brothers continuously played the same type of near-lethal games on each other. They rarely got mad but instead would let out a string of curses and vow to get even. Joe realized that most people wouldn't want to be around such a band of dangerous clowns, but he saw the black humor in it and found it enjoyable. He wanted to fit in.

Waking out of his daydream, Joe picked up his pen and resumed working on the illustration laid out on his drafting table. It was just after one o'clock and he was ready for a coffee break, but that would have to wait. The mail pouch would be leaving soon, and he had to get this diagram finished for it to be included. Being one of three men in the art department meant they were always on a tight schedule, as they had to put out a detailed, technical, electronics magazine every two weeks. Joe had been employed by Western Publishing Company for the past six years and had risen to the post of assistant art director. At times he enjoyed what he did, but lately he found himself daydreaming more and more.

At twenty-seven years old, he was beginning to feel that he had jumped into marriage and this job too quickly after college. He felt his youth slipping by and any challenge this job offered him was long past. Jim, the art director, ten years older than Joe, was already turning gray and had the beginnings of an ulcer, undoubtedly from the stresses of the job. That was a future Joe did not want for himself.

He had enjoyed drawing since he was very young, even entering a contest he saw once in a magazine. The contest was sponsored by a mail-order art school that contacted talented applicants, offering them the opportunity to enroll and be trained by their professional art instructors. Joe was thrilled that his drawing was good enough to be offered this opportunity, but when the representatives came to his home, his father flatly refused to even consider it and pretty much threw them out. His father thought art was a waste of time that offered no way to make a living. He believed the only way for a man to support his family was to learn a trade. That was something Joe had heard many times since he was very young. Joe thought maybe he was right, but since he had no desire to follow in his father's footsteps working in a welding shop, he decided to pursue an art education regardless. He graduated with a degree in commercial art, then immediately started job hunting.

He thought about his instructors, mostly retired art directors who had spent their careers working at various advertising agencies in Manhattan. He remembered one of them telling the class that the students across the hall taking painting instruction were wasting their time. Here was where the money in art was to be made, he said, meaning the commercial end, which meant magazines, illustration, and advertising. That all made sense, so Joe landed this job and settled into his new career. He married his high school sweetheart that same year and began the rest of his life. Or so he thought.

Jim had started bringing to work some of the paintings he was creating at home to show around the office with the hope of maybe selling them. Joe was interested and began asking him questions about his techniques. Even though Joe never had a painting lesson in his life, he felt he could do it and wanted to give it a try. After a while, Joe bought some cheap paints, some canvas boards, and an aluminum easel. He began to paint, soon discovering that he loved it. This was it. This is what he wanted to do for the rest of his life. However, with bills to pay, a wife, a three-year-old daughter, and another child on the way, that dream seemed far off indeed.

Joe increasingly felt trapped and stifled and wanted to break out of the box he found himself in, which helped explain why he secretly enjoyed playing practical jokes on the engineers who made up the editorial staff for the magazine. His imaginative impulses had to break out somehow, and the dull, stuffy engineers were the perfect targets. One of the best pranks he pulled off was the time he spread phony pencils around the art department, placing some in the cubicles occupied by the engineers. He brought in some wooden dowel rods cut to the length of an average pencil. He then sharpened one end in a pencil sharpener, colored the tip with pencil lead, and drew a small circle on the back end. When he colored the shaft with a yellow marker, it looked exactly like one of the many real pencils lying around the office. Joe sat at his table quietly watching whenever one of the engineers, who were always in a hurry, picked one up and tried to write with it. Failing to write anything, he would look at it closely, try again, then in frustration pick up another one and get the same result. They would finally ask loudly, "What's wrong with all these pencils?" Jim said didn't know where they came from and could offer no explanation.

That gave Joe a few days of amusement. He never fessed up or took any credit for the stunt, so it remained a mystery.

However, he needed more than a little office fun to lift his spirits, which is why he enjoyed spending time with Rizzo and his brothers. They were an adventurous tight-knit family and always had Joe marveling at their clownish antics. He really enjoyed the weekends spent at their family cabin in the Catskills, along with the hunting trips, including a fishing trip to a remote lake in Canada. It was just the thing he craved in his somewhat boring, repetitive everyday life, and trips with Rizzo's family were anything but boring. They were always engaging in some outlandish behavior, like the time Big Al drove his and Rizzo's elderly parents up to the cabin one weekend for a family gathering. Joe wasn't present, but Rizzo told him the story. Big Al had brought along a Ruger .44 Magnum revolver he had just purchased and wanted to try it out. As he and his brothers took turns shooting the high-powered gun, Al asked his mother if she would like to give it a try. She reluctantly agreed and held the heavy gun in both hands. As she fired, the recoil was so great that the gun flew back and struck her hard in the forehead. She dropped the weapon and everyone laughed at her as a stream of blood flowed down her face. Joe couldn't believe they would put their own mother in such a dangerous position and then laugh about it when she got hurt. He really had to question some of the things they did.

There was another aspect of their behavior that made Joe uncomfortable. Rizzo was forthcoming and transparent about it, which confused Joe somewhat. He thought those explicit tales should not be uttered so freely; in case the wrong person might overhear them. In a way, he felt flattered that Rizzo trusted him to that extent, including him in the inner circle. Even the fact that Joe's father-in-law was a captain on the city police force didn't stop Rizzo from revealing details of the jobs they pulled off. Joe thought it humorous to be in this position. On one hand, his father-in-law was a high-ranking city cop; on the other, his brother-in-law's family was a crew of professional burglars.

Joe finished the drawing, then dropped it into the mail pouch. Now it was time to get that coffee. He was about to head down to the break room when the telephone rang. He knew Jim would answer it, so he paid it no mind. As he started to leave the art department, Jim turned to him and said, "It's for you, Joe. It's your wife."

Joe's wife, Janet, hardly ever called him at work. He thought maybe she wanted to wish him a happy Valentine's Day.

He reached for the receiver and said, "Hey, what's up?"

He immediately knew something was very wrong.

"You have to come home now!" she said.

Joe stood there for a few seconds wondering what had happened. Was she all right? Was it Marie, their daughter? Was there a problem with her pregnancy?

With all these questions running through his head at once, he asked, "Why, what happened?"

She said again, more urgently, "You have to come home now!"

"Tell me why—what's going on?"

"I can't tell you, just come home now," she answered firmly in a low voice.

Joe turned, stretching the phone cord as far as he could to try to get some privacy.

"Look, I can't just come home. I'm at work, remember? And besides, Jim drove us in today. How the hell am I supposed to tell him I have to leave?" he whispered.

By now, Jim and the other illustrator, Louie, had stopped working and were looking at him with some concern. He still had no idea why Janet was doing this, so he asked her again what was wrong.

She paused for a few seconds, then said, "Rizzo got arrested today and the cops are searching all over the city for something. Sandy is here with me at your mother's and just told me. She said we'd better get those goddamn things out of our house before they find them. If my father ever finds out he will kill me, so you have to come home now!"

A bomb went off in Joe's head. All he could think to say was, "Oh, shit."

Rizzo got arrested and the cops were searching all over the city for something. Searching for what? Joe really hoped it wasn't what he had hidden away in his apartment. Trying to remain calm, he told Janet he would be home as soon as he could, and then hung up the phone.

Suddenly, Joe felt sick to his stomach as he visualized his father-in-law, police captain Dominic Marino, watching the men of his precinct ransacking his daughter's apartment and finding over seventy stolen rifles and shotguns stuffed in closets, under the bed, and behind the sofas. Joe knew that had to be what the cops are looking for. Janet was right. Her father would kill her, but first he would kill him.

Joe's relationship with Dominic Marino had always been a little strained. Marino had attained the rank of captain after twenty-five years of rubbing elbows with the right people and busting lots of heads on the job. He stood over six feet tall, weighed in at almost 240, and had the look of a half-crazed Indian chief. But he knew how to make the right friends and quickly learned the politics of the job. At home he hardly ever spoke, but would make you feel that he was analyzing you and didn't like what he saw. He never called Joe by name, but always referred to him as "boy." Do you want some wine, boy? Do you like the food, boy? Better stay out of trouble, boy.

At home he was a tyrant, but on the outside, Marino could have run for mayor. He marched in parades and belonged to all the right social clubs in town, always attending their functions. He sometimes even enjoyed cooking for the boys at some private club. One thing was for sure—he really loved being a cop.

During one of his rare mellow moods, he told Joe how much he missed the old days when a cop could beat up on a suspect without any retribution. He would remember with a smile the time as a rookie when he walked into the precinct house and asked what happened to a man he saw lying on the floor in a pool of blood. The desk sergeant answered, "Oh, him? He hit a cop."

Joe had heard many such stories of rough treatment of prisoners and suspects, and he believed every one.

The day Marino found out who Joe's sister had married, his face turned beet red with rage. He glared down at Joe and said, "That no-good bastard is a fucking thief, and his whole fucking family are thieves, including his old man. He was busted dozens of times for bookmaking and I'm going to lock up the rest of the bastards before I'm through." Then he moved a little closer, his face as red as a cherry tomato, and said, "You'll join them if you ever get involved."

Joe knew if the cops found those guns in his apartment, this was going to be a really bad day.

After he hung up the phone, he paused for a moment, then turned to his boss and said, "Uh, Jim, I have to go home." Thinking fast, he added, "Janet isn't feeling too well, and she wants me to take her to the doctor."

With genuine concern, Jim asked if it was the baby and if Janet was all right. Being a father of two boys, he knew what living with a pregnant woman was like.

Joe answered, "I don't think it's anything serious. She just feels a little funny and wants to get checked out. She's afraid to drive and wants me to take her."

Jim took a quick glance at his watch, thought for a moment, then said, "Okay, sure. Let's go."

After showing an annoyed Louie what needed to be completed by the end of the day, they both left.

***

They crossed the snow-covered parking lot, got into Jim's car, and headed east on Route 80 toward the George Washington Bridge. The ride to Mount Vernon on a good day would take about 30 minutes, but more often than not, they would be stuck in traffic, stretching that time to hours, sometimes many hours. Today looked like it was going to be one of those days.

The slow going gave Joe plenty of time to think. Jim could tell he was worried, though he didn't have a clue why, so he didn't say much. Joe was thankful for that. His mind was racing, trying to figure out what zo got arrested. Well, he was sure that came as no big ybody. With all the crimes they committed, it was only a e before they got busted for something. But right now, all Joe was concerned about was that the cops were searching the city, looking for something. The only score Rizzo had made recently that Joe knew about was that damn gun store, and he had all the goods at his apartment.

Jim must have sensed his anguish and said, "Hey, don't worry, it's probably nothing. She'll be okay."

Joe gave him a look, as if to say what the hell are you talking about. Then he remembered. "Oh, yeah, yeah—I'm sure everything is going to be just fine," he said.

***

Captain Marino's office was in high gear. After over a three-month investigation into the Max Santoro murder, the grand jury had at last handed down the indictments that would finally put the Buccelli brothers away for a long time. To Marino, the case was iron-clad. They had three eyewitnesses, taped conversations along with phone wiretaps, and the Buccellis knew the victim. In fact, they were rivals, which gave the case a plausible motive.

The fact that the investigation had failed to turn up any physical evidence was of little concern to Marino, but what he really would like to have was the murder weapon. He had his detectives looking all over for it, including the suspect's homes, their vehicles, their hangouts, and anywhere else they were able to obtain a warrant to search. He had been waiting for this day for over fifteen years, and he was sure they would not evade him this time. To him it was personal. He had followed the Buccelli wake of destruction for years as a detective, investigating their burglaries and interviewing the scores of terrified victims. The police knew from many sources who was behind the break-ins, but they could never get the evidence needed to indict them. Marino also found it ironic that the Buccellis had done him a favor by taking out the head of the other major burglary ring operating in the city. Max Santoro had been on their radar for many years as well. Not just for burglaries, but also for assaults with his favorite weapon, a baseball bat, which had earned him the nickname "The Turban" for all the cracked skulls he had inflicted. That one group of this vermin had taken out the other was just fine with Marino. He could now retire with the knowledge that he had finally won in the end.

***

Joe sat there watching the traffic build up as the car slowed to a crawl. Less than an hour ago, the biggest problem he faced today was getting Jim to let him off at the drugstore near his apartment so he could buy a Valentine's Day card for his wife. Janet would be pissed if he came home without at least a card. He sat there amazed over how fast things can change. The empty feeling in his stomach wouldn't leave, and was in fact getting worse. He could feel a cold sweat coming on as he pictured his father-in-law glaring down at him saying, "I always knew you were no good" as he slapped handcuffs on him.

Enough of that; he had to get hold of himself. He had to think. There really wasn't any reason for the cops to search his apartment, and without a good reason they couldn't get a search warrant. They would have to show probable cause or some such bullshit, and they really didn't have any. But then he remembered what had happened two summers ago, and suddenly wasn't so sure.

Rizzo, Sandy, Janet, and he had been returning from a weekend at the upstate hunting cabin owned by Rizzo's parents. As they crossed the Tappan Zee Bridge, they were spotted by two detectives who recognized Rizzo's car and plate number and decided to tail them. The cops followed them right to Joe's apartment and watched as they unloaded suitcases and guns from the car. The next day, Marino heard the report, and recognizing the address, went crazy with rage. He drove to where Janet was working at the time and pulled her outside into the street. He proceeded to scream at her, saying that the police had followed her to her house while she was riding in that scumbag Rizzo's car, and she had embarrassed him in front of the whole precinct. She was still shaking when she told Joe about it later that night. Joe thought for sure that he was going to hear about it next, but Marino never said a word about it to him. When Joe told Rizzo what happened, he thought it was the funniest thing he had ever heard and almost fell over laughing, but Joe noticed later on that week that Rizzo was driving a different car with new plates.

As they inched along Route 80, Jim kept trying to make small talk, but Joe's mind was miles away. They always talked about many things on the way to and from work, but Joe thought it best not to tell Jim anything about Rizzo's profession, or that he hung around with a crew of burglars. Jim knew that Joe went on hunting and fishing trips with Rizzo and his brothers, and Joe had even told him of some of his experiences, but not all. He could never tell him everything that happened. For one thing, Jim would never believe him. Jim lived in a world where there was a clear line between good guys and bad guys, and the good guys always won.

He would never believe some of the things Joe had heard and witnessed over the past five years, like the time Joe was with Rizzo at a shopping mall when a uniformed police officer approached them. At first, Joe thought his brother-in-law was about to get pinched for something, but then could not believe what he was hearing. This cop was telling Rizzo the names and addresses of people who were going on vacation. Those people had given the police their vacation schedules to ensure their homes would be watched over during their absence. The police were there to protect us, not rob us—or so everyone was supposed to believe. This cop didn't know who Joe was and didn't care. He didn't even look at him. Joe guessed the cop thought he was just one of the crew. When Joe asked Rizzo about it later on, he laughed and said that guy was always feeding them information. In fact, at times he even parked his squad car in front of buildings they were ransacking and acted as a lookout. Rizzo added that of course, the cop always got a cut of the take.

Some people would never believe stories like that, and Jim was one of them. Besides, Joe didn't want Jim to know the type of people he was associating with. Hell, that was the real question. Why was he associating with them? Shaking his head, he knew the answer. He had never known people like this. They were exciting and fun to be around. They laughed and joked all the time, and yet there was a definite air of danger about them. But now Joe was worried that maybe he had gotten a little too close.

Jim saw him shaking his head and said, "I know, this traffic is unbelievable."

Joe turned to him and smiled, saying, "Yeah, well we're stuck in it now."

It was going to be a long ride.

CHAPTER TWO—BOYS WILL BE BOYS

Joe didn't think of himself as a criminal. He may have been involved in some minor scrapes when he was a kid, but nothing serious, never any jail time. He was taken downtown once in the back of a police car, but since he was only 14 and wasn't handcuffed, he figured it wasn't really an arrest. The police just wanted to know how the 50-pound sack of gunpowder stolen from the explosives shed in the stone quarry near Joe's house had been taken. When Joe entered the police station and saw the bag of gunpowder on the next table, he figured he'd better tell them everything. To his relief, he wouldn't be asked to rat out his two partners in crime because they were already there. The boys were taken to different rooms and interrogated separately.

During his interrogation, Joe told the detectives that he had heard Roger was asking around the school if anyone knew where he could get some gunpowder for making fireworks. Joe knew where some might be found, so along with Cliff, they forged a plan. Although Cliff was two years older than Joe, they were attending the same classes, as Cliff had been left back a couple of times. That should have tipped off Joe that his buddy wasn't too bright.

Their plan was to wait for the right evening when Joe would be able to sneak out of the house undetected. That opportunity came one night when Joe's parents were both in the basement, occupied with trying to repair the washing machine. Joe called Cliff, then took a hacksaw blade from his father's toolbox and quietly left. The two met up and proceeded to make their way down to the stone quarry. Joe had seen the red metal sheds many times over the years and always assumed they held explosives. One such shed was located at the end of a parking lot that contained a few small buildings and some heavy machinery. They approached the shed, then knelt down in the shadows in front of the small, locked iron door. Cliff kept watch as Joe began to saw through the lock with his hacksaw blade. Suddenly, a large German shepherd appeared behind a chain-link fence that stretched behind the shed. It stared at them. They both froze, waiting for the dog to begin barking the alarm. To their surprise, the dog just sniffed at them a few times and then walked away. What a great watchdog, Joe thought, as he continued to saw through the lock.

After about fifteen minutes, the lock was sawn through and Joe slowly opened the door. The inside of the shed was pitch-black, revealing nothing of its contents. To Joe's terrified astonishment, Cliff lit a match and with it, reached into the black interior. Joe immediately grabbed his arm and asked him if he had completely lost his mind. Cliff then realized that maybe that wasn't such a good idea. Shaking his head, Joe reached in, grabbed the first thing his hand touched, and pulled it out. It was a large plastic bag containing black chips that he assumed to be blasting powder. Their mission accomplished, they quickly left the area, carrying the heavy bag between them. They dumped it in a grassy vacant lot near Joe's house for the night. Cliff said he would pick it up the next day, deliver it to Roger, and receive their payment.

They never discussed the amount of that payment, and Joe didn't really care. To him this was a *Mission: Impossible* type of adventure that was nothing more than a bit of fun. He never considered the theft would be taken so seriously and investigated by the police. The officer questioning him said the amount of blasting powder was enough to take down a good-sized building, so the theft was considered a major threat to public safety.

Joe then found out that Cliff was the reason they were all caught. A few days after the theft, a teacher saw him trying to light some of the stolen gunpowder in a school hallway, surrounded by a circle of students. The teacher went to the principal, who then called the police, and that was that. When the police came to the school and arrested Cliff, he wasted no time blaming the whole caper on Joe and Roger. Being over 16 years old, Cliff spent that night in jail when his father refused to bail him out.

Joe and Roger were driven home separately by detectives. When the police car pulled up to Joe's house, he saw his father working in the yard. He told the two cops that he was really going to get it now. To his surprise, the two officers went over to Joe's father and asked him not to be too hard on the boy, that he was a good kid who just made a stupid mistake. Joe was thankful for that. His father didn't give him the beating he was expecting. The only thing he ever said about it was that he was disappointed and would have to keep Joe busy from now on. When the owners of the quarry found out it was a bunch of kids who stole the gunpowder, they dropped the charges. Joe had to make a brief appearance in juvenile court, but since he was underage, he wouldn't have a criminal record and could just put it all behind him. He stayed away from Cliff from then on and didn't have much to say to Roger either. He thought it best not to get involved in any more criminal activities.

That is, until his sister married into the Buccelli family. Rizzo really enjoyed playing the big man and lived for all the attention it brought, especially when he waved around the big wad of cash he always seemed to have on hand. Joe was always impressed when the waiters at one of Rizzo's favorite restaurants would trip over themselves to see that his party was seated in their section. He would start off by handing the waiter a C-note just to get things rolling. Of course, he got the best service and sometimes the owner himself would come over with a bottle of wine and sit with them for a while. One night, a restaurant owner asked Rizzo how he got his name, as it sounded a little different. Laughing, he said his real name was Lorenzo, but his brothers started calling him Rizzo when he was young and the name stuck. His family was always ready to pin a nickname on someone. Whenever anyone asked Rizzo what he did for a living, he would simply say he "worked nights." If they persisted in questioning him about his job, he would ask, "Why? Are you writing a book?" In his own way, Rizzo had a celebrity status and Joe, by association, was enjoying it as well.

However, it bothered Joe when Rizzo mocked him about being some kind of *gavone* for going to a crappy job every day for a lousy paycheck and a few weeks' vacation a year. It was true that Joe wasn't making a lot of money for all the time he spent at work, but he had many considerations to ponder that Rizzo would never understand. He didn't like the thought of getting arrested, going to jail, facing his father-in-law, and probably losing his wife and kids. Rizzo never seemed to worry about any of that, even for himself.

Rizzo kept trying to get Joe to see the folly of being a dumbass and going to work every day by always bragging about all the money he was making. He was confident he could convince Joe that his way was best if he just put out the right bait. One night he thought for sure he was beginning to win him over.

It was after 10:00 p.m. when Rizzo called and insisted that Joe and Janet come over to see something they would not believe. Joe said he couldn't, as it was too late. He had to get up early for work in the morning, and Marie was already in bed sleeping, but Rizzo would not take no for an answer. He told Joe that what he would see would change his life. It was something he had never seen before and would most likely never get to see again.

Sometimes Rizzo had the qualities of a snake charmer, and of course, Joe was now intrigued. He said okay, then told Rizzo they would be right over, but couldn't stay long.

"Don't worry, it won't take long for you to get the message," Rizzo chuckled.

When they arrived, Rizzo opened the door, beaming. Joe was holding Marie, still asleep, and Rizzo motioned for him to place her in the bedroom. Joe moved quietly so he wouldn't wake her or Rizzo's two kids, already asleep in the room. A smiling Rizzo led him and Janet into the kitchen. Sandy, Joe's sister, was by the stove brewing tea, but what caught their immediate attention was what they saw spread out over the kitchen table. They both stared wide-eyed for a few moments when Joe finally blurted out, "What the hell!"

Rizzo and Sandy both began to laugh as Joe and Janet started walking over to the table. There before them, spread out over the entire table surface, was more money than they had ever seen in their lives. Rizzo was right. It was indeed something they had never seen before. There were stacks of money, each with a hundred-dollar bill on top, filling the entire table.

As Joe's eyes scanned the incredible sight before him, he finally asked, "How much is this?"

Rizzo proudly announced there was over eighty-four thousand dollars there, then he added, "Not bad for a night's work, eh?"

Then in his familiar mocking tone he asked Joe, "How long would it take you to make this much money . . . tax-free?"

Joe mumbled it would take a lifetime. It did give him something to think about.

One day a while later, Rizzo offered him the chance to make some real money of his own and Joe almost took the bait. It seemed simple enough. All Joe had to do was drive Rizzo and his brothers to some destination, drop them off, and return to pick them up in forty-five minutes. For that simple act he would make ten thousand dollars. Ten thousand dollars! That was more money than Joe made in a year. He could have it all at once and in tax-free cash just by saying yes. He almost hated Rizzo at that moment for putting him in such a position. His mind raced as he weighed the possibilities. That was an awful lot of money, and he remembered well seeing all that cash on Rizzo's table, and now here was a chance for him to make some for himself. He could buy a new car or put a down payment on a house or any number of things. On the other hand, something could go wrong and he could lose everything.

Rizzo sat there with a smug look on his face, enjoying the conflict he had inflicted, but he was confident Joe would jump at the chance. In Rizzo's mind, who wouldn't?

When Joe declined, Rizzo stared at him in wide-eyed disbelief and said, "What are you, *oobatz*? Are you shittin' me? You're gonna turn down ten grand just like that? Jesus Christ, I didn't realize I had a wackadoo for a brother-in-law."

It was a tough decision for Joe, but the money aside, deep down he knew it was the wrong thing to do, and he feared the easy money might lead to a slippery slope into criminality. That was somewhere he didn't want to go, but for days he thought about all that money he could have had. Still, he was confident he had made the right decision. Later that week, he saw this skinny young punk who worked at a gas station where Rizzo hung around drive through the neighborhood in a late-model Cadillac. After Joe turned him down, Rizzo offered the job to that guy, who obviously grabbed it and now was playing the big man driving around in his shiny car. Joe thought he looked like an asshole.

***

This ride was taking way too long. Why did this fucking road have to be backed up like this today? He hated this road, he hated his job, he hated his life. Right now, he hated everything. How did he get himself in this situation? He had tried to steer clear of trouble, not get involved in Rizzo's criminal world. But here he was. He took the bait. He had told himself just this one time. After all, it had been too much to resist and it had seemed safe enough.

It started with a phone call about ten o'clock last Friday night. Joe was watching television, and Janet and Marie were both in bed. When Joe answered the phone, Rizzo asked him what he was doing. With Rizzo, that was never a good start to a conversation.

Joe answered, "What am I doing? Nothing, why?"

"Mind if I come over?" Rizzo asked.

"You want to come over now? Everybody's in bed," Joe said.

Then Rizzo asked, "Are you in bed?"

"No, I'm not in bed. I'm watching TV."

"Okay, then I can come over," Rizzo said, no longer asking. He added, "I got something to show you, and believe me, you're really gonna like it."

Pausing for a moment and somewhat intrigued, Joe said, "Yeah, okay, sure. Come on over."

CHAPTER THREE—GOT GUNS?

Rizzo knocked on the door about twenty minutes later. After Joe let him in, he looked around the apartment a little and then sat down.

He asked, "You got how many closets in here? Three, four?"

Joe thought that was a weird question, but he smiled and said, "There's three—two in the bedroom and one out here. Why?"

Smiling back, Rizzo said, "I got some things outside I need to keep somewhere for a couple of days. Two, three days at most. I already got 'em sold. I just need someplace to keep 'em until I meet with the guy."

Leaning back in his chair, still smiling, Joe asked, "What things?"

Rizzo got up and said, "Sit there. I'll show you."

He went outside and Joe heard him talking to someone whose voice he couldn't quite place, but felt he knew. Rizzo came back in holding a Winchester rifle. He knew about Joe's love of guns, especially old Winchesters. What he held in his hands was a Model 73, a true classic, one of the most sought-after rifles by serious collectors. It was the gun that won the West and one that Joe probably would never be able to afford. Rizzo knew which one to bring in first.

With an ear-to-ear grin, he handed the gun to Joe and said, "Here, this one's yours."

He had Joe hooked. All Joe could say was, "Holy shit, are you serious?"

Still grinning, Rizzo said, "I got a few more outside, different ones. Some new, some old, and a few shotguns too. So, can I bring 'em in? Oh, and for your trouble, you can pick out a couple more for yourself."

That did it. Rizzo knew Joe would not refuse him this time. No way. He played it beautifully.

Joe, still looking at the rifle in his hands, said, "Yeah, okay, bring them in. But be quiet, Janet's sleeping."

Rizzo went outside to the van parked next to Joe's door, returned with an armload of rifles, carefully laid them on the floor, then went out again. Then the guy whose voice Joe thought he recognized came in with another load. It was Dingo, that little creep with the Cadillac who worked at the gas station near Joe's mother's house. He dropped off his load and without saying a word, went out again. When Rizzo came back in with another armful, Joe asked him, "Damn, how many do you have?"

Rizzo started to laugh and said, "Just a few more."

Then Dingo came in again with another armload and they both started laughing. They went out again, but this time Joe followed them to see for himself how many more they had out there.

Walking over to the open side door of the van, Joe looked inside. "Holy Christ, you gotta be fuckin' shittin' me!"

The two of them just continued laughing and carrying armloads of guns into Joe's apartment. Following them back inside, Joe saw Janet standing in the doorway of their bedroom. She looked like she was about to pass out. Her eyes and mouth were both wide open as she looked in horror at the growing pile of guns on her living room floor.

Finally, she found her voice and asked rather loudly, "What the hell is going on? What is all this?"

Quickly walking over to her, Joe pulled her back into the bedroom, shut the door and said, "Look, it's only for a couple of days. He already has them sold. They won't be here that long."

"I don't want them here at all! Are you crazy? Do you see what's out there?" she said in a frantic whisper.

"Yeah, I know, there's more than I thought there would be. I'll go out there and see how many more they have. Stay in here, don't come out. I'll be back," Joe said as he shut the door behind him.

He could hear Janet yell after him, "I want them all out of here now!"

They were still bringing them in. The pile on the floor had grown larger and they were now stacking the guns against the wall. Rizzo looked at Joe with a grin and said, "Only a few more" and quickly went back outside.

He came back in with the last load, looked for a place to stack them, then sat down at the kitchen table. Joe heard the van start up and back out of his driveway. He asked Rizzo if that was his ride, to which he answered that his car was in the lot next door. He then laughed and said they drove in separate vehicles.

"I told that *stugots* to follow me here," Rizzo said. "I drove my car in case he got pulled over with all those guns in the van. That way I would just keep going and he'd take the rap, and he knew if he ever mentioned my name he would end up in the river. You got some tea?"

"Tea? Yeah, sure," Joe said, getting up to fill the kettle with water. "Shit, man, how many did you get?"

"Seventy-six. We cleaned the fucker out. That *gavone* will be in a coma when he walks in there tomorrow."

"Where did they come from?" Joe asked.

"Far from here, and that's all you need to know," Rizzo answered.

Joe was glad it was not a local gun shop. That meant the local cops would not be looking for them, or so he thought at the time. Then he remembered Janet was waiting for him in the bedroom. Slowly opening the door, he peeked in and saw her in bed with the covers pulled up over her head. As he came back out, Rizzo asked, "What did she say? Why is she all freaked out?"

"Why is she all freaked out? Look around," Joe said. "You never said what you were bringing over or how many. There's enough guns in here to outfit a Mexican revolution. Damn right, she's freaked out. She's acting like she's asleep in there, but she's not. Ah, she'll be okay. She's always worried about her old man finding out."

Smiling, Rizzo asked, "How is old Tonto doing anyway? He still trying to bust my ass?"

"You know it. There's nothing that man would like better than to bust you guys," Joe said as he got out the teacups. "He's always on me to give him information about what jobs you guys have pulled and where you keep all the shit you robbed. Boy, would he love to be here now. Trouble is, he'd throw my ass in jail with you."

"He still asks you about the jobs we pull, huh? You know I should give you some bullshit story to tell him about some big score and where we have it stashed, then watch him make an ass of himself when he shows up with half the police force. That would be a pisser."

Joe answered, "Yeah, but then he'll come down on me for giving him bad info. I don't think you should fuck around with him like that. Just let him be. I don't tell him anything, period. He's going to retire soon anyway."

After bringing the steaming teacups to the table, they each took a sip and looked over at the arsenal in the living room. Joe had to know. He asked Rizzo how much would he get for the guns when he sold them.

Rizzo put down his cup and said, "I got them sold to a guy for ten grand. And the guy knows the owner of the gun shop. How about that shit? You can't trust nobody these days. I told that numbnuts Dingo that I got them sold for five grand and we'll split it fifty-fifty. He's happy with that, and what he don't know won't hurt him, unless he ever opens his mouth. I know some of them are probably worth a lot, but I gotta move 'em fast."

Rizzo always made threats like that, but Joe never knew of him actually hurting anybody. He was certainly big enough and his outgoing personality always seemed to keep people in check so he would not have to make good on his threats. One time, however, he did show that he was quite capable of violent behavior if pushed too far, and Rizzo loved to tell the story.

It seemed some guy owed Rizzo money and was not making any effort to pay it back. Rizzo was tired of asking for it, so he started watching the man's movements, especially where he liked to hang out at night. This was called "hawking" a victim, whether it be a business, a home, or a person. All the brothers were adept at it and it became almost a nightly ritual for them. When this fellow parked his Cadillac in just the right spot one night, Rizzo pulled up near it and proceeded to empty a thirty-round magazine from an M2 automatic carbine into the man's car. That little stunt made the papers, and although the case was never solved, word got around who the shooter was. Rizzo made his bones that night, as they say, and he also got his money.

After Joe and Rizzo drank their tea, they started to hide the guns behind the sofas and in the closet in the living room. Joe wisely thought it best not to disturb Janet, and he waited until the next day to hide the remainder in the two-bedroom closets. Tomorrow was Saturday and Joe would have all day to take his time and look them over.

The next morning, Janet announced that she was taking Marie shopping and she didn't want to see any guns lying around when she got home. Well, at least she wasn't screaming for them to be gone like she did the night before, Joe thought. After they left, Joe locked the door and began looking them over more carefully. Rizzo said he could keep a couple for himself, so Joe decided on keeping three. It took him quite a while to pick two others besides the one Rizzo originally gave him. He would have liked to keep more, but knew he couldn't and probably shouldn't keep any of them, but what the hell. He put his three aside and started to stuff the rest into the bedroom closets and under the bed, hoping they would all be gone soon.

***

That was only a few days ago and now he wished he had never seen any of them. The traffic on Route 80 was still backed up and the clock was ticking. He almost felt like getting out of the car and running the rest of the way home. Anything was better than sitting here. Now traffic was completely stopped in all three lanes, so Joe stared out at the snow-covered landscape and thought how good it was to be free. Was this his last day of freedom?

Jim was telling him about a painting he was working on, and any other time Joe would have been interested, but not today. He totally didn't give a shit what Jim was babbling on about and wished he would just be quiet. He had to think. The worst part was not knowing what was happening at home, or even to Rizzo. Were his brothers arrested as well? As far as Joe knew they were not involved in the gun heist, if that was indeed the reason Rizzo got busted. He wished he had spoken more with Janet and got more information about what happened. Too late for that now; he would just have to wait. Waiting and thinking, that's all he had right now. He sat there thinking about some of the crazy ideas Rizzo tried to get him involved with in the past. Things Joe didn't want any part of.

CHAPTER FOUR—THE MIDAS TOUCH

One day last summer, Rizzo called Joe at work with one such crazy idea. Jim answered the phone and handed it to him, saying he didn't know who was calling. Joe was surprised to hear his brother-in-law's voice on the other end. Rizzo then asked a question that didn't make any sense.

"You went diving once, right? You know how to dive underwater?"

Surprised at the question, Joe asked, "What do you mean?"

"You went diving you said, right? So you can dive underwater, right?" Rizzo asked again.

"I went that one time a couple of years ago. Why?" Joe asked.

"What I want to know is if you know how to dive underwater, yes or no?"

Joe started to laugh and said, "I dove once, that one time, I'm no expert. Why do you want to know?"

Rizzo said, "I'll call you back," then hung up.

Joe sat there not knowing what to think. Asking him if he knew how to dive . . . what the hell did that mean? Ten minutes later, Rizzo called back. Jim handed Joe the phone and he heard Rizzo ask, "Okay, what I gotta know is if you can dive underwater. Dive down and get something?"

Joe turned to face the wall and said, "Look, what the hell are you talking about? Dive where? Get what?"

"Christ almighty, it's a simple fuckin' question. Can you dive underwater or not? That's all I gotta know."

Exasperated, Joe asked, "Look, it depends. Where am I diving? What am I getting? And besides, I don't have the stuff I would need, you know, the air tanks and all that shit," Joe said, starting to lose his patience.

"Okay, if you had the tanks and all the other shit, could you do it then?" Rizzo asked sarcastically.

At this point Joe gave up and said, "Yeah, I suppose so."

Rizzo added, "Good. See, was that so fuckin' hard? I'll talk to you later," then hung up.

Joe handed the phone back to Jim, who asked what was that all about. Joe said he didn't have any idea, then turned around and went back to work.

That night about ten o'clock, Rizzo knocked on the door of Joe's apartment. Joe hadn't told Janet about the weird phone call, and had forgotten all about it himself until he saw Rizzo at the door. Rizzo told Janet he wanted to show Joe something in the car and they would be right back. When they were both in the car, Joe asked if he was fucking around with him today with that phone call. Rizzo laughed and said no, they lost something and wanted to get it back.

Rizzo said he might as well tell him the entire story. Joe wasn't sure if he wanted to hear it.

About a week before, Rizzo said, he and his older brother, nicknamed "Nazabeep," received a tip about a certain warehouse near the river that was being used as a sort of gold repository. Joe wasn't sure, but he thought Nazabeep— "Naz" for short—had acquired that nickname due to his odd-shaped nose, which hooked down to almost cover his upper lip. It made him look like a typical Hollywood gangster. The tipster had told both brothers that there was a room full of gold chain on large spools stored in there. He wasn't sure how long they would be stored, but believed they would have limited time and had to work fast. The building was old and had an outdated alarm system that could be bypassed easily by someone who knew how it worked. That so happened to be one of Rizzo's talents. He prided himself on it and bragged about it often. The only catch was that the building was directly across the street from the city jail. The whole area out front was lit up like the Vegas strip, but the back of the building, which sat along the bank of the Hudson River, was lit by only a few floodlights. Obviously, someone thought that all the activity at the jail meant the area would be safe and secure.

They decided to go for it, and made their plan of attack like it was a military operation. They would have to get a good-size boat somewhere and slap one of Big Al's outboard motors on it, pack it with the tools they would need, wait for dark, and then go. They had a small problem with Pete, Rizzo's younger brother. Pete could not swim and was rather apprehensive about boating on the Hudson River in the dark. Naz assured him that they would stay close to shore, and they would find him a life vest if he really wanted one. Of course, he knew he would be laughed at by his brothers for being a pussy, so he declined the vest.

Rizzo's youngest brother, Bugsy, was the one most intrigued by the endeavor, and he took over the planning. He had served a tour in Vietnam and was anxious to use some of the skills he had learned in the military. His nickname came from Big Al, who called him Bugsy because of his sometimes-unusual behavior. Being a Vietnam vet, he had stories about his wartime experiences, and many of them were gruesome and brutal. He seemed to relish telling them. Other than that, he never said much of anything.

Rizzo usually didn't tell Joe, or anyone else, about such a recent job. He always waited a few weeks or months before bragging about a score. But Joe could see that he was very excited and couldn't wait to tell all, plus he needed Joe's help on this one.

Rizzo continued the story.

The four of them—Naz, Bugsy, Pete, and Rizzo—shoved off in a stolen boat that was not as large as they were hoping to find. They left near midnight from a public launching ramp a few miles downriver from their destination. They were all dressed in black, and even blackened their faces like commandos. They brought along canvas sacks, a grappling hook, rope, assorted tools, and a set of two-way radios. Joe thought that seemed like a lot to pack into a small boat along with four grown men, but didn't say anything.

The river was calm as they proceeded slowly, trying to be as quiet as possible. As they approached the backside of the three-story brick warehouse, they were surprised to see the large rocks that lined the shore. As they drew nearer, the water became a little choppy and they had some difficulty finding a place to land. Bugsy finally jumped into the water, pulled the boat in, and tied it to an iron bar that protruded from a block of concrete. They threw their gear onto the rocks and then carefully stepped out of the boat. After pausing to look around, they crept up to a chain-link fence that surrounded the property. Taking a bolt cutter from their tool bag, they cut a hole in the fence, then ran one by one to the back of the warehouse. As they were told, the back of the building was not as well-lit as the front, and provided them with deep shadows to hide in. There was an old fire escape attached to the back of the building that would be their stairway to the roof. Bugsy used a grappling hook to grab hold of the fire escape, which was about twenty feet over his head. He quickly climbed the rope, then lowered the raised iron ladder to the ground. The others followed in quick succession and made their way to the roof. So far, so good.

Joe was listening intently and slowly shaking his head. He felt as if he were listening to a movie script. Rizzo talked on.

Once on the roof, Bugsy took one of the radios and crept over to the edge overlooking the front of the building. He could plainly see the front of the jail and all activity around the entire area. Police cars were parked on the street, as well as in the parking lot off to the side of the jail. His job was to keep watch and give a warning on the radio if he noticed any suspicious activity by the cops below. The other three picked a spot and began to chop a hole in the roof.

Joe thought about how Rizzo was always saying that going through the roof of a building was often the best way of getting inside. Doors, windows, and sometimes even walls can be alarmed, but no one ever thinks to alarm a roof. And it doesn't take very long to chop a hole big enough for someone to drop through. Shingles, tar paper, wood boards, or plywood and that's it. Fifteen, twenty minutes at best, and you're in.

Rizzo continued the story, explaining how they used folded rags to muffle the hammering sounds and soon had a hole big enough to get through.

Then Naz shined a flashlight into the hole and said, "There's a drop ceiling about two feet down. Hold my feet while I punch through it and see what we got." As the ceiling tile gave way, he said, "Good, it's open and clear to the floor."

He then secured the grappling hook around a vent pipe and lowered the rope into the black hole. Before any of them climbed down, Naz called over to Bugsy on the radio to see if everything was okay on the street.

Bugsy replied, "Yeah, everything's cool. One car pulled up and two cops got out. They took a couple of coons inside, but other than that, nothing."

Naz slid down the rope into the darkness, followed by Pete and then Rizzo. They each carried a small flashlight and a couple of canvas sacks. They began to search the nearby rooms, being careful not to shine their lights near any windows. They rounded up some tables and piled them on top of each other like a pyramid under the hole they came through so they could climb out easily and quickly. Then they went looking for gold.

Rizzo often talked about the great feeling he would have when he was in a new place, be it a warehouse like this or someone's home. He said it felt like Christmas every time. There were treasures to be had and you never knew what you would find. They mostly worked on tips given to them by "friends" of the victims, but there was always the unexpected. Like the time they were searching a house and found one of the owners hiding under a mattress they flipped over as they looked for money. They all got scared and left quickly. It was their policy never to enter a home or business if they thought someone might be in there. They never carried guns with them didn't want to meet anyone who might have one. Also, the last thing they wanted was to have any witnesses who could identify them later.

Joe could see the excitement build on Rizzo's face as he told him about searching the rooms looking for the hoard of gold they had been told was there. The tipster had said the gold would be in the form of chain wound on spools. Not heavy chain, but the type used in necklaces and other jewelry. There might even be gold bars in there like at Fort

Knox, who knows? Their imaginations ran wild with anticipation. This was going to be a very big score.

They went from room to room, carefully opening doors and peering inside with their pencil flashlights in their mouths. Rizzo said they saw only packing material and boxes on the third floor, so they found the stairs and walked down to the next level. There was some dim lighting on this floor, so they were careful not to pass in front of any windows. At this point, Naz again called on the radio to Bugsy to see if everything was okay outside.

Bugsy answered, "Everything's okay out here. How are you guys doin'? You find anything yet?"

Naz answered, "Not yet. Just keep your eyes open out there."

Rizzo paused and told Joe how he thought it was so damn funny that they were robbing the place right in front of the police station, or better yet, the city jail. A building full of cops and right across the street, the jewelry warehouse gets robbed. Boy, are they gonna be pissed. Joe thought yeah, it would be a major embarrassment for the entire police force. Then Joe thought it was strange that this happened about a week ago and there had been no mention about a gold robbery in the newspapers.

He asked Rizzo, "How come it wasn't in the paper? I mean, a job like this should make the news, don't you think?"

Rizzo said they probably didn't want the knowledge of what the warehouse was used for to get out, and besides, the cops didn't want the embarrassing news to get out either. So they figured the whole thing was kept quiet and not reported to the papers.

Rizzo continued with the story. On the second floor, they hit pay dirt. They entered a room with a row of tables against the far wall. On the tables were spools that lit up as the flashlight beams hit them. The sparkle on those spools could mean only one thing—gold. The informer was right; here was a room full of spools of gold chain. After their initial shock wore off, Naz approached a table and picked up one of the spools. He was surprised at the weight and immediately realized they had a problem.

He started cursing, "Fuck! Did we ever screw up. We can't carry all these out of here in these fuckin' bags. And that fuckin' boat isn't big enough for all this weight. We can't come back in here after tonight, and there's no time to get another boat, so it's now or never. Shit, we're not prepared for this. That asshole never told me how much was in here. I'm gonna be sick."

Pete scanned the room and said, "Fuck it. Let's just take what we can carry and get the hell outta here."

Rizzo said he started to pull chain off the spools and stuff it in his pockets. Forgetting about the sacks they brought, they started to place the spools by the door. They then carried the dozen or so spools up the stairs to the third floor.

They each made several trips over to the stacked tables under the hole they had punched in the roof. Rizzo wanted to go back down and carry up another load, but Naz stopped him.

"What, are you fuckin' stupid?" Naz said. "We can't take any more. We fucked up. The boat can't handle the weight."

Rizzo didn't say it in those exact words, but Joe figured that's what Naz had said.

41

Rizzo was sick about having to leave any of the gold behind. Even with his pockets stuffed full, he still wanted more.

Naz called to Bugsy on the radio, "Get your ass over to the hole now!"

Bugsy replied, "You guys find it?"

"Never mind. Just move your ass!" Naz shouted back.

Pete climbed up the tables under the opening in the ceiling. Rizzo went halfway and Naz stayed on the floor. They began a relay and started to pass up the spools to Bugsy on the roof. They guessed the spools weighed about sixty pounds each. They were cutting into their hands even with the gloves they were wearing. After all the spools were on the roof, the three men climbed up and sat down to catch their breath.

Bugsy asked, "Is that it, that's all of it?"

Naz spat back, "No that's not all of it, most of it's still down there. This is all we can handle. It's a fuckin' shame. Get back over to the ledge and keep a lookout."

They began to carry the spools over to the fire escape one at a time. Naz called to Bugsy to come on over and give them a hand getting it down to the ground. Pete and Rizzo climbed down the ladder and set up a relay down the fire escape to Naz on the ground, but it was slow going. They were getting pretty tired and took many rest breaks. Rizzo wondered why gold had to be so heavy. Plus, he had probably another thirty pounds of chain in his pockets. Once all the gold was on the ground, Pete and Rizzo climbed down. They were completely exhausted. Bugsy, still on the roof, picked up the tools and grappling hook. After scanning the area to make sure they left nothing behind, he climbed down and joined his brothers.

After a brief rest, the four of them carried their haul through the fence and down to the shoreline. Rizzo climbed over the rocks and into the boat. The others passed the gold spools to him as he carefully placed them in the boat to balance out the weight evenly. With all of it loaded, Bugsy threw in the tools and the other three climbed into the boat. The downriver current was strong, and the water rougher than it had been earlier. Naz decided to let the current carry them away for a while before starting the motor.

They all came to the conclusion at the same time that they were in trouble. They were being pulled away from the shore and the boat was taking on water. Pete began to panic and told Naz to stop fuckin' around, start the motor, and get closer to shore.

Naz replied, "Shut the fuck up. Keep your voice down."

"Fuck you, asshole. Get closer to the shore!" Pete yelled.

Naz started the motor and the boat lurched forward, making matters worse. Water splashed over the bow and sides. Pete grabbed the side of the boat and let out a string of curses as Naz tried to steer the boat toward the shore. It was no good. They were going down.

Bugsy was the first to jump off, and without looking back, started to swim for the shore. Naz started to laugh at this crazy turn of events as he tried in vain to steer the boat to shallow water. He thought for a brief moment he would make it, but then the boat sank. It happened fast. In a moment, the boat was gone. He was in the water, as were Rizzo and Pete. Pete was in full panic mode as he choked and gurgled, slipping below the chop. Rizzo was being pulled down by the weight of the gold in his pockets and immediately removed his coat, letting it sink out of sight to the bottom. He grabbed for Pete and held him up, telling him to stop thrashing around and calm down. They were joined by Naz, who helped Rizzo get Pete to shore.

Bugsy was already there, sitting on a rock, taking mental notes of where the boat sank and already planning some sort of salvage operation. They all sat there shivering in silence for a while, not believing how they totally fucked up a once-in-a-lifetime golden opportunity. They thought the cops would be embarrassed by this heist, but as it turned out, they weren't looking too good either.

So now Joe knew what all the questions about diving were about.

He slowly asked Rizzo, "So what you want me to do is dive in the river and bring up the gold, is that it?"

"Yeah, that's it," Rizzo said. "We know about where it is. It should be easy enough. Don't worry about the air tanks or nothing, we can get those if we need them. Bugsy thinks you might not need them at all. Maybe you could just hold your breath. The water's not that deep."

Joe couldn't believe what he just heard. He stared at Rizzo, not believing the total stupidity of this whole thing. He really didn't know what to say, so he just blurted out, "You guys are fuckin' crazy."

Rizzo, surprised at his answer said, "What do you mean, crazy? There's a lot of money down there. We broke our asses trying to get it. We're not going to just leave it there."

Joe said, "Well, why don't you guys go down and get it. Send Pete down to get it."

"Send Pete! That chickenshit won't even get into a bathtub after this. You're the one who knows about diving. Tell me why. What's the problem?"

"What's the problem? The problem is that you're trying to get me killed. That fuckin' river is treacherous with the strong currents, and besides, it's so dirty you can't see your hand in front of your face. People jump in there to commit suicide, not swim around looking for buried treasure. There's no way I'm going in there. No fuckin' way."

Rizzo never mentioned it again. As far as Joe knew, it was all still down there somewhere.

***

Joe still couldn't believe they thought he would actually dive into the river on some stupid-ass mission like that. Whatever. That was history, this was now. Jim was still trying to make small talk to pass the time, but at least the traffic was moving again. Joe gave Jim simple answers and comments to his questions, but his thoughts kept going back over the years to all the experiences he had had with the Buccelli family.

Last summer, they invited him to go along on their annual fishing trip to a remote lake in Canada. That's when he really got to know the whole family, as well as some of their closest friends. Rizzo assured Joe that to be invited was indeed a special kind of honor; they wouldn't take just anybody along with them. He then added that many who went once never went again. Joe wasn't sure what that meant.

When Joe asked where the lake was, he was surprised to hear that it was about five hundred miles north of Montreal, way up in the Canadian bush country in the middle of an Indian reservation. That piqued Joe's interest enough, making it easy for him to agree to go. He had recently begun painting Western subjects and researching Indian history and culture, so the chance of visiting an Indian reservation was too good to pass up. He planned on taking many photographs of the countryside as well as actual Indians. He attended the pretrip meeting, where he was told what to bring and how much the trip would cost. It all sounded reasonable. One thing they stressed was not to bring any alcohol whatsoever. That was one of the puzzling things about Rizzo's family. They never drank alcohol of any kind as far as Joe knew. Whenever they were together, or even separately, they drank tea. No beer, no wine or whiskey, only tea. These rough-and-tumble burglars who were avid outdoorsman drank only tea. It was almost comical. But Joe agreed and said fine, he wouldn't bring any alcohol. Then they told Joe some of the stories from past trips, and he understood why some people never made the trip again, if those stories could be believed. At the close of the meeting, Joe asked Bugsy what the name of the lake was. Bugsy answered, "Mistassini."

When Joe got home, looked it up in his atlas and saw that the lake was indeed way up into Canada, his excitement grew even more. He had two weeks to get ready.

CHAPTER FIVE—THE INVASION OF CANADA

On the day of their departure, they were all to meet at Big Al's house north of the city to load up the three vans they would be traveling in. One van, belonging to a family friend named Rocky, was pulling an aluminum boat on a trailer. Rocky was employed as a butcher for a national food chain and had known the Buccelli family for years. He had made the trip before, and this time decided to take his sixteen-year-old son along. The boy's name was Alberto, which quickly turned into "Fat Alberto," as he weighed well over two hundred pounds. Joe saw right away that the kid would not catch a break with this crowd, especially when Rocky announced that he brought along a large bag of "sangwedges" and two roasted chickens for when they got hungry. Joe guessed they were to keep Fat Alberto well fed and happy.

Another family friend who arrived was called "Snake Lips." Joe guessed he earned that nickname because his lips were very thin, almost not there at all. He was short and stocky, with a full head of jet-black hair. Joe noticed that his squinty eyes darted back and forth whenever he spoke, as if he was constantly studying his surroundings. He seemed to know the brothers well, but Joe right away felt uneasy around him. Rizzo's fifth brother, Sonny, was going along as well, as he had done for many years. He and Big Al were the only brothers not involved in the "family business." They both had real jobs working for the city and spent time together only on trips such as this. Sonny was a big man, tall and solid, but he had an innocent, almost childlike, look about him. He was very likable and laughed easily and was also the butt of many jokes and pranks played on him by his brothers. He was sometimes referred to as "Puff" because of his habit of exhaling gusts of air instead of speaking actual words when asked a question.

Pete arrived, driven by his wife, Donna. Pete was a little shorter than the rest of his brothers, but still had a solid frame, which seemed to be a family trait. He also was not as outgoing as the others, but his reserved personality didn't preclude him from enjoying the many pranks they played on each other.

As Pete unloaded his gear from the car, Donna made sure to tell all of them in a loud voice not to bring along any girlfriends on this trip. Pete's brothers didn't like this loud, obnoxious bitch who always accused them of hooking up with whores whenever they went on hunting or fishing trips. Joe heard stories on how that may have happened in the past, but he never witnessed anything like that himself.

Before they left, Big Al invited all of them into his home for a cup of tea. To look at Big Al, you would never expect him to live in such a well-appointed home. Obviously, it was his wife, Penny, who kept it that way. She had the look of an English aristocrat and was totally mismatched with Big Al, who was always unshaven and looked as if he had just crawled out from under a car. Penny escorted the motley group into the dining room, which easily accommodated all of them, and served the tea. Joe was astonished as he looked around at the elegant setting that included carved busts of famous men displayed on marble columns. He then looked over at Al and could not imagine him living in such surroundings, looking like some turd in a china bowl. He could not understand at the time what Penny saw in him, but later on in Canada he would discover a clue. The lively talk around the table was mainly about past trips, leading Big Al to comment about Sonny's mishap the previous year.

"So, tell us, Sonny, you gonna fall out of the boat again this year?" Big Al said.

Everyone started to laugh as they retold how Sonny lost his balance and fell out of the boat in waist-deep water, completely soaking himself along with his wallet, which was in his back pocket.

Smiling, Sonny thought he had a good response. Pointing to his head, he said, "Ah, this year I'm gonna be smart. I'm keeping my wallet in my shirt pocket. See, you gotta use your head. Then it won't get wet."

He then proceeded to take the wallet from the back pocket of his pants and slip it into his shirt pocket to show everyone his great idea. Then he took a big gulp of tea, and to everyone's astonishment, tea dribbled out of his mouth and went directly into his shirt pocket.

Sonny yelled out, "Whaa happened?" He took the soggy wallet out of his pocket and threw it on the table.

Everyone busted out with howls of laughter, as Penny came running in to see what had happened. Rizzo was laughing so hard he had to leave the room. Joe joined him in Big Al's den. They both sat down in two overstuffed leather chairs, trying to regain control of themselves.

"Sonny's always pulling stupid shit like that, the guy can't help himself. He could fuck up a wet dream," Rizzo said as he wiped tears from his eyes.

Joe again marveled as he looked around at the furnishings in the large room, complete with deer mounts on the walls and a wide, ornately carved gun cabinet containing an assortment of rifles and shotguns. There were scores of books on shelves along one wall. Joe smiled as he doubted that Al had read any of them. He then noticed, sitting precariously on the molding over the double French doors, easily over fifty evenly spaced brass shell casings. Rizzo and Joe both sat there, still chuckling at Sonny's clumsiness, when he entered the room

49

with a large grin. Seeing Sonny's tea-stained shirt, Joe and Rizzo started to laugh again.

Then Rizzo said, "What the hell is the matter with you? What are you, *stunad* or what?"

Sonny puffed, then answered, "Whaddya mean? Why, you never spilled nothin'?"

"Christ, you're always spilling shit all over yourself. You gotta smarten up," answered Rizzo.

Sonny just grumbled, "Ahh," then glanced around the room. He turned his attention to the shell casings lined up above the French doors.

Rizzo nudged Joe, pointed to Sonny, and whispered, "Watch this."

Just as Rizzo suspected, Sonny went to reach for one of the shells. He very carefully removed it to take a closer look and then went to put it back. Rizzo was about to lose it again when Sonny's fat fingers knocked down two other shells to the floor. Sonny let out a sigh and bent over to pick them up. He very slowly tried to return them, and in doing so, knocked four more to the floor. Both Rizzo and Joe were now laughing hard as more shells hit the floor.

It didn't stop until Big Al came into the room and said, "What the hell are you trying to do, wreck the place? Get the hell out of here, for Christ's sake."

Rizzo had tears running down his face again from laughing so hard as he and Joe quickly left the room. They joined the others outside and Rizzo told them the story so everyone could enjoy another episode at Sonny's expense. No one got a break with this crowd.

More invited people started to arrive, bringing their total number to an even dozen. One was a friend of Big Al's called Gilly, a short, fat man who seemed to have a jovial personality. Another newcomer was a friend of Bugsy's named Johnny. He also was a Vietnam vet who barely said a word to anyone. After all the introductions were made, they began to board the vans. Watching as the men passed him, Snake Lips laughingly remarked that this bunch looked like a traveling circus.

As Sonny passed, he said, "Here come the clowns!" Then as Gilly and Fat Alberto passed, he added, "and there go the elephants."

Joe thought, "Oh, yeah, this is going to be fun" as he boarded Sonny's van along with Rizzo and Gilly. Rocky's van had Big Al, Naz, and Pete aboard. Bugsy drove his van with Snake Lips, Johnny, and Fat Alberto. All three vans had the rear seats removed and were loaded with fishing gear, gas tanks, outboard motors, clothes, and canned goods. All of that was covered with a mattress so the guys in back could either sit or lie down. It was over nine hundred miles to their destination, and there would be no stopping except for pee breaks, gas, and food. They would sleep in the vans and take turns at the wheel if the driver needed a break.

Rocky's van took the lead, with Sonny second and Bugsy taking up the rear. Joe settled in the rear of Sonny's van, making himself comfortable for the long ride. The trip was uneventful until they reached the U.S.--Canadian border. Sonny stopped his van at the customs gate. Rocky's van had already gone through. The border guard approached and began to ask the standard questions: How many were in the vehicle? Where were they going and for what purpose? What equipment did they have? Did they have any firearms or alcohol? To each question, Sonny mumbled, shook his head, and made a puffing noise. The guard stopped talking and just stared at Sonny. Rizzo quickly leaned over and answered the man's questions. The guard then

51

asked to see all of their IDs, and while staring at them intently, asked each man his name. For a minute, it looked to Joe as if they wouldn't be allowed to the cross the border at all. The guard finally gave them back their IDs and waved them through, telling them to enjoy their stay. The third van had no trouble crossing.

Rizzo looked at Sonny and said, "When are you going to learn to talk like a human? What's all that 'ahh' and 'ohh' and all that blowin' bullshit you always do. You gotta talk words! Words—not sound like some fuckin' whale with a pole up his ass. You better smarten up."

Sonny answered, "Whaddya mean?"

"Ah, leave him alone. He's just a little different, that's all. Ain't that right, Sonny?" Gilly said.

Sonny mumbled what vaguely sounded like, "Go fuck yourself."

A few miles up the road from the border crossing, Joe was looking out the back window at the following van when he thought he saw the side door suddenly open. Then he saw something big and red fly out. As he watched it tumble and roll down the grassy embankment, he realized what it was.

"Hey, they just threw Fat Alberto out of the van," he said.

Rizzo turned and asked, "What?"

Joe repeated that someone just threw Fat Alberto out of the van behind them.

Rizzo laughed and said, "You're shittin' me. Sonny, pull over."

All three vans pulled over and everyone got out to see what had happened. Fat Alberto picked himself up and walked slowly back up the embankment, looking like he was about to cry. He stood there waving his arms, his face beet red, saying that Snake Lips had thrown him out the door. Everyone looked at Snake Lips, who shrugged his shoulders and calmly said, "I got tired of listening to his stupid shit, so I threw him out."

That started everyone laughing, including Rocky, his old man, who said, "Well, the kid's got to learn some time."

Joe was amazed that the kid's own father would say that, and laugh along with the rest of them, after his son got thrown out of a moving vehicle. Big Al suggested that maybe they should leave him here, where he might have a better chance of survival than spending the next week with them in the bush.

Snake Lips said, "Tell him to keep his stupid mouth shut or I'll throw him out again."

With that, they all returned to the vans, and Joe could not believe that Fat Alberto got back in the same van with Snake Lips. What a dumbass, he thought.

They continued their journey and quickly forgot about Fat Alberto. Rizzo was telling Sonny to be sure and stop at the small tackle shop they went to last year. They liked that shop because they found it easy to steal fishing lures and other small items from the shelves. Rizzo would steal things just for the sake of taking them. Joe heard him say once that he didn't feel right if he went into a store and didn't steal something. It didn't matter what. It might be just a pack of gum—he just had to steal. And he was really proud of that statement. Joe thought when they got to that store, he would wait in the van.

Things quieted down as they drove through the night, so Joe tried to get some sleep. He was awakened by Rizzo's voice telling Sonny, "Pull up next to the pump and be quiet." Joe sat up and looked out the window to see that they were at a gas station. It was well after midnight and there was no one around except for the teenage attendant, who was fast asleep in a cubicle near the gas pumps. Rizzo got out of the van. He very slowly lifted the nozzle from the pump and began to fill the van's gas tank. Joe could tell that Sonny was getting nervous and heard him mumble, "Okay, that's enough" a little too low for Rizzo to hear.

When the gas tank was full, Rizzo returned the nozzle and got back in the van, telling Sonny to get going. At that moment, the attendant woke up and ran toward the van, waving his arms. Rizzo jumped out of the van and proceeded to ask the kid for directions to the next large town. The kid was still half-asleep and so befuddled by the question that all he could do was give Rizzo the directions he asked for. Rizzo said thank you and quickly got back in the van as Sonny sped away, mumbling something that sounded like "illegal." As they drove away, Joe watched the station attendant stand there staring at them. Joe wondered if he would check the pump to see if they took any gas and if he had enough sense to get their plate number. Joe asked where the other vans were and Rizzo said they stopped at a different station to gas up. Rizzo, never one to pass up an opportunity, had noticed the kid was sleeping and told Sonny to pull in there. Joe wondered if they would get through the week without winding up in some Canadian jail. This was only the first day.

***

Night became day as they as they traveled north, deeper into Canada. They stopped for breakfast at a small restaurant in the town of La Tuque, taking every available table with their small army. In true ugly American fashion, the boys had a great time screwing around with the waiters, who seemed to speak only French. Joe had his doubts about that and wondered if they were going to spit in their food or worse. The other patrons stared at them the whole time, not knowing what to make of these big, burly, loud Americans all dressed up like cowboys.

The next stop was the little tackle shop Joe had heard so much about the day before. Joe thought that based on past visits, the owner would surely call the cops as soon as they stepped through the door. Not all of them went in at once, which was a good thing. Joe decided to go in following Rizzo and Naz. Rizzo told Joe to be on the lookout for a certain lure called the "Red Devil." Rizzo said it was the best one to get and to be sure to get plenty of them. However, Naz found them first and took them all. Joe was sure he would pay for only a fraction of what he had.

Later, outside the store, Naz told Joe, "You'll need plenty of these lures because you lose a lot of them on the rocks, and this is the only place to get them." Laughing, he threw one to Joe and said, "Here, good luck."

Joe sarcastically answered, "Thanks."

Naz replied, "Don't thank me, thank God you got it."

Rizzo said, "Hey, don't worry, we'll just rob his tackle box. He's got dozens in there."

Naz quickly replied, "Don't touch my fuckin' tackle box or I'll cut your hands off and use them for bait. You can't get this shit in the bush. You have to get what you need now or you won't have it. *Capeesh?*"

Rizzo answered, "How can anybody get them when you got them all?"

He turned and winked at Joe, then got into the van. Some of the others were still in the store doing God knows what, but Joe was confident the store owner got the worst of it.

They drove on for most of the day, finally coming to a small town named Chibougamau. This would be the last town where they could buy—or steal—anything for the next week, so it was now or never. They bought gas, cigarettes, and anything else they thought they might need. Joe looked around for some of the Red Devil lures, but didn't see any. After shopping, they went into a restaurant to have lunch. They filled the counter, taking every available stool. Like before, all the locals stared at them. Rizzo pulled a stupid stunt when Big Al, sitting a few seats away, asked him to pass down a plate of toast. He passed the plate so fast that the bread flew off and landed on the floor near the cook. The man stared at Rizzo like he was a complete idiot, but Rizzo didn't care. He was laughing hard, as were most of the others, except for Big Al, who asked, "Are you stupid or what?"

After lunch, Joe learned that from this point on, they would have to drive on a dirt road into the wilderness to their final destination, a small Indian village on a river leading to Lake Mistassini.

Many miles of dirt road can really work on the nerves with the jarring and swerving, and everyone bitching about the choking clouds of dust. They were forced to shut the windows, but dust still got in, making it almost impossible to breathe. Through the dense air, Joe could hear the laughing and jeering coming from the van in front that was creating the blinding cloud. Everyone but Sonny had their shirts pulled up over their faces, trying to filter out as much of the dirty air as possible. Joe looked back to see how the van behind them was doing and noticed that they had fallen far back, almost out of sight. Joe thought, "Why the hell are we following so damn close?" and then realized why the guys in the front van were laughing. They knew that

Sonny was driving behind them and lacked the sense to fall back out of the dust cloud. Sonny just kept on driving, not caring at all as the van filled up with dirt and grit.

Finally, Rizzo shouted, "Jesus Christ, Sonny! Back off, will you? Slow down, let them go on before you kill us all. Come on, use your fuckin' head."

Sonny started to slow down and let the lead van pull away. The air immediately became cleaner and Rizzo opened the window to let it circulate. All of their faces were white and everything else in the van was coated with a fine layer of grit.

Sonny rolled down his window, let out a sigh, and said, "They should pave this road."

Rizzo answered, "Yeah, they're gonna pave this road just for you. You're not supposed to follow so close on a dirt road, asshole. You can get a rock through your windshield or through your radiator, then we'd really be fucked."

Smiling, Sonny said, "What rocks?"

"What rocks? The rocks in your fuckin' head, that's what rocks," Rizzo said.

Rizzo told Joe to open the side door of the van to let more air in, and as he watched the scenery go by through the open door, he wondered if Fat Alberto was still in the van behind them. They drove on until they saw Rocky's van pull over onto the shoulder and stop. They pulled up behind him, followed by Bugsy's van, and they all got out for a pee break.

Rocky then noticed that both his boat trailer and the underside of his boat were pretty well beat up and dented by the rocks kicked up by his van. "Damn, will you look at this. I hope there's no holes punched through or this boat's gonna be useless," he said as he examined the damaged hull.

Sonny noticed that the front of his van also suffered some damage from following too closely to the van and boat trailer ahead of him. He started to complain, "Yeah, well fuck that, look at my van!"

"Serves you right for being so stupid by following Rocky up the ass like you did," Rizzo said.

"I should charge you guys riding with me a dollar a mile to pay for the damage," Sonny mumbled with a smile.

Rizzo laughed and said, "Yeah, hold out both hands and shit in one—see which one fills up first."

Everyone laughed, then went over to see if Rocky's boat had any holes punched through the hull by the rocks. Seeing only dents but no holes, they were satisfied the boat was fine. They boarded the vans to continue their journey, but at a slower pace.

Many miles later, they approached a small wooden shed next to a lift gate that blocked the road. On the gate was a sign that read "*Arret.*" A uniformed man stepped out of the shed and stood in front of the gate with his arm raised. He waited for the three vans to reach the gate before he walked up to them. He began to speak in French, but quickly changed to English when he realized they were Americans. He informed them that they were about to enter an Indian reservation and certain rules would apply. Alcohol of any sort was forbidden, as were any firearms. They would have to pay a fee for fishing rights and were strictly forbidden from fishing in waters beyond the posted boundary.

He showed them on a map where the boundary was, as Big Al and Naz both gave him a knowing smile. He then gave them the map and turned to lift the gate, waving them through. Joe knew that except for a small bottle of whiskey Big Al had hidden away for "medicinal" purposes, they didn't have any alcohol, and he was pretty sure they didn't have any guns with them either. But he wasn't so sure about that forbidden boundary. The way Big Al and Naz smiled at the mention of it, he had a feeling that warning didn't mean shit. They drove on with still another fifty miles of dirt road to go before reaching the river that would lead them to the lake.

For Joe, driving through the Indian reservation was a great disappointment. He wasn't sure what to expect or what he would see, but he had imagined something a whole lot better than this. As they approached the village near the river, they rode past ramshackle cinder-block houses, abandoned and stripped cars, and all sorts of rusted junk scattered all around. When they passed what looked like a small grocery store, about a dozen young Indian kids dressed in rags came running up to the vans, yelling for them to stop. They didn't.

They drove on until they came to a wharf area on the banks of a small river, then pulled up and parked on the long dock. Several large, eighteen-foot wooden boats were tied to the dock in a row. Big Al and Naz said they were going to find someone who would rent them the three boats they needed. The rest of them started to unload the gear and pile it up near the boats. They took Rocky's boat from the trailer, put it into the water, and tied it to the dock, again checking it for possible leaks. After the vans were unloaded and parked in a small adjacent lot, everyone sat down to await the return of their fearless leaders. A few of them noticed that they didn't see any people around anywhere. No men or women—in fact, the only people they had seen so far were those kids by the store they passed.

Rizzo, Pete, and Joe decided to go after Big Al and Naz and find out what was going on. They walked past a few of the junk-filled yards and called out, "Hello, is anybody here?"

They heard Big Al answer from around a corner, and went over to see him and Naz talking to a kid about twelve years old. They said the kid told them they needed to see the chief about renting any boats, and that he lived in the red house down the street. They could see in the distance a cinder-block house with faded red paint, so they walked toward it, with the kid following behind. They reached the house and walked through a torn screen door onto a trash-filled porch.

Big Al knocked on a faded blue door and called out, "Hello, anybody in there?"

After a few more knocks and hellos, they heard some movement from inside, then the door slowly opened, letting out a gust of fetid air. The chief slowly stepped out, and was truly a sight to behold. This was not what Joe thought an Indian chief should look like. He was rail thin, bent over, violently shaking, wearing dirty, loose-fitting clothes, and had a nose that looked like a beet-red cauliflower. His hair was white and cut very short. His watery eyes squinted in the light and seemed not to be able to focus on anything.

Big Al, raising his hand and smiling broadly, said, "How, Chief."

The rest of them just smiled and shook their heads in disbelief. Big Al tried to converse with the old chief about renting the boats, but all he got was a series of mumbling sounds. Finally, in disgust, he turned to the kid and asked if there was anyone else he could talk to around there. The kid said, without any embarrassment, that everyone else in the village was like the chief. It was unbelievable. The whole town was either drunk or passed out. And here was their chief, who bent down farther with each mumbling sound he made.

Big Al decided to do business with the only sober person he'd met so far, the twelve-year-old, who was very willing to take their money. When they returned to the dock, however, they saw two adults talking to the rest of the group. It was a relief to see that, because besides renting the boats, they also needed to buy gasoline, a lot of gasoline, and didn't want to buy it from some kid.

Big Al asked the two men where everyone else was in this town, and they said that many of the old people were either drunk or indoors. As Big Al talked to them, a few more men came out and stood around to watch as they negotiated a price for the three boats. After the deal was made, the group began loading their gear into the boats. They attached the motors they had brought with them and bought a fifty-five-gallon drum of gasoline. The big drum was dropped into the wooden boat that Rizzo and Joe would occupy. Since there wasn't room for anyone else, Gilly rode with Big Al. Joe wasn't too happy about having to ride with all that gas, but there was nothing he could do about it. The other boats were loaded with the rest of the gear and the food they brought along. Naz, Pete, and Sonny were in another rented wooden boat, and Bugsy, Johnny, and Snake Lips were in the third one. Big Al, Gilly, Rocky, and Fat Alberto were in the boat they had brought with them.

Before they could leave, they were told to proceed to the small log cabin nearby to register their names with the "government man." The cabin served as a small office and housed a desk, some bookshelves, and a few file cabinets. The only light in the windowless room came from a small ceiling fixture. On the walls hung an assortment of animal pelts, some of which were stretched on wooden hoops. Sitting behind the desk in the only chair was the government man, the superintendent

61

overseeing the lake region. No more than two at a time could enter the small room, so they took turns going in, showing their identification, and signing the register book. The man was very friendly and asked them many questions about where they were from and if this was their first time at Lake Mistassini. The group told him of their past trips to the lake, but said this was the first time they had come to this jump-off point. Joe wondered why, but he didn't ask.

When the last two had signed the book, the government agent came outside to explain how to reach the main lake by following the small river they were on. He warned them to be careful not to take one of the wrong forks, or they could be lost for a long time. Then he turned very serious and said that even though it was June, the water temperature was thirty-eight degrees, and if any of them fell overboard they would be dead in minutes. He added that they should be aware of the fishing boundary line and be sure not to cross over into that area.

Big Al smiled and said, "Sure thing. See you next week."

They cranked up the motors and started off down the narrow, winding river. It didn't take long for the arguments to begin about which way to go. The route seemed simple enough when the agent explained it, but now it proved to be much more difficult. There were many small islands and the river forked off in many directions, making it almost impossible to choose the right channel. In addition to that, no one could agree on what the man had said only a few minutes ago. They were already lost. Joe thought they probably couldn't even find their way back to the dock at this point. All the islands were covered with small pine trees and looked identical.

Finally, Naz got the brilliant idea that they should split up and each go in a different direction to find the lake. Of course, there was no way of communicating with one another if one group did indeed find the lake. Regardless, everyone thought that was a good idea, so they split up and went off in different directions. No one asked Joe for his opinion, which didn't matter, because he figured he would never see any of them again. In minutes, they were all out of sight.

Moments ago, there were four boats and twelve guys all together, and now Rizzo and Joe were all alone in the Canadian wilderness. They proceeded along what they thought was the main channel for about thirty minutes without seeing or hearing anyone. The river was widening, which gave them hope they were on the right track. Joe used Rizzo's binoculars to scan the shoreline, looking for any sign of the way out to the main lake. As they passed a large cove, Joe told Rizzo to stop while he searched the far side for an opening.

Seeing nothing, Joe said, "I don't see a fuckin' thing but trees, no way out in there. How are we supposed to know where everybody else is anyway? I think we should have all stayed together."

Rizzo answered, "Don't worry, we'll find it. We'll find it—and besides, we have all the gasoline."

Joe laughed and said, "What the hell does that mean? We could build a big bonfire so they can find us? Fuck the gasoline."

Joe decided to give the cove one last look as Rizzo gunned the engine, when he noticed something.

"Whoa, whoa, whoa, I see something," Joe said. "Looks like a canoe. Where the hell did that come from?"

Rizzo turned to look into the cove and said, "You see a canoe? Where?"

Joe answered, "Back in the cove, way on the other side. I swear it wasn't there a minute ago. Looks like it's headin' toward us."

"I thought you said there was nothing out there," Rizzo said.

"There wasn't. This is spooky. I don't know where it came from."

Minutes later, Joe could make out that two men were in the canoe, and one of them was operating a small motor, pushing the canoe toward them. They waited in silence as the canoe approached. Joe was hoping the men could direct them to the main lake.

As the two men pulled up directly alongside, Rizzo and Joe saw that they were both Indians and their small canoe contained nothing but two shotguns lying across the seats. The Indians said nothing as they looked them over carefully. Joe started to get a bad feeling.

Rizzo broke the silence by asking, "So, are you guys hunting?"

No response.

"Fishing?"

No response.

"Nothing?"

Again, no response.

It would have been funny if it wasn't so scary. Here these two were, armed and not very friendly, eyeing everything Joe and Rizzo had and knowing it was all theirs for the taking. The Indians could have shot them both. That's what Joe was thinking, anyway, as he slowly reached for one of the oars. Then Rizzo asked if they knew the way to the lake.

Joe expected the same silent treatment and was not disappointed. However, this time one of them pointed to the far side of the cove.

Rizzo asked, "Is there a way out to the lake back there?"

They again said nothing, just gave them another looking over, then pushed off and sailed away. No hello, no goodbye, no wave, nothing, not a word.

Joe said, "Boy, that was weird, I thought we were in trouble for a minute there."

Laughing, Rizzo said, "Yeah, I saw you reaching for the oar, so I thought I'd better ask for directions. That always seems to work in a tight spot. Besides, you would have whacked one with the oar and I would have stabbed the other fucker in the heart before he got his gun up."

Joe said, "You really think that's the way it would have played out? Or would both of us be at the bottom of the river with our guts blown out? I'm just glad they're gone."

They decided to go and see if there was a way out of the cove. Those Indians had to come from somewhere. As they approached the far side, Joe, using the binoculars, still could not see any opening. He was scanning the shore, and then as he turned his head to the left, he saw it.

"Son of a bitch, look at that," he said as he lowered the binoculars.

Rizzo looked over and said, "See, what did I tell you? I knew we'd find the way."

Joe said, "Yeah, right. If it wasn't for those two wackadoo Indians, we would be on this shithole river forever."

The narrow opening to the lake could be seen only from where they now were, and not from anywhere else in the cove. The angle had to be just right. They never would have found it on their own. It was just pure luck that those two Indians happened to be coming through when they did and Joe turned to look one last time. The opening was so small and shallow they almost had to get out and drag the boat through. Rizzo cut the motor and raised it so they could row and pole their way over the rocky bottom into a much larger body of water. They still were not on the main lake, but Rizzo noticed a gap in the distant shoreline. He recognized it from last year and said, "There it is. That's the way in."

Joe was surprised that this wasn't the main lake; it sure looked big enough for him. For one thing, the water was a lot rougher here than it was back on the river. The weight of the drum of gas was making the boat sluggish, and they started to take on a little water. Joe started to bail it out with a small plastic cup, remembering the warning they got about the water's temperature. He suggested that maybe they should keep closer to the shore just in case.

"Just in case of what?" Rizzo asked.

"In case the boat sinks. We have a lot of weight in here," Joe shot back.

"This boat ain't gonna sink. Besides, we make better time going straight than following the shoreline," Rizzo answered with a big grin on his face.

Joe thought this was the second time in the past hour when he might get killed.

As they passed through the gap, the great expanse of Lake Mistassini opened up in front of them. It looked like a vast inland sea dotted with hundreds of little islands. One thing they noticed right away was that the water was even rougher out here. The boat slowed as it battled the waves and almost seemed to be standing still. The big gas drum was rolling between the seats and very cold water was splashing over the sides.

Once again, Joe asked Rizzo to get closer to shore and this time Rizzo wisely agreed, then steered the boat toward one of the islands. He decided that they would island-hop their way up the lake, always keeping near a shoreline. Relieved, Joe thought that was a great idea. Then Joe asked Rizzo how far it was to the campsite and Rizzo answered, "Hell, I don't know."

Joe yelled, "What do you mean, you don't know? Weren't you here before?"

Rizzo yelled back, "We can't stay at the same place we did before, Al didn't say where we were going this year."

Shaking his head, Joe continued to bail out the water that was collecting in the boat. Just then, the motor cut out and Rizzo began to change gas tanks.

"This is our last full tank," Rizzo said. "We're using a lot of gas because the water's so rough."

Joe put down the cup he was bailing with and picked up the binoculars to see if any of the other boats were out there. They weren't.

Here they were, all alone in the middle of a giant lake, running out of gas, not knowing where to go, the boat filling with ice-cold water.

On top of that, the sun was getting lower in the sky. Joe was coming to realize why some guys who went on this trip never wanted to go again.

Joe started to bail water again when Rizzo yelled out, "I see a boat. I think somebody's out there waving. See if you can tell who it is."

Joe answered, "I just looked and didn't see anything."

Rizzo answered, pointing to his right, "Well, look again, over there by that island."

Joe could make out a small speck that had just passed from in front of the island, making it visible. Picking up the binoculars, he could see who he thought was Big Al, waving his arms.

Joe said, "Looks like Big Al waving hello."

Rizzo answered, "Yeah, but maybe he's out of gas. We better go see."

Joe knew he was probably right, but he surely didn't want to cross that great expanse of open water away from any nearby island. Rizzo steered the boat toward the waving figure and gunned the engine. A wave crashed over the bow, soaking Joe with icy water, then another, and another. Joe began to frantically bail with one hand while trying to steady the rolling gas drum with the other. He yelled at Rizzo to slow down, to no avail. Joe kept bailing, wondering how all this was going to end.

When they finally were alongside Big Al's boat, they learned that he was indeed out of gas. As the two boats rose and fell, banging against each other, Rizzo and Big Al tried to figure out a way to siphon gas out of the big drum.

Luckily, the cap was on the upper end of the drum, which allowed Big Al to remove it and insert a rubber hose to siphon out the gas. He sucked hard on the tube, then spit out a mouthful of gas into the lake.

With a big smile he said, "Ah, nectar of the gods."

Rizzo and Rocky held the boats together while Joe kept on bailing out water.

Gilly handed Big Al the tanks to be filled. Fat Alberto, wearing a bright orange poncho, just sat there hunched over, looking like an oversized pumpkin.

"Hurry up, damn it," Rizzo said, then yelled out in pain as his hand was crushed between the two boats.

Big Al smiled and said, "Not for nothing, genius, but why don't you use the rope?"

Rizzo shot back, "Yeah, yeah, fuck you! Just hurry up. Where is this fuckin' camp, anyway?"

"What do you mean? Don't you know? What are you, lost already?"

Rocky then added, "Yeah, come on, Daniel Boone, tell us the way."

"Rizzo yelled back, "You got the fuckin' map, I don't!"

"Ha! What good would the map do you, anyway? You can't read the fuckin' thing. How did you get this far anyway? We thought we'd never see you again," Big Al said with a toothy grin.

Just then, Rocky noticed another boat heading toward them in the distance, with the occupants waving and yelling. As the boat came closer, they saw that it was Naz, Pete, and Sonny. They, too, were almost out of gas and were getting worried about being stranded out there in the dark. Now there were three boats banging into each other as they tried to fill the gas tanks without someone falling overboard. Big Al asked them if they knew where the last boat was. Naz answered that they hadn't seen them since they all split up on the river.

Big Al said, "I don't care so much about those three clowns, but they have most of the food with them and that might be a problem."

Joe thought it was ironic that Bugsy and Johnny, the two Army vets who had seemed to be the most capable ones out here, were nowhere to be seen. As Big Al and Naz were discussing where they might be, Fat Alberto piped up, "Maybe they came another way."

"This is the only way to come, you dumb fuck," Big Al yelled. "This is the big lake. What, are you worried about not eating tonight?"

Everyone looked at Fat Alberto as he again hunched over, pulling his orange hood over his head. He hadn't learned yet not to say anything on this trip. Joe almost felt sorry for the poor kid.

Big Al then said they had a few more miles to go before reaching the camp, and they should make it without having to refuel again. Checking the map, he said they had to pass two more large islands, then turn to the left. By this time, the sun was almost setting, and Big Al knew the camp would be almost impossible to find in the dark. They couldn't waste any time waiting for the fourth boat. Those boys were on their own. It took almost another hour before the camp came into view in the twilight. From a distance, the abandoned commercial fishing camp looked pretty good, but as they got closer, Joe could see that it was in bad shape.

The camp consisted of two large, gray wooden buildings a short distance from the lakeshore. They were situated on the left side of a beautiful little cove that had a narrow opening to the lake. On each side of the opening was a low, sturdy wooden dock connected by a bridge over the entrance to the cove. They beached the boats in front of the larger building and began to unload their gear.

That's when the attack came.

Suddenly, they were enveloped in a swarm of buzzing, stinging mosquitoes, millions of them. They hadn't noticed or felt any out on the water, but as soon as they landed, they were covered in them. They scrambled through their baggage to find the bug spray that was on everyone's list to bring. A few of the guys found theirs first, spayed themselves, and passed the cans. Rizzo found his and told Joe to watch as he sprayed his face while folding in his lips so the spray would not get into his mouth. The other brothers also knew that trick, but some of the new guys didn't and got the bitter chemicals on their lips as they sprayed their faces. The brothers laughed as they watched them spit on the ground and try to wipe their mouths to get rid of the taste of the spray.

Big Al said with a grin, "You think this is bad, wait until the black flies find out we're here."

After they sprayed themselves over and over, the mosquitoes hovered about two inches away from their bodies, allowing them to unload the boats and bring their gear into the larger building. They climbed the five wooden steps onto a porch, then went through the open door into what was once an ice house for storing fish. The few small windows had no glass and would have to be covered quickly if they were to stay in there. Some of the walls were stripped of wood, exposing thick foam insulation, and others showed evidence of being hit by shotgun blasts. Against the back wall were three large tables piled with trash, some of which had spilled onto the floor. Off to the left side was a small cooking area with a busted-up stove and sink, and three large cardboard drums filled with more trash. Not exactly the Ritz, but it would be home for the next week.

Big Al brought in a bundle of folded plastic and dropped it onto the floor. Looking at Joe, he said, "Here, make yourself useful and cover the windows so the mosquitoes don't suck us dry."

Joe looked down at the plastic and said, "How do I attach it to the walls?"

Big Al answered as he went back outside, "You're a college boy, right? Use your head."

As the other guys brought in the rest of the gear, Joe cleared a spot on the floor and began cutting large squares of plastic with his knife. He looked around to find some way of attaching the plastic and noticed scores of nails scattered on the floor in a small back room. Joe then went outside to find a rock suitable for use as a hammer and began covering the windows. When he was finishing the last one, Rizzo came over while spraying himself with bug spray.

"Well, at least you learned something useful in college," he said.

Joe didn't remember taking any courses in hanging plastic, but didn't say anything. With all the windows covered over, they then went around killing any mosquitoes that had gotten inside. After they thought they had gotten them all, each one cleaned up an area along a wall for their cot and personal belongings. Big Al and Naz pulled two of the long tables into the center of the room, cleared off the trash, and told everyone to start bringing it all outside. Those who brought coolers put them around the tables to serve as chairs. Everyone else had to search for something to sit on or just stand.

They left the third table against the wall, to be used to store their food. Of course, at this point, except for a few boxes of crackers, there wasn't any food, all of it being in the missing boat. Joe went outside to bring in the rest of his gear and was immediately attacked by a swarm of stinging mosquitoes. The spray must have worn off a little, because he was being stung on the back of his neck and some were even trying to get into his mouth. He wondered how they were supposed to survive the week in this buggy hell. He sure hoped there would be enough bug spray. He quickly collected all his gear, his fishing pole, duffel bag, and tackle box to bring them in for the night. As he entered the building loaded down with everything, Naz looked at him and laughed.

"Hey, here comes Joe Shoes," he said. "Look at him bringing all his shit inside. Don't you know all the thieves are in here!"

Everyone burst out laughing as Joe stood there and thought, yeah, Naz was right. The place was full of thieves and all his stuff would probably be safer outside. He put it all down by his cot anyway. He asked Rizzo what was the bit about "Joe Shoes." Rizzo said Naz started calling him that because of the new hiking boots he was wearing. That's all it took to earn a nickname with this bunch. Joe thought, oh well, it could have been worse.

After the laughter died down, Big Al went outside, lit a lantern, and placed it on top of the bridge over the cove opening. Being the only light for miles, it would be easily spotted from out in the lake. The water was now as black as ink, as were the distant shores. They blended together into one black sheet. Without that light, no one would be able to find the camp.

When Big Al came back inside, quickly shutting the door behind him, he saw Naz busily hooking up the propane tank to the camp stove they brought along, Rizzo and Joe lighting the other lanterns, and the others cleaning up the place to make it more livable. Then he looked over by the food table and saw Fat Alberto rummaging through the few boxes of crackers.

Big Al shook his head and said loudly, "Look at him, he's like a bear in a garbage dump. What's the matter, you fat fuck, you can't wait for the food to get here?"

Rocky then told his son to get away from the table and help pick up some of the trash still lying around.

Big Al then said to everybody, "You know the food, when it gets here, is for everybody. We all chipped in to buy it, and I don't want to see any asshole hanging around that table filling his face with whatever he wants. We got to sit down and plan the meals or it's not gonna last the week."

He looked right at Fat Alberto when he finished, then asked Sonny to help him clear out some debris from the kitchen area.

Rocky took his kid into the back room and was overheard telling him, "Look, don't embarrass me in front of these guys again."

In a high, whiny voice, Fat Alberto pleaded, "I don't want to be here. I want to go home."

His old man replied, "Look, you wanted to come on this trip, now you're here. You gotta grow up. You got to be a man. These guys are men and they're not going to put up with your bullshit or cater to you in any way. Stop acting like a fucking spoiled *gavone*, keep your mouth shut, and help out. Do something useful."

Rocky came back out shaking his head. "The kid's got to learn," he said.

Fat Alberto stayed back there for quite a while. They didn't see him again until they heard the sound of an outboard motor approaching. Big Al opened the door, stepped out, then immediately came back in to spray himself with bug spray. They all did the same and went outside to greet their missing compatriots.

They heard Bugsy's friend Johnny yell out in the darkness, "What's with all these fuckin' mosquitoes, man!"

Big Al tossed him a can of bug spray and said, "Welcome to paradise. Where the hell you been?"

Bugsy, Johnny, and Snake Lips climbed up onto the dock, but didn't say anything about where they had been or why they were so late. And the funny thing is, no one asked them again. Joe looked down into their boat and saw that they had three gas tanks and could have made it without refueling. Joe thought that maybe they wanted to get a jump on the fishing, but he didn't see any fish. It was mysterious, but no one seemed to care. They all pitched in to unload the boat and bring the supplies inside. As Joe stacked the boxes of food on the table, he asked Rizzo where he thought those guys were all this time. He answered there was no telling where they were or what they were doing.

"Maybe they robbed some guys they met along the way," Rizzo added with a laugh.

Joe asked in a hushed tone, "Do you really think they did?"

"You ain't gotta worry about that. Who the fuck knows? But if they did, I hope they had enough sense to kill them and sink the bodies. I didn't come up here to get in trouble," Rizzo answered in a serious tone.

"Holy shit, are you kidding me! All you guys do is shit that can get you in trouble. You know we're in a foreign country. They've got different laws up here. Holy shit, you don't really think they killed somebody, do you?" Joe asked in a hushed tone.

Rizzo looked around to see if anyone was near enough to hear and said, "I've known Bugsy since he was born. That guy's fuckin' *oobatz*. He goes off alone a lot when we go deer hunting. Once I tripped over him in the woods. He was sleeping under a pile of leaves. He didn't even wake up, or maybe just pretended he didn't. You ever hear him tell what he did in 'Nam? Let me tell you this—don't ask where they were. You notice no one else did? Hell, Al didn't even ask him twice. Just forget about it."

Joe said, "Hey, no problem," as he put a box of Frosted Flakes on the table.

After the three latecomers set up their cots on the far wall near each other, Naz began to heat up some large cans of chili for supper. They all sat or stood around the long table while they ate and talked about how good fresh trout is going to taste. No one talked about why those three guys were so late, and that was okay with Joe. After supper, all the paper plates were put in a plastic garbage bag and thrown outside. Naz put on a large kettle of water for tea while Big Al got out the map of the lake to plan the route for tomorrow. Navigating around the hundreds of small islands in this lake could be very tricky. All the islands look alike and it's easy to get turned around and suddenly feel as if you're lost in a maze. Big Al and Naz seemed to know the lake pretty well, but Joe wasn't too sure about the other guys.

Then Big Al announced, "Okay, ladies, lights out. We get an early start tomorrow."

Rizzo went around the room spraying everyone one more time with bug spray. Joe lay on his cot, stinking of chemicals and hoping to fall asleep soon.

***

Traffic was moving again on Route 80, making Joe more anxious than ever to get home. He knew what he had to do. He would have Jim drop him off at the gas station near his mother's house, go in, and ask if they knew anything about Rizzo's arrest. Then he would go to his mother's house, pick up Janet and Marie, and get home as fast as he could. He would then load up all the guns and get the hell out of town. Where was he going to go? Well, he hadn't figured that out yet. Of course, all that depended on the guns not yet being found. How much time did he have, anyway?

***

The week at the lake seemed to be going by quickly. They arose early each day and Naz made breakfast, after which they loaded up the boats and took off in different directions to go fishing. Some days they were in sight of each other, and other days they totally split up. The lake was incredibly beautiful, with water so clear you could see the bottom up to twenty feet down. The weather was so warm that Joe almost felt like diving in for a swim, but he knew that would be suicidal. The water was so cold, yet so inviting.

He got the urge to dip his face in the water one day when they all stopped for lunch on one of the islands. He immediately regretted it. The water was so cold that he felt as if it were burning his face. The

77

shock momentarily paralyzed him, and he had to force himself to pull his face back out. He never tried that again. The water may have looked clear and beautiful, but it was deadly. That same day, Sonny took off his boots so he could wade out into the ankle-deep water. He immediately started hopping on each foot, as if he were walking on hot coals. That government agent back at the dock was right about how dangerous these waters were. The weather was wonderful, though. So far, they had not had a single day of rain. They ate the fish they caught every day, sometimes for lunch over an open fire on a deserted beach. They seemed to have the whole lake to themselves, as they had not seen a single person or even another boat all week.

One day while Rizzo, Rocky, and Joe were out on the lake, Rizzo beached their boat on one of the larger islands so they could take a break from fishing and do a little exploring. They fought their way through heavy underbrush and swarms of mosquitoes until they came upon a good-sized body of water. Joe found it funny that this island in the middle of a lake had its very own lake. Looking around, he wondered if any other human in history had ever walked on the same spot where they now stood. In an area as remote as this, it could be possible that no one ever had, and Joe was amazed at the thought. Rizzo suggested that maybe they should drag their boat over there and do some fishing in this newfound lake. Rocky and Joe didn't think that was a good idea. So, after exploring the lakeshore for a while, they left the island they discovered, returned to their boat, and resumed fishing.

Later that afternoon, their boat was almost rammed at high speed by a boatload of laughing idiots. They were fishing in a beautiful, peaceful little bay when Joe saw the other boat approaching fast. As it bore down on them, he could see Naz at the helm, and Pete and Sonny grinning from ear to ear. At the last possible moment before a devastating collision, the boat veered off, spraying them down with a sheet of icy cold water. Rizzo yelled curses at the retreating boat and immediately tried starting the engine to begin a pursuit. By the time he got it running, the other boat was long gone. Back at camp that night, everyone got a good laugh at the hilarious prank. It was just another one of the near-deadly jokes they all enjoyed playing on one another.

Rizzo was the target of another prank late the next afternoon, to the amusement of all. The day's fishing was done, so everyone was just sitting around when Bugsy and his friend Johnny started to throw their knives at the side of the smaller wooden building. The others quickly joined in and it became a contest, with everyone eager to show off their knife-throwing skills. Scraps of paper were attached to the wall to serve as targets, and everyone tried to hit them, or even just get their knives to stick, which most times they did not. After one hard throw, Bugsy's knife hit the wall sideways, causing the handle to split in two. Joe could tell Bugsy was embarrassed by the failure of both his knife and his throwing skill. He stood there and stared at the broken pieces on the ground, while his brothers began to tease him about the cheap Japanese knife he was carrying.

Rizzo, laughing along with the others, walked forward to retrieve the broken handle. He was about to pick up the pieces when Big Al threw a large stick of wood that hit Rizzo hard in the middle of his back. Thinking it was a knife that hit him, he screamed loudly while frantically reaching behind him to feel if he had been stabbed. After the laughter died down, Big Al was declared the winner of the match and the games ended, at least for now.

About midweek, they started running low on gas. The fifty-five-gallon drum was about three-quarters gone and would not last them for the remainder of the week. They also needed to be sure they would have enough gas for the return trip to their jumping-off point at the Indian village. After filling all the tanks, they decided that Rizzo, Joe, and Bugsy would make the trip back to refill the drum. Bugsy knew the way to the dock area where they had left from last year, and where gas was readily available. Big Al made sure Bugsy remembered where it was, and with a toothy grin, bid them all farewell. Joe didn't mind going along because it was getting boring sitting around camp listening to the same stories, which by now he knew by heart. He did wonder why they hadn't left for the lake from the same dock this year. It was another unanswered question that no one wanted to talk about.

It was near dark when they tied up at the dock. This area was much easier to find and seemed to be in better shape than the one they had left from this year to get to the lake. Again, Joe wondered why they hadn't left from here. Bugsy jumped out of the boat and hurried off to purchase the gas. A small group of Indians gathered around the boat and stared down at Rizzo and Joe, not saying anything. That seemed to be the way these Indians behaved around strangers. Joe again got an uneasy feeling, while Rizzo sat there with a slight smile on his face. Something must have happened here last year by the way everyone was acting.

Joe was relieved when he saw Bugsy retuning with a man wheeling a dolly carrying a full drum of gas. Rizzo and Joe lifted the empty drum onto the dock without any offer of help from the onlookers. They started to slowly lower the full drum into the boat when they lost their hold, causing it to drop down hard.

One of the Indians smiled and said, "You better watch out, you'll put a hole in your boat."

Well, at last one of them finally had something to say, thought Joe.

The others smiled as well as Rizzo pushed off from the dock, and Joe looked to see if they had put a hole in the bottom of the boat. As

Rizzo gunned the engine, Joe looked back to see the Indians still standing on the dock, staring at them as they sped away.

Joe had to ask, "What the hell was that all about? What happened there last year?"

Rizzo said, "Nothin'—forget about it," then started to laugh.

Bugsy stayed silent, and Joe had learned just to let it go.

As they rounded a bend out of sight of the dock area, Bugsy yelled at Rizzo to pull over to a small island just ahead. Rizzo carefully beached the boat as Bugsy jumped out onto the shore. He quickly ran up to a tree and cut the bindings holding three bear skulls. He handed the skulls to Joe, then pushed off, telling Rizzo, "Go, go, go!" Joe looked down at the skulls, wondering if they had some sacred religious purpose and would be missed, causing a general uprising among the Indians. He looked behind to see if they were being followed by a howling war party, but saw nothing, at least not yet. Bugsy asked for the skulls, looked them over, then tossed one to Joe saying, "Here, you can have this one." Joe was ready to pitch it overboard if he saw anyone following.

On the way back to their campsite, the dark sky was suddenly filled with lightning, indicating a massive storm was approaching fast. Joe wondered if they had offended some Indian spirit over the theft of the bear skulls and would now be struck down. Whatever the reason, he felt they were now in extreme danger, riding on open water with a large drum of gasoline during a lightning storm. Adding to his concern, Bugsy was holding up an oar, saying it would act as a lightning rod. Joe wasn't sure if the oar would attract a lightning strike, but knew if it did, the fireball they made would be quite impressive.

81

Joe was relieved when he saw the light from the lantern in the distance. As Rizzo beached the boat, the others came out to see how it went.

Big Al asked with a smile, "Well, did you get the gas?" as if he wasn't sure that they could.

Bugsy answered, "Yeah, no problem. The same guys weren't there."

He then showed off the bear skulls, quickly changing the subject. Joe wasn't sure how he felt about being told to go on a possible suicide mission, but at least he was safely back. He put his bear skull under his cot and tried to go to sleep, hoping no bad spirits had followed him.

The next night, Bugsy's boat got back well after dark, guided in by the lantern on the dock. As he approached the camp, Bugsy called out, "Hey, everybody, come out! You got to see this."

They all went outside and immediately looked up. They saw an incredible sight as the aurora borealis filled the entire sky. It looked like a huge, blowing curtain of different colors that stretched horizon to horizon. Everyone doused themselves with bug spray and sat on the porch to watch the spectacle. Everyone, that is, except Fat Alberto, who quietly went back inside to probably raid the food table while he had the chance. Joe sat there listening with interest to the different theories put forth as to the cause of the mysterious lights. Big Al suggested that it was reflections off the polar ice caps. Naz said it was probably light from a city somewhere reflecting off the clouds. No one pointed out that the sky was crystal clear. Then Bugsy said that he read somewhere that it had something to do with the earth's magnetic field.

Rizzo turned and scoffed, "What do magnets have to do with it?"

Big Al said, "Not magnets, you dumb shit, the magnetic field. You ever hear of that, Einstein?"

Rizzo answered, "Yeah, well I know about magnets, and magnets don't give off light."

"Yeah, Al, I guess the genius told you," laughed Naz.

Everyone else was laughing as well when Rizzo, trying to deflect the attention away from himself, turned to Joe and said, "You went to college, right? Okay, smart guy—you tell us what makes the lights."

Joe paused for a moment, not liking being put in this position with these guys. Then he thought, what the hell, he would tell them the little he knew. "Well, Bugsy's right," he said. "It's caused by radiation from the solar wind reacting with the Earth's magnetic field. The sun is a boiling ball of gas and sometimes it shoots out a huge flare into space. When the flare reaches us, it interacts with our magnetic field and the ionization causes pretty colors across the sky. The colors depend on which gases in our atmosphere the radiation reacts with."

"What kind of a bullshit answer is that?" Rizzo said. "What, did you go to college to get stupid?"

Joe thought it best not to say anything else while the others continued debating the question.

Rizzo, still not satisfied and wanting to put Joe on the spot, then asked, "Okay, you're so smart, tell me this: Where does the sun go at night?"

"What?" Joe asked, thinking he hadn't heard the question correctly.

"Yeah, the sun. It comes up in the morning, right? Then it goes down at night, right? So where does it go?"

"Are you kiddin' me?" Joe asked, starting to laugh.

He looked around at the other guys and could see their white teeth as they smiled at him in the darkness.

Rizzo asked again, "So where does it go? I thought about it a lot. It's got to go someplace."

The last thing Joe wanted to do was to make Rizzo feel stupid in front of everybody. But he couldn't believe he had asked a question like that. This was a question a three-year-old might ask, not a grown man in his thirties. Joe knew that Rizzo had been "asked" to leave school when he was seventeen and still in the eighth grade, but he had no idea of the depth of his ignorance. He was not a stupid man. He had extraordinary mechanical abilities with all kinds of things, from fixing cars to cutting off burglar alarms and opening safes. He was naturally streetwise and had survived all these years by his wits. Rizzo knew the kinds of things that cannot be taught in a school. So here Joe was, surrounded by Rizzo's family and friends, and he was supposed to tell him where the sun goes at night.

Joe finally said, "Okay, the earth is round like a ball, right? Well, the sun is a ball too, only much bigger and it's far away, about 93 million miles. The earth revolves around the sun and at the same time, it spins like a top. When it spins, the side that faces the sun is in daylight and the other side is dark like now."

"Get the hell out of here! You didn't answer my question. I want to know where it goes. It goes down at night, so where does it go? And here's another thing—what would happen if it fell?"

"If it fell?" Joe knew he wasn't going to get anywhere here, so he just shrugged and said, "Well, if it falls in the water, I guess it will go out."

"Yeah, then we'd all be fucked. That's enough of this bullshit" laughed Big Al as he got up to go inside.

The others followed him, including Rizzo, who for the time being gave up his quest for answers. Joe stayed out a while longer, looking up at the colorful sky and wondering if all of that had been a joke. He hoped it was.

The next morning began pretty much as all the others had. Naz cooked breakfast, usually oatmeal, hard-boiled eggs, and tea, while everyone else got themselves together for another day of fishing. Joe stepped outside to relieve himself off the dock, and while scanning the rear of the small cove, he thought he saw something he hadn't noticed before. Upon a closer look, he thought it resembled a boat like the ones they'd been using all week. Curious, he made his way around along the beach, fighting the brush as well as the bugs, until he saw that indeed it was a boat. It was covered over with brush and branches, but it looked to be in good shape.

Joe went back inside to report his discovery, and everyone came out to see for themselves. Naz, Rizzo, Pete, and Joe went back around the cove, removed the branches and pulled the boat out into the water. They pulled it around to the side of the dock, and while Big Al and Rizzo held it, Pete stepped in to give it a closer look. Pete said it looked pretty good and maybe they could use it somehow. No one seemed to care why the boat hadn't been noticed before now.

Then Naz picked up an oar and said, "I'll bet this boat's dry-rotted" and proceeded to punch a hole completely through the bottom, letting in a stream of water. He rapidly punched three more holes. A torrent of water filled the boat and it began to sink. Pete, unable to swim, quickly tried to get back on the dock. Big Al and Rizzo started pushing the boat away, and Naz stepped on Pete's hands as he tried to pull himself out of the sinking boat. The others were yelling and laughing as Pete was fighting for his life, finally throwing himself up onto the dock, knocking Rizzo off his feet.

Pete got up and looked really pissed as he walked off, telling them all to go fuck themselves. They all laughed at the big joke as Joe watched the boat sink beside the dock in about nine feet of water. The water being crystal clear made the boat plainly visible lying on the rocky bottom of the cove. When they returned that evening from fishing, Joe noticed the boat was still there. When he went outside the next morning, however, he was surprised to see the boat was gone. He searched the cove side of the dock, as well as the outside facing the open lake. There was no sign of the boat anywhere.

He went in to the others and announced, "The boat's gone."

Rizzo asked, "What boat?"

"The one we found yesterday, the one we sank, remember?" Joe answered.

Rizzo said, "What do you mean, it's gone? How could it be gone?" he asked as he pulled on his pants and zipped them.

"I don't know. It's not there, it's gone," answered Joe, smiling.

Rizzo asked, smiling back, "What did you do, move it?"

"Yeah, I'm going to dive down in nine feet of freezing-cold water and move a hundred-pound boat underwater to where? I'm telling you, it's nowhere around. I looked."

Rizzo followed Joe outside, convinced it was some kind of joke, but then said, "What the fuck? Where is it?"

They both went back inside to tell the others, but everyone thought they were just bullshitting around and trying to be funny. Finally, their curiosity got to them and they started coming out to see the big joke. But when they saw that the boat was gone, they began presenting different theories about what had happened. Sonny suggested that the boat was rotten and just broke up and drifted away. Naz said maybe the current pulled it out into the lake. But there wasn't any current inside the cove, and besides, how would it get through the opening under the bridge? Snake Lips suggested that Rizzo and Joe moved it somewhere and most of the others agreed. But Rizzo and Joe both knew that wasn't true. Big Al said with a grin that maybe the Indians came in the night, raised it, and pulled it away. Then he added with a laugh that maybe they hid the boat there for us to find since no one noticed it until yesterday. No one liked the idea of Indians prowling around their camp at night, but it did sound plausible when really nothing else did. They began to wonder if they were being watched the whole time they were out there. What if Indians had in fact watched them drag the hidden boat out of the brush, float it, then sink it? Not one of them had seen a single person all week, not once. Maybe those Indians were watching them right now, laughing at the stupid white men trying to figure out what happened to the boat.

Snake Lips and Bugsy still thought that Rizzo and Joe had hidden it somewhere, and they searched the area for a while before giving up. The boat was gone, and that was that. There was no easy answer for this one and they never did find out what happened, but that night all the guys brought their gear inside, even though they all remembered when Naz had said, "All the thieves are in here." The icehouse may have been full of thieves, but they were no longer certain about who might be lurking outside in the dark of night.

At the end of the week, Big Al, Naz, and Sonny came back to camp with a boatful of walleye, laughing and bragging about finding the best fishing spot on the lake. Everyone decided to follow them back there the next day. It would be their last day on the lake and a great way to end the trip. The guys couldn't believe all the fish they caught and hoped to do as well. Early the next morning, they all set out, following Big Al's boat up the lake. It was a beautiful day. The sky was deep blue, the lake was as smooth as glass, and the cool air was scented with pine. Joe noticed that they were traveling much farther up the lake than they had before, but it all still looked the same. It was so easy to get lost up here, he thought again.

In a few hours, they steered off to the right and entered a large bay dotted with many small islands. As they approached the first island, they saw a large weathered sign posted on the shore. The sign read in English and French, "Rupert River Fishing Reserve," and under that was "No Trespassing."

As they passed the sign and continued on, Joe guessed this was the boundary they had been told not to cross by the two Canadian officials a week ago. Big Al knew from previous trips that this area had a fishing fee of $100 a day, as opposed to the $10 fee on the lower lake. Without the least bit of concern, Big Al flipped the finger to the sign as they passed it by. They headed to the back of the bay and anchored off an island near a high, rocky cliff that towered above them, where two ravens were circling and croaking over their heads.

Naz then said in a loud voice, "Okay, everybody, watch this!"

He dropped his line in the water and started counting. When he reached four, he yanked his line and pulled up a good-sized walleye. "You can do this all day long," he said as he removed the hook and dropped the fish into the boat.

Everyone dropped their lines in and immediately began catching fish.

Rizzo looked over the side of the boat and said, "Oh man, look down there."

They all looked and saw hundreds of fish eyes glowing in the depths below them. They were catching so many that after an hour or so they had to take a break and rest. The ice chests were full, as were the bottoms of the boats, which they couldn't even see for all the flopping fish. They knew they would have to stop fishing, but it would be hard to do. They had never seen a place like this.

And now Rizzo showed a part of himself that would seem to be totally out of character. Given his gruff appearance and demeanor, no one would ever suspect his total aversion to touching anything the least bit slimy. Every time he caught a fish, he had the person nearest to him remove the fish from his line. Even though he was ridiculed by the others, he still couldn't bear to touch them. When the guys were posing for pictures holding the fish they caught, Rizzo would hold his by some fishing line he'd tied through its mouth and gills.

Years ago, Joe had seen firsthand how Rizzo's brothers teased him about his squeamishness. One day when they were all target shooting upstate at the sand pits, they went to visit a nearby farm whose owner they knew. The farmer was showing them around the barn area when he mentioned that he had a large wooden barrel full of trout. The brothers walked over to the barrel filled with thick, slimy water to see the fish.

Rizzo, leaning over to look, said he couldn't see any fish, and then Big Al said, "Here, take a closer look," and shoved his head into the filthy water.

Rizzo jumped back, cursing at Big Al as he tore off his shirt to wipe the slime from his face and head. He was pissed off for the rest of the day as his brothers continued laughing and joking at him. Joe had noticed many more examples of Rizzo's little quirk over the years.

They were still fishing when suddenly they heard what sounded like a small-engine aircraft approaching. When the plane was overhead, Big Al and Naz waved to it as it circled the cluster of boats a few times. After a few minutes, it flew off in the same direction it came from, and everyone thought the same thing. They just got busted. They were well inside the forbidden boundary and they got busted. Some of the guys wanted to dump the fish and get out of there.

Naz stood up with some difficulty and said, "What, have you lost your fuckin' minds? Are you serious, dump the fish? They saw us. They know we were fishing here. Dumping the fish won't make no difference. If they're gonna fine us, they're gonna fine us, fish or not."

Big Al then said he and Naz found this spot last year and nobody said a thing about it then, so fuck 'em. "So what can they do?" he added. "Fine us for one day, that's all. Nobody saw us out here yesterday. So the most they can get is a hundred bucks from us." Then he smiled and said, "I got my hundred. How about you guys?"

Joe didn't know about anybody else, but he sure as hell didn't want to hand over an extra one hundred dollars. He hadn't counted on that and wasn't even sure he had that much extra on him. It was a perfect ending to a beautiful day.

On the ride back to camp, everyone was subdued when they should have been ecstatic about the amount of fish they had caught. When they arrived, they decided to make a feast on their last night and eat as many of the fish as they could, fillet the rest, and then pack them for the trip home.

Naz and Big Al started to dismantle the smaller building so they could use the wood to build a huge bonfire. Joe learned that the building they had camped in last year suffered the same fate, which was the reason they had to find a new spot. Big Al remembered seeing this camp last year and headed straight for it, hoping it was still there and unoccupied. The fire burned well into the night, as some of the others kept feeding it until the smaller building was nearly consumed. At one-point, Big Al started doing some sort of made-up Indian war dance, stepping into and across the fire while taking a swig of whiskey from the small bottle he had smuggled across the border. It was the only time Joe saw any of them drink alcohol. Big Al then stopped to pee into the fire, and Joe realized one reason why Peggy was still married to him. The nickname "Big Al" now made sense; Joe swore the man's penis hung clear down to his knees. As the night wore on, more wood was thrown on the fire, and Joe wondered where they would stay next year if they continued to burn down their camps.

The next morning after packing everything into the four boats, they said goodbye to their idyllic, smoldering campsite and began the journey back down the lake. The big gas drum was again dumped into Rizzo and Joe's boat, but now being empty, it was not such a problem. The water was calm and they made good time, much better than their trip out a week ago. Big Al led the way, and now knowing which channels to take, they made the return trip to the dock without getting lost. Joe couldn't understand why there had been such a problem last week when they all decided to split up.

91

Upon reaching the dock, they tied up and began unloading the boats. A small group of adult Indians stood around watching them while talking and laughing among themselves.

Big Al said, "I'll bet some of those guys were clocking us the whole time we were out there."

Naz answered, "Why not? What else do these assholes got to do?"

"Fuck 'em," Big Al said. "Alright, boys, it's time to pay the piper."

It was time to pay the fishing fees for the week to the Canadian government, which would then distribute some back to the Indians whose land they were on. Big Al walked over to the small cabin where the government agent was and walked through the door. The rest of them gathered outside around the door to hear the verdict.

The uniformed official stood up from behind his desk, extended his hand to Big Al, and said, "Well, it's the Americans. Did you have a successful trip?"

Big Al answered as he shook the man's hand, "Yeah, we did. The mosquitoes were pretty bad, though."

"Yes, they are this time of year. I do hope you brought along enough repellent to ward them off? Some people can be driven mad by them if they are not prepared," the officer replied.

"Yeah, we had enough. I guess we need to settle up so we can hit the road. We have a long drive ahead of us," Big Al said, eager to get to the point.

The officer, not quite ready to end the conversation, said with a smile, "And the fishing—was the fishing good? I hope you all did well."

Big Al smiled back and said, "We did okay. We ate a lot of them during the week. But we still have some packed away to take home."

The officer stood smiling at Big Al for a moment before saying, "We had a report the other day that there were four boats fishing beyond the Rupert River boundary. We figured it might be the Americans."

Big Al decided not to deny the accusation and said, "We did see a plane circle us overhead once. We waved at it, then it flew away."

The officer replied, "Yes, they reported that you waved at them. They figured that you did not realize that you had crossed the boundary. I assume you didn't realize it or see the posted warnings."

Big Al, seeing an opening, replied, "We didn't know where we were most of the time. It's easy to get turned around out there. You know, we were lucky we found our way back here."

Still smiling, the officer said, "Well, we have decided to overlook the trespass. You do realize that the fees for fishing in that area are very much higher than for the lower section of the lake. If you decide to come here again, be sure to study the maps and heed the warning signs. But for now, the fees of ten dollars a day will apply."

Big Al gladly paid the eighty dollars due and thanked the officer with a handshake.

As he walked out the door, he wiped his forehead with his hand, saying, "Phew, alright boys, pay up and let's get the hell out of here."

They entered the cabin one at a time and each paid their eighty-dollar fee. When Joe's turn came to go in and pay, he saw that Snake Lips was still in the room lurking around. Joe watched as he walked behind the seated officer and stopped near a small metal box on a shelf next to some books and a shortwave radio. Joe continued watching him in disbelief as he carefully opened the box, which Joe could plainly see contained American and Canadian currency. Without a moment's hesitation, Snake Lips emptied the box and stuffed the bills into his pocket. Joe could not believe what he just saw. How stupid can someone be? How for a minute did he think he was going to get away with that? Snake Lips winked at Joe as he brushed by him and stepped outside.

Joe thought, well that's it, now they were all going to jail for sure. He didn't know what to do. Should he tell someone? Who should he tell? The guys would really be pissed that Snake Lips put them all in jeopardy, and Snake Lips would really be pissed at Joe for ratting him out. That guy was not right in the head and Joe didn't know what he might do. Joe also thought it was pretty low to rob this man, especially after he didn't fine them for fishing over the boundary. He really didn't know what to do.

After he paid his fee, Joe went outside and saw the snake talking and laughing with the others. A few more guys had to pay, so there was still time to do something. Then Joe saw Bugsy and Johnny coming out of a nearby storage shed, carrying an armful of axes. Rocky saw them too and ran over to get some for himself.

Big Al saw what they were doing and said, "What the hell are you guys doing? What, are you stupid? You want to get us all pinched over some fuckin' axes. Let's just finish paying up and get the hell out of here."

Joe thought, axes, hell—what if they all knew what Snake Lips just pulled off in the cabin? Joe decided he wasn't going to say anything. No one else knew what happened, so he was going to become one of them. If they were caught, they would all turn on Snake Lips anyway, but it wouldn't be Joe's doing, so he could not be blamed. In fact, Joe wanted that son of a bitch to be locked up for what he did.

As they climbed into their vehicles to leave, Joe kept looking back at the cabin, expecting the officer to come running out, pointing at the van and shouting, "Thieves, thieves, stop them!" But he never did.

They drove out of the village, then headed south on the seventy miles of dirt road to Chibougamau. The others in the van were talking and laughing about events of the past week, but all Joe could think about was what that snake-lipped bastard had done. Once the officer discovered the missing cash, all he had to do was get on the radio and send out the alarm. They would be stopped for sure at the Indian reservation checkpoint. They would be met there by carloads of police or Mounties or whatever with drawn guns, ordering them to stop. Joe would have to call his father for bail money, that is, if they even had bail in Canada. Joe looked at the others enjoying themselves, totally unaware of what was probably going to happen. It was the longest fifty miles of Joe's life.

When the checkpoint came into view, Joe was surprised to see no one waiting for them. Just the one man came out, raised the gate, and waved as they drove by. Joe could not believe the strange sort of luck these guys had. They never seemed to get caught, no matter what they did.

When they reached Chibougamau, they stopped for lunch at the same restaurant where they had eaten over a week ago, this time without incident. When they lined up to pay their bills, Snake Lips

95

winked at Joe, took his bill, and paid for his lunch. Joe still wished him dead.

After leaving the restaurant, they purchased as much ice as they could fit into the packed ice chests to cool the fish for the ride home. Joe rode in a different van this time, along with Rizzo, Naz, and Rocky. Naz drove, and Rizzo rode in the front passenger seat, while Rocky and Joe sat in the rear on the lumpy, dirty mattress covering their gear. Joe didn't know Rocky all that well, even though they had just spent the past week together, as he had mostly ridden in one of the other boats. Joe thought he was a nice enough guy, even though his son, Fat Alberto, was such a loser. Joe thought it a bit funny that they were not riding together, and wondered why Fat Alberto was again in the same van with Snake Lips. Joe realized that Rocky was right: The kid's got to learn.

This van had no windows in the back, which made it seem like a dark cave, so it was easy for Joe to doze off for a while. When he awoke, Rizzo was driving, with Naz sitting beside him, asleep. Joe had no idea what time it was or how far they had gone. Just then, Naz woke up, looked around, and asked Rizzo where they were.

Rizzo answered, "Hell, I don't know."

"What do you mean, you don't know? You're driving, ain't you?" Naz said. "Who are you following?" he asked, pointing to the van in front.

Rizzo answered, "Sonny."

"Sonny!" Naz shouted. "Do you realize you're following the stupidest man in the world? Pull over now," he said as he reached over and started beeping the horn.

Rizzo pulled onto the dirt shoulder, and the other vans followed suit. Everyone came over to find out what had happened and to get an answer to the nagging question some of them had. No one was certain they were going in the right direction, but they had faith that the man driving the lead van knew the way. Joe looked around at the desolate landscape, not seeing anything but stunted pine trees. No buildings or any other signs of civilization could be seen in any direction.

Naz and Sonny were deep in conversation that would have been funny if it wasn't so worrisome. They were lost, really lost.

Naz asked Sonny, "Where are we? What road is this? Do you have any idea where you're going?"

Sonny mumbled, "What? This is the way home."

Naz yelled back, "The way home! How the hell do you know that? You don't even know where the hell we are. I don't recognize anything around here. What was the last town we passed through?"

Sonny answered, "I don't know. I didn't see no town."

Big Al walked over while looking at a map, trying to figure out where they were, but without any point of reference, the map was useless. Big Al had been asleep as well, trusting in the others to be able to follow a map, or at least be able to retrace their route southward.

Naz said, "And the rest of you *gavones* just keep following Sonny, no matter where he goes. He could be taking us to the North Pole, for Christ's sake. What a bunch of screwups."

Rizzo didn't say anything, and neither did anyone else. They all felt pretty stupid at this point, except for Sonny. He still thought he was going in the right direction.

Off in the distance, Big Al saw a car approaching. "Don't let that son of a bitch pass us," he said. "Fan out across the road and make sure he stops. Maybe he can tell us where the fuck we are and how to get back on the right road."

Joe wondered what that guy would think when he sees a dozen big men standing across the desolate road, blocking his path. He might just panic and speed on through. Joe thought that's what he would want to do. As the car neared, Joe could see two men sitting in the front seat, and the car was slowing down. It finally stopped about thirty feet from the human shield blocking the road.

Big Al and Naz walked toward the car, telling everyone else to stay put. The driver rolled down his window and began speaking in French to the two approaching men. Big Al asked him if he spoke English, and thankfully, he did. After consulting the map and several minutes of hushed conversation, both Big Al and Naz started shaking their heads. Naz walked back to the others, still shaking his head, as he glared at Sonny, who had a wide grin on his face.

Finally, Naz said, "Well, the pathfinder here got us about seventy miles off in the wrong direction. We'll have to backtrack or continue on this road all the way to Quebec City, which is pretty damn far out of the way. Hey, Sonny, why didn't you pay attention back at Lake Saint-Jean and get on Route 155? That's the way we came up, numbnuts. You got us on Route 169, and there ain't shit on this road from here to Quebec. I hope we got enough gas to get us back. Do us all a big favor and don't drive no more."

Big Al came back over and told Sonny to find his ice chest and take out some fish to give to the two men for their help. Sonny mumbled something about how he was heading the right way as he walked off to find his cooler. Big Al gave the men the fish and thanked them again, after which they sped off in a hurry.

Big Al looked over at Sonny and said, "I thought you knew where you were going. I mean you been up here how many times now? Four, five times?"

Sonny answered that he was following the signs that said south. He knew that was the right direction.

Naz shot back, "That's not good enough, genius! You got to know the right road to take south, or we wind up like we are now, shit out of luck, miles from nowhere. We might not have enough gas to get us out of here."

"He said there was a small town called Mont-Apica, or some such shit, a few miles down the road," Big Al said, repeating what the driver of the car had told him. "It puts us further in the wrong direction, but they got a gas station there, so we can fill up and then head back the way we came. It's still a lot shorter that way than driving down to Quebec, and I sure as hell don't want to fight our way through a big city where all the signs are in French."

Some of the men rolled their eyes, while others were cursing under their breath. Sonny let out a big puff of air as they walked back to their vehicles.

After filling their gas tanks in Mont-Apica and retracing their route back to the correct roads, they finally arrived early the next morning at the United States border crossing. Their vehicles were lined up, one behind the other, as they were questioned by the border guards before being allowed entry. This time, Rizzo was driving, while Sonny sat in the passenger seat, thankfully remaining silent without emitting any blowing or puffing noises. After everyone's IDs were checked and they answered a few basic questions, they were allowed to proceed across the border. They had no trouble getting through and neither did the van behind them.

However, something triggered one of the guards to conduct a search of Bugsy's van, and he was instructed to drive over to a side lot so his van could be inspected. The others noticed this and were apprehensive about why he was selected to be searched and what might be found.

Rizzo drove on for about one hundred yards past the border station, then stopped. Big Al pulled up alongside. The brothers began to discuss whether they should wait or just drive on.

Joe was touched by the sudden concern they were showing for their detained brother. A better word might be "surprised" after witnessing the total lack of concern they had showed for one another during the past week. As Joe heard them discussing what Bugsy might have hidden away in the van that could pose a problem, he remembered that Snake Lips also was in that van. Was it possible that the money he stole back at the lake had finally been reported, along with a description of the thief? Besides the money, there were all those axes that were taken from the storage shed, and some of them were piled next to where Joe was sitting. If that was the case, wouldn't all three vans have been stopped? Joe quickly dismissed that theory, thinking it was highly unlikely that a handful of cash and a few axes taken from a remote cabin in the Canadian backcountry would be reported this far away, and then cause an international incident at the border. He laughed at himself for letting his imagination run away with him.

His confidence quickly evaporated when he saw two black vans with flashing lights bearing down on them. All conversation stopped as everyone stared at the rapidly approaching vehicles. Joe half-expected Rizzo to floor the gas pedal and take off and was very relieved when instead he cut the engine. For a moment, Joe thought he should hide the axes under some blankets, but then realized they would be found easily if the van was searched.

Here he was back in his own country, almost home, and still in danger of possibly being arrested. This trip just did not seem to end. He again decided to keep his mouth shut and take his lead from the others more experienced in these kinds of circumstances. Or maybe he should just fling open the door, make a run for the tree line, and hitchhike home. But it was too late for that. They were surrounded.

It seemed at first to be a lot worse than it was. The officers approached them because they had stopped too close to the border crossing, which looked suspicious, as if they had stopped there to pick up people who had made their way across the border undetected. Rizzo and the others probably didn't notice the "no stopping" signs posted everywhere, and if they did, they were ignored. The officers asked them all to produce identification and say their names, as they listened carefully to their accents. The officers then gave the vans a quick look to see if any other occupants were hiding inside.

Big Al explained that they stopped there to wait for their brother's van, which was being detained back at the crossing. The officers said they could not wait there and to drive on immediately. Big Al and Rizzo started the vans and drove away, leaving Bugsy and friends to their fate. Joe lay back and closed his eyes, then taking a deep breath, began to count the miles to home. Well, he thought, this was just another wacky incident among many others that had happened on this trip. After all the narrow escapes from the law and even the possibility of death, the adventure, along with the physical beauty of the place, outweighed everything. Joe felt that he would still like to make the trip again, but that was not to be.

***

As Jim drove across the George Washington Bridge and exited onto the northbound Major Deegan Expressway, the traffic flow picked up and they were now making good time. Joe would be at his mother's house in about fifteen minutes or so. Jim was still prattling on, but Joe hadn't heard a word he'd said the whole time. As they approached Joe's neighborhood, he asked Jim to drop him off at the gas station at the corner just ahead.

Jim dropped him off and said, "Let me know how it goes. I'm sure everything's alright. Do you think you'll be able to drive us in tomorrow?"

Joe answered, "Yeah, I'm sure I will. Thanks, see you tomorrow." He hoped.

Joe went inside the station and asked the owner, Tony C., if his brother Dingo was around. Tony said Dingo had cut out that morning, running out the back door like a scared rabbit when the police showed up. The cops had presented Tony with a search warrant and tore the place apart, looking for God knows what. They were there for over an hour, asking him when he last saw Rizzo and if Rizzo ever left anything there. They warned him that he'd better cooperate or risk being arrested for obstruction of justice and tampering with evidence.

"Tampering with what evidence?" Tony recalled. "I told them I didn't know what the hell this was all about and that I wasn't hiding anything."

"Do you have any idea where Dingo went?" Joe asked.

"No, I don't. Do you know what's going on? Is Dingo involved in some kind of shit? I'll kick his ass if he is," Tony said.

Joe answered, "Naw, I don't think so. Do you know what the cops were looking for?"

"They didn't say, but they were sure busy," Tony said. "I'll tell you what—they sure scared the hell out of me. I didn't know what they might find. The way my dumbass brother took off, I was really worried that he did something or was hiding something in here. That little prick could have jeopardized my business, you know? I know he does some shit with Rizzo now and then, like when he drove up in that Caddie. He wouldn't tell me how he got it, so I said, 'Well, it's your ass, not mine.'"

"Well, alright, yeah, I'll see you later," Joe said as he left.

Joe quickly crossed the street and walked the three blocks to his mother's house. He saw his car parked in front of the house and his sister's car across the street. He thought good, they were still here. Maybe now he could get some answers.

As soon as he stepped inside, Janet jumped up from the kitchen table and yelled, "Where the hell have you been? I called you almost two hours ago!"

"Hey, I got here as fast as I could!" Joe yelled back. "Traffic on that fuckin' Route 80 was backed up. What the hell is going on?"

Sandy got up and said, "Rizzo, Naz, Pete, and Bugsy were all arrested this morning. They surrounded my house at five o'clock with their fuckin' guns drawn. There were six police cars out in the street with their lights flashing. My landlady almost had a heart attack, for Christ's sake. She came out the front door with her arms up in the air screaming, 'Don't shoot, don't shoot, please don't shoot!' Rizzo told her to shut up and get her rusty twat back in the house and go lay down. Now I'm going to have to move."

Joe, almost laughing, asked, "Okay, okay, why did they arrest him?"

"Murder," she said.

"Murder! Aw, come on, murder? Joe asked.

"Remember that guy Max Santoro, who got shot at the Riverside Diner last November? The cops said they killed him," she said as she sat back down in her chair.

"They tore my whole house apart," Sandy continued. "They threw all our clothes out of the closets, emptied all the drawers, took off the mattresses, everything. They took all of Rizzo's guns and knives. And I know the bastards took some of my jewelry. If I didn't hide some money in a potted plant, they would have taken that too. They're going around to all the places Rizzo hung out, doing the same thing. I've been getting phone calls all day from people we know asking what the hell is going on. You'd better get those guns out of your house before they go there, and get the ones he's got downstairs out of here too."

"He had some guns here as well?" Looking around, Joe asked, "Where's Ma?"

"She's downstairs cutting up the guns," Sandy answered.

Joe stared at her for a moment, then rushed down to the basement to find his mother standing over her ironing board with her hair flying out in all directions, wearing two sets of eyeglasses and cutting a rifle barrel in two with a hacksaw.

"Ma, what are you doing?" Joe yelled.

She looked up at him, her eyes magnified to the size of walnuts through the double lenses she was wearing, and said, "If I cut them up they'll be easier to hide, no?"

"No, stop that, don't do that. It won't make any difference," Joe said as he stopped her and picked up the ruined rifle.

"Aw, Ma, this is a sin," he said as he looked down at the engraved, gold-plated John Wayne commemorative Winchester in his hands.

The badly scratched and marred barrel was nearly cut in two. The gun was probably worth a lot of money moments before, but was now just a piece of worthless garbage. He asked if there were any more guns down there and his mom pointed to a bench with a hinged lid. He looked inside and pulled out an automatic 12-gauge shotgun with a drum magazine. It looked like some sort of riot gun, just the thing Rizzo would have to keep for himself.

Joe asked, "Is that it? Are there any more?"

His mother answered, "I don't know. Sandy just told me about these, but never mind that. You'd better get home and get the other ones out of your house."

"How do you know about that?" Joe asked with surprise.

"That's all Sandy and Janet have been talking about all afternoon. I'm getting *agita* listening to all this. You better get moving," she said, waving Joe up the stairs.

Joe's mother was a typical Italian housewife of her time. Her concerns were her children, cooking, and keeping Joe's father in the dark about the goings-on during the day while he was at work. She would never tell her husband about the stray cats she was feeding in the basement or the baby robin that was convalescing in the small downstairs bathroom. And she surely wouldn't ever tell him what was going on there today. Joe's father worked hard all day in his welding shop, and when he got home, he was only interested in a glass of vermouth and reading the paper while he ate his dinner. He never asked her about what she did all day, and his mother didn't volunteer any news either. She would never knowingly engage in any dishonesty or criminal behavior and would never approve of her children doing so. But if they somehow found themselves involved in such a situation, she would strongly defend them publicly and then read them the riot act later on in private. She didn't fully understand what was going on concerning these guns she had just heard about, but she knew Joe had to get rid of them quickly. She also had just learned about Rizzo's possible involvement in a murder. It was all too much for one day. She would have to wait for things to quiet down before insisting on learning the whole story.

Joe took the ruined Winchester and the riot gun upstairs and told Janet to get ready to leave. He threw the two guns into the trunk of his car, went back inside, and sat down at the kitchen table.

He asked Sandy, "So, do you think they really killed that guy?"

She quickly answered, "No, they didn't kill anybody. It's all a bunch of bullshit. They just want to bust them for anything they can, that's all. The bastards have been harassing them for months. Detectives kept picking them up, asking them questions about the murder, then letting them go. They picked up Rizzo three or four times in the last couple of weeks, always the same shit, the same questions over and over again. They steal stuff, sure, but they don't kill. They had nothing to do with that murder."

Joe didn't know that Rizzo and his brothers were being grilled about the Santoro murder. There was nothing on the news about it and Rizzo and Sandy never brought it up. Joe couldn't understand how Rizzo could still be pulling off jobs while being investigated by the police. Rizzo told him the guns came from far away, and that must have made him feel that he would not be a suspect in the theft. He still took an awfully big chance, and now he had dragged Joe into it as well.

Joe got up and said to Janet, "Come on, let's go." Then he turned to Sandy and said, "So what are you going to do now?"

"I'm going home to start cleaning up the mess the cops made, then feed my kids and hope I don't see my landlady," she said.

Joe told her he would stop by later that night to see how she was doing.

Joe turned to his mother and said, "Hey, Ma, you know if the cops come here, you don't know anything, right?"

She answered, "Who, me? I don't know nothing, what do I know?"

Joe said, "Good, keep it simple."

"But I don't know what I'm supposed to tell your father when he gets home. The paper didn't come yet, and you know all this talk about murder is gonna to be in there. You know how he hates Rizzo. He still yells at me about Sandy marrying him, and I know he's gonna hit the roof when he reads about it. And if the cops ever come here, oh, *Madonn*,he's gonna break something, I know it. I got to hide the paper, that's all. I can't let him see it. I'll put it under a cushion in the living room and say the kid never delivered it," she said in a panic.

"You know he always wants that goddamn paper as soon as he gets home," Joe reminded her. "He's not going to be very happy when it's not here. You know you can't hide this from him forever—he's going to find out. What are you going to do? Hide tomorrow's paper too, and the next day? You might as well let him see it now and get it over with."

"I don't want to hear it, not tonight, not now. I got enough aggravation today already. My *agita's* getting worse," she said as she started belching. "*Uffa,* the whole neighborhood is gonna know about it anyway, but I'm still not going to show it to him. I'm just not ready. *Madonn!* I could kill that stupid Rizzo," she said as she waved Joe to the door.

"Yeah, well, don't go talking about killing anybody, okay? We've got enough of that already. I gotta go. I'll check back later on," Joe said as he left with Janet and Marie.

All the way home, Janet kept bitching about Joe getting involved and putting them all in danger by taking in those damn guns. Joe thought she had a good point, but ragging on him now wasn't going to help. He had to decide where he was going to take them, and fast. Ideas raced through his head. There were too many to take behind his apartment building and stash in the woods. His mother's house obviously was out. This was a real problem; there was no one he could really trust to help him with this. For a moment, he thought he could wait until dark and throw them in the river, but then realized the river was frozen over. That was a bad idea anyway. Someone would surely see him, and Rizzo would probably want him to pay up the ten grand he would have lost. Then in a flash he had the answer. He would drive them up to the family hunting cabin in the Catskills.

That was it! It was perfect. The cabin was on a nearly deserted road, hours away from here, and no one would be around in the middle of winter to see what he was doing. The guns would be safe and Rizzo could go collect them whenever he wanted to or whenever he could. Joe chuckled at the thought that now Rizzo would need the money for a lawyer, but then realized that wasn't at all funny. He wasn't out of this mess yet.

CHAPTER SIX — A RIDE IN THE COUNTRY

When they arrived at their apartment, Joe was relieved to see the house not surrounded by police cars. He drove down the driveway then turned around and drove back up halfway opposite his door. They lived in a three-family home owned by an elderly Italian couple who rented out the middle and ground floors. Joe was thankful, now more than ever, that they occupied the ground floor, which made it easier to come and go without being seen. The landlord kept to himself. The only time Joe saw him was when he came around for the rent.

He parked beside the door and told Janet to take Marie inside while he loaded up the guns. There was a large apartment building next door with a parking lot between it and Joe's house. Joe hoped no one would be looking out through any of the windows facing him, but then he noticed a man washing his car in the parking lot. He was using a bucket full of soapy water to wash his car in the middle of winter. Joe couldn't believe his luck. What kind of an asshole washes his car on a day like this? The man, only about twenty yards away, would have a clear view of what Joe was doing.

"Fuck it," Joe said. He couldn't wait, this had to be done. He opened the trunk of his car and went inside.

He pulled one of the sofas away from the wall, picked up three rifles, then laid them on the floor. He went to the window and glanced outside.

"That fuckin' *stugots* is still out there. Damn him. I don't have time for this shit," he said loudly.

Thinking fast, he told Janet to bring him some towels.

"What are you going to do with my towels?" she asked.

"I'm gonna have to wrap the guns in them so that asshole out there won't see what I'm putting in the trunk," Joe answered.

"You're not gonna ruin my towels!" she yelled back.

"Look, damn it, I'm not going to ruin your precious towels. If they get dirty, you can wash them, okay? Don't give me any shit. Please, not now."

Joe went into the bathroom, grabbed a towel, and began wiping down one of the rifles.

"What are you doing now? You're rubbing grease all over my towel!" Janet yelled.

Joe said, "My fingerprints are all over these things. I got to wipe them off. Go get me a pair of gloves and don't touch any of these."

Janet answered, "Oh, don't worry, I'm not touching anything. And get your own fucking gloves!" She went into the bedroom with Marie and slammed the door.

The last thing Joe needed now was a fight with his wife. He called out, "Look, we have to get these damn things out of here, so give me some help, alright? Or maybe we should just sit here and wait until your old man shows up, how about that? Now, please get me some more towels. We have to hurry."

She came out of the bedroom, went over to the linen closet, grabbed an armload of towels, and dropped them on the floor, saying, "Just hurry up."

"Brilliant," Joe thought. That's what he'd been trying to do since she called him at work.

He retrieved his gloves from the bedroom closet, then picking up a towel, furiously wiped each rifle as he laid them on the floor. He wrapped up five in a bundle and walked out to his car, carrying them in his arms. He dropped them into the open trunk, then glanced over to see if the car washer was still there. He was, and he was looking right at Joe. The man gave Joe a small wave, stared at him for a moment, then went back to washing his car. Joe ignored him, turned and went back in for another load, surprised to see that Janet was actually wiping off a rifle.

"Good," he said. "If we work together, we can get it done a lot faster."

She said, "You know, I really hate you for this. I can't believe this is happening. I can't believe this," and then she started to cry.

There was no time to console her, not now. He wrapped up another bundle and went out to dump it into the trunk. While he was relieved to see that the car washer was gone, he suddenly realized he had a major problem. The trunk of his Volvo was not going to be big enough to handle the load. Joe hadn't given that a thought. He had just visualized all the guns in the trunk as they drove away. He had only twelve in there and over sixty were left to fit in somehow. He went back inside, and the reality hit him as he saw the huge pile in the middle of the living room floor. Janet had been pulling them out from their hiding places and wiping them off. Well, at least she had stopped crying and was helping him. He said nothing as he wrapped up five more rifles.

After three more trips, the trunk was full, and that was less than half of them. After closing the trunk, he started to lay them on the floor of

112

the car and then continued, stacking them on the back seat. He kept wondering if anybody was observing his suspicious behavior as he went in and out of his apartment carrying the heavy bundles into his car. But he was certain that no one could possibly know what was in those bundles. When they all were finally loaded, the wrapped-up rifles reached the level of the rear windows. Joe then covered the guns as best he could with bed sheets and blankets. Quickly, he went inside and told Janet to get herself and Marie ready to leave.

Janet asked, "Why do we have to leave?"

Joe answered, "I don't know, but I think it would be better if we all left together. Just in case we get stopped, it will look better if you two were in the car and not just me."

"Oh, sure, then we all get arrested, right? And where are we going, anyway?"

"We're not going to get arrested, okay? With you and Marie in the car, no one is going to suspect anything. I thought a lot about where to take them and decided the best place would be the cabin."

"The cabin! That's three hours from here!" she exclaimed.

"I know how far it is, that's why I want to go there. It's far away from here and nobody's up there this time of year. We'll take it nice and easy, drop these things off, grab some dinner, and come home. No problem," Joe said.

"Yeah, no problem," Janet said sarcastically. "What time are we going to get back?"

"I don't know. It will be late," Joe said as he looked out the window. "The sooner we get going, the sooner we get back, so come on, let's go."

Joe would never admit it, but he wanted Janet with him for another reason as well. He didn't trust her to keep her cool if the cops did show up and start to question her. He knew she would crack and spill out the whole story. It was better they stay together.

When Joe entered the car, he could feel the extra weight, and hoped his little Volvo could handle the strain. Janet and Marie got in, and Joe said to put Marie in the back, seated on top of the pile of guns. Her head just cleared the roof of the car, but the thickness of the blankets made her comfortable enough. Joe thought that with a little girl and a pregnant wife along, they would look innocent if they were stopped by the police.

Joe had no idea how prophetic that thought would prove to be.

***

As Joe pulled out of the driveway, he felt the car bottom out and scrape the pavement at the entrance to the street. With the car riding that low, it would be obvious to anyone that they were carrying a heavy load. Joe just hoped that some cop wouldn't notice and become curious enough to stop them.

Joe headed for the Thruway, thinking that would be the fastest route upstate, but then he remembered always seeing state troopers patrolling back and forth, looking for speeders. He decided to take the older, less-traveled roads that had been the main routes before the Thruway was built. It would take a little longer, but might prove to be the safer choice. They all rode along in silence.

Joe thought about the last time he was at the cabin, during deer hunting season last November. It was just after the Santoro murder, which, of course, was the main topic of conversation. Everyone there tried to guess what had happened and who might be responsible. Besides Rizzo and his brothers, seven or eight other guys were there, most of whom Joe did not know. Some were just spending the weekend, while others would be there for the entire week. Bugsy brought a friend along, but the two of them didn't have a lot to say and pretty much stayed by themselves. Joe remembered a few of the guys from the Canada trip and was glad that Snake Lips was not among them.

After hunting all day, most went to town for supper, while the rest cooked something simple and ate in the cabin. Again, there was a total absence of alcohol of any kind. They drank tea or coffee, all of them. Joe brought along a six pack of beer, but was mocked and ridiculed to the point that he left it in his car. They made comments like, "What are you, some kind of rummy? Don't you know that alcohol and gunpowder don't mix?"

Joe didn't think a couple of beers would pose a problem, but it sure did with this crowd. After supper, the boys talked, joked, or played cards, but the conversations always returned to the Santoro murder. Rizzo and his brothers denied any knowledge of it, and guessed along with the others about who the killers were and what the motive was. At the time, Joe had no reason to suspect they were involved, and even now he was finding it hard to believe. After spending so much time with them, he really felt that these guys weren't killers. Burglars for sure, but not killers. But then again, indictments had been handed down, so the cops must have something on them. Joe was somewhat relieved that Rizzo's arrest was not over the load of guns he was carrying. For the first time today since that phone call, he was starting to relax a little.

115

They pulled over at a small gas station to fill up and let the girls use the restroom. There he again noticed how low the overloaded car was riding. Soon they would be approaching the mountains, and Joe worried the car might have trouble making the grade. They also would be getting on the interstate for a few miles to make the connection to Route 24. Joe hadn't spotted any police so far, and he was sure not to speed and to make a full stop where required. Route 24 was a single-lane country road winding its way through the mountains. It might pose a problem for Joe's four-cylinder overloaded Volvo, but he had no choice. It was the only route he knew.

When they reached the entrance ramp to the Thruway, Joe floored the accelerator pedal to get the car up to speed to merge into traffic. He stayed in the right lane and cruised along for the twenty or so miles to the next exit. He gave out a sigh of relief as he put on his blinkers to exit the interstate. While making the long, wide turn on the exit ramp to Route 24, he saw him.

The car was sitting in a gas station at the end of the ramp. Joe would have to pass right in front of it. He slowed down as he merged onto Route 24 and looked straight ahead as he passed the state trooper. He glanced over at Janet, but she apparently didn't notice the cop. He was glad for that. If she had seen him, she probably would have stared at him with deer-in-the-headlights eyes and then he would have grown suspicious and stopped them for sure. Joe kept driving, careful not to exceed the speed limit, all the while looking in the rearview mirror. He started to get a little nervous when the trooper pulled onto the road about one hundred yards behind him. He started to sweat when he saw the trooper put his hat on his head. He almost vomited when the flashing lights came on. They were being pulled over.

Joe told Janet they were being pulled over. She looked at him and said, "What!"

Joe had been pulled over before. He had gotten a few speeding tickets over the years, especially when he was riding his motorcycle. That bike had been stolen some years back, which probably saved Joe's life. He found that he was a little too reckless on that bike. After a few spills, the last of which resulted in two cracked ribs and a few missing teeth, he began to lose interest in riding. So when the bike was stolen, he wasn't all that upset. Although he maintained his motorcycle license, he had no desire to purchase another one. Whenever he was pulled over in the past, mainly for speeding, he always maintained his cool. He never argued with the cop and always remained polite. This time, however, he was so nervous, he was about to shit his pants.

He said again that they were being pulled over, and told Janet to just sit there and not say anything.

She started to shake and said, "Oh, my God. Oh, my God, what are we going to do?"

"I'm going to pull over, what do you think? I'm not going to try and outrun him, that's for sure. Just sit there and don't say a word, you hear me? Not a fuckin' word!"

Joe turned around and saw Marie sitting on the pile of guns, licking a lollipop and smiling back at him. He thought, what have I done? My whole family is screwed. Joe resigned himself to being caught, and then a strange, sudden peace washed over him. He almost wanted to burst out laughing over the ridiculousness of the whole situation, but he didn't. This was serious, really serious. This whole day seemed like one big nightmare, and this just topped it off.

Joe pulled over with the trooper directly behind him. He turned off the ignition and quickly got out of the car. He wanted to keep the trooper as far away from the car as he could, so he walked back toward the approaching officer. The trooper brushed past him and walked to the front of Joe's car, looking at the windshield. That's when Joe realized why he had been pulled over. The inspection sticker on the windshield was expired. He'd had the car inspected the week before, but neglected to put on the new sticker, and now that oversight had gotten him into some real trouble. Joe was never one to comply with the letter of the law, and usually had his cars inspected after the due date, which in his case was the last day of January. It had never been a problem before. It really was no big deal, at least not until today, not until this screwed-up day.

Not believing his bad luck and trying to remain calm, he said, "Oh, yeah, my inspection sticker is expired. I just forgot to put the new one on. I have the new one at home. I promise I'll put it on tomorrow."

The officer coolly responded, "Well, that's fine, but you are getting a ticket today."

Joe said nothing as the officer walked over to the driver's-side door and asked to see Joe's license, registration, and insurance card. Joe opened the door while reaching for his driver's license and asked Janet to get the other documents out of the glove compartment. She was as white as a ghost, and her hands were visibly shaking as she opened the glove box and reached inside. Her hands shook so badly that the entire contents of the glove box spilled onto the floor of the car. My God, what the hell are you doing? Get a grip on yourself, Joe thought. He reached into the car, found the documents among the spilled litter, and handed them to the officer. His wife just sat there, staring straight ahead as if she were catatonic.

"This insurance card is expired as well," the officer said.

Without a moment's hesitation, Joe replied, "Oh, yeah, that's at home next to the inspection sticker, really it is. I had them both together to put on the car, but I just forgot."

Joe thought that sounded pretty lame, and he could not believe how stupid he was not to remember to take care of this. It was true he had them both at home, but this time his negligence just might have cost him his freedom.

The officer asked, "Are you sure you have insurance on this vehicle?"

Joe insisted that he did and invited the officer to call his insurance company to verify the fact, not knowing if he was going too far. He knew that cops were used to hearing every kind of excuse imaginable, so when Joe said he forgot the documents, he knew it wouldn't go over well.

The officer glanced into the car at Janet and said, "Your wife seems a little nervous."

Joe answered, "She always gets nervous if we get pulled over. Her father's a cop and she's afraid he will find out."

Glancing in the car again, he asked, "What do you have in there?"

There was the question Joe was waiting for and hoping he wouldn't get. At this point, Joe thought he was caught and there was nothing he could do but face the inevitable. He didn't care anymore. He had been scared all day since he got that damn phone call from Janet, and now it was over. He was standing in front of a firing squad and almost glad.

Without thinking, he blurted out, "My father owns a welding shop and I'm taking some scrap metal up to a friend of mine in Woodstock. He's an artist and welds the metal into sculptures."

Joe didn't have a plan for what to say if he was stopped and asked about the heavy load he was carrying. He didn't think he would be stopped. He had never considered it, never even thought that far ahead. He just wanted to get rid of these guns and go home.

The officer glanced into the car again. He looked at Marie licking her lollipop, and then over at Joe's pregnant wife, before walking back to his patrol car.

Joe stood there on the side of the road, watched the cop get into his car and wondered what he was going to do. Would he call for backup, or call to have Joe's car impounded because he had no proof of insurance? He glanced over at Janet, who remained staring ahead, wide-eyed in her catatonic state, no help at all. The cop was seated in his car, looking down like he was writing something, and for a moment Joe thought he might get off with just a ticket or two. Could he be that lucky? Was that possible? Did that silly scrap metal story really work? Or was this cop about to get lucky and bust a major gunrunner and probably get a promotion? Joe looked into the back of the car, and to his dismay, he could plainly see some of the gun barrels sticking out from under the blankets and sheets. He wondered how the cop could have missed that. How could he have not seen them? He now thought there was no way he was going to get away with this.

The officer got out of his car and walked over to Joe, looking him straight in the eye. He handed him two citations.

"These are for no proof of insurance and an expired inspection sticker," he said, still looking Joe in the eye. "Get these things taken care of tomorrow."

Joe answered that he definitely would and thanked the officer, then immediately regretted the impulse. Not wanting to say anything else that might make the officer suspicious, he quickly got back into the car. Joe sat there watching the officer as he smiled at Marie and then walked back to his patrol car. Janet was still looking straight ahead as she asked, "Is he gone?"

Joe looked in his rearview mirror and answered, "Not yet, he just got back into his car. He's sitting in there looking down, like he's writing something."

"Let's go, let's go," Janet said, still not moving a muscle.

Joe agreed and turned the key in the ignition. The engine turned over, but didn't start. Joe tried it again with the same result. He tried a third time, and still the engine wouldn't start.

Janet said loudly, "What's wrong? Why won't it start? What are you doing? I want to leave now."

Joe answered, "I don't know why it won't start. This is fucking unbelievable. Come on, you fucking piece of shit, start!"

Joe was having some trouble with the SU carburetors lately, but he thought he had fixed the problem. He couldn't believe this was happening. If the car wouldn't start, then what would he do? He looked in the rearview mirror and saw the officer was now looking at them. Joe prayed to God to please let the car start. He tried it again and the car sputtered to life. He revved the engine a few times and dropped it into gear. Looking in his rearview mirror, he slowly pulled onto the road. As he drove away, he kept his eye on the trooper as he also pulled out onto the road behind them.

CHAPTER SEVEN—A HUNTER'S PARADISE

As Joe drove on, he thought back to the first time Rizzo had invited him to go deer hunting with his brothers at the family cabin. It was Thanksgiving weekend and the beginning of deer season. The upstate area they hunted was remote and very mountainous. The cabin was a small wooden structure with a main room, a small kitchen to one side, a bathroom, and a back room with four sets of bunk beds. The only source of heat was a fireplace in the main room. The bathroom had a sink, toilet, and a shower stall that was being used as a storage space. Hanging on the walls of the main room were nearly a dozen mounted deer heads attached to wooden plaques. Written neatly on each plaque in white paint was the name of the hunter, the caliber of bullet used, and the location of the kill. A pullout sofa that opened to a double bed, assorted chairs, a large round table, and a few lamps comprised the furnishings.

It was a rustic setting that Joe always enjoyed visiting, but that time it was very different. All of Rizzo's brothers were there, along with a host of invited friends, which filled the cabin to capacity. The double bed was claimed by Big Al and Naz, while the other brothers and friends filled the eight bunk beds. The remaining guests slept in sleeping bags on the floor. Joe felt privileged to have one of the bunk beds.

In what seemed like the middle of the night, Joe was startled awake by the loud clanging of two metal pots being banged together along with Naz yelling, "Okay, ladies, it's time to get up. Everybody up!"

Joe checked his watch and saw that it was 4:00 a.m. He thought, why the hell did they have to get up so early? Big Al already had coffee made as the others stumbled out of the bunk room and stepped over the scattered sleeping bags on the floor. Rizzo's brothers dressed quickly, while some of the others lay about, and a few even went back to sleep. Joe thought it would be great to go back to sleep, but he followed Rizzo's lead and got dressed.

Joe collected his gear and his rifle, then grabbed a half-cup of coffee and joined Rizzo outside. The early-morning sky was full of stars and the air was bitterly cold. Joe followed Rizzo and his brothers to a battered, old Jeep wagon they kept on the property. The license plates had expired many years ago, and there was no insurance on it, but they kept it here as an off-road vehicle for driving up mountain trails and across rocky, fast-moving streams. It was full of rust and dents from hitting many trees and boulders over the years, but Rizzo kept the engine fine-tuned.

Everyone piled in as Rizzo started the engine to let it warm up a bit before they headed out. It was very crowded and overloaded with six men and all their gear and rifles. Joe wondered if it could move at all, let alone climb a steep mountain trail. The others in the cabin would find their own way and hunt where they wanted, if they hunted at all. Joe learned later that some of them just wanted to get away from their wives for the weekend and didn't give a crap about hunting. They would stay in the warm cabin until the restaurants in town opened, where they would spend most of the day.

Rizzo drove the Jeep down to the county road and continued for about five miles before turning off onto a dirt road leading into the woods and up a mountain. Joe tried to pay attention to the way they came, but it was still too dark to see much of anything. There wasn't much talking during the ride, just a few comments about one of the guys sleeping on the floor, whom none of the brothers seemed to know. They all laughed about how anyone could have come in and gone to sleep unnoticed in that crowd. Then Big Al made a comment on how clear the sky was and the number of stars that were visible. Rizzo said that it was easy to see the North Star up here because it was the brightest one.

"Actually, the North Star isn't the brightest star in the sky," Joe said.

Rizzo quickly said, "Bullshit! If that's not the brightest one, then which one is it, smart guy?"

"It's called Sirius, It's in the constellation Canis Major.

Rizzo laughed, then said, "Sirius? You get serious. You're so full of shit. Canis who? I never heard such bullshit. So where is this serious star?"

The other occupants of the Jeep were agreeing with Rizzo that the North Star is the brightest one in the sky.

Joe, sorry now that he ever brought it up, answered, "You can't always see it. It depends on the time of year."

Everyone laughed along as Rizzo said, "Oh, it depends on the time of year. I get it. I think it's time you got some brains."

Joe was ready to let it drop, so he said nothing. Rizzo's attention was back on his driving as the Jeep bounced and slid up the narrow trail, almost getting stuck more than once. Rizzo, while not knowing anything about astronomy, was adept at driving in this type of terrain after having done it for years. No one complained about the bumpy ride.

After about forty-five minutes, the trail ended and the Jeep stopped.

Rizzo announced, "Okay, this is it. This is where we get out."

Big Al answered, "It's still early and I'm not ready to start freezing my ass out there yet."

The others agreed, so they decided to sit in the warm Jeep awhile longer. About a half hour had gone by when they heard a loud, shrill cry come from somewhere nearby.

"What the fuck was that?" asked Naz.

Everyone remained silent for a moment, then they all started to feverishly load their guns. Bullets were dropping all over the Jeep as they fumbled in the darkness.

Finally, Sonny said, "It sounded like a woman."

"What the fuck is some twat doing up here in the middle of the night? Are you stupid, or what?" answered Naz.

Big Al said, "Well, it did sound like a broad, but I don't think that was it. It might be an owl."

"I never heard no owl scream like that," Rizzo said.

"Screech owls scream like that," answered Big Al, "but that sounded like it came from something big."

"It might be Bigfoot," Pete said in a low, soft voice. "I heard some people spotted them in these mountains."

"What the fuck is Bigfoot doing around here? That was no Bigfoot," Naz said.

"How the hell do you know? What do you think it was?" said Big Al.

"Bigfoot? What's a bigfoot?" asked Rizzo, then added that maybe it was just a dog.

"A dog! You think that was a dog," Big Al shot back. "What the fuck is wrong with you, you ever hear a dog scream like that? Are you *stunad*, or what? That was no fuckin' dog."

The conversation continued as they sat in the Jeep, looking out the windows while cradling their rifles. Joe said nothing, but sat there quietly remembering an incident from the previous summer when Rizzo, Sandy, Janet, and he were at the cabin, and one night something very strange happened. Rizzo and Sandy were sleeping on the pullout bed while Janet and Joe shared one of the bunks in the back room. During the night, Janet was awakened by a noise coming from the other room. She raised her head and saw in the bedroom doorway a short, brown, hairy creature staring at her. She said it had yellow eyes. Terrified, she laid her head back down, then after a few moments, looked up again. It was still there, not moving, just staring at her. She closed her eyes, too scared to move or yell out. When she got the courage to look again, it was gone. She was still too scared to wake Joe, who was sleeping beside her, so she just lay there until she fell asleep.

In the morning, they found the door to the cabin wide open, and one of the heavy Adirondack chairs in the front room was turned over. Rizzo was skeptical of Janet's story, but Joe and Sandy were not so fast to dismiss what she said she saw. After all, they couldn't explain the overturned chair or the open door.

The conversation in the Jeep went on about what could have caused the scream. They waited to hear it again, but didn't. As the sky began to lighten, they decided to do what they came to do. Stepping out of the warm Jeep into the cold morning air, they split up, each one going off in a different direction to hunt. They planned to meet up back at the

Jeep in late afternoon before dark and ride back together. Rizzo said he would stay back to turn the Jeep around to get it ready for the return trip.

Joe wasn't too happy about walking off alone, but he knew the ridicule he would suffer if he made that known to this crew. He slowly picked his way through the dense woods in the gathering light until he found what he was looking for. He spotted a large cliff face with a ledge large enough for him to comfortably sit with his back to the cliff wall. He pulled up dead branches and brush to cover him in front. He felt he was well hidden and decided to stay there until the night jitters left. He sat there thinking about Bigfoot and the cold, deciding maybe he might stay there all day.

He heard the woods slowly come alive with the sunrise. Birds, squirrels, and other small creatures moved about, rustling the leafy forest floor. The rising sun did little to warm the air as the hours slowly passed without any sign of deer. Joe sat there shivering until he decided it was time to leave his safe haven and brave the wild forest. At least if he moved around, he might warm up a bit. As he got up, several deer jumped up near him and ran off in different directions with their tails flashing. They were no more than twenty yards away from him the whole time. He was angry with himself for not being more alert and realized that he must have dozed off for a while. Checking his watch, he saw it was a little past three o'clock, so he decided to slowly walk back in the direction of the waiting Jeep. Maybe he would come across those deer again and get a chance at a shot. About hour later, he was at the spot where the Jeep had been parked, but it wasn't there. He was sure this was the spot. He saw the tire tracks in the mud where Rizzo had turned the Jeep around. This was about the time when they all were supposed to meet up and ride back, so he sat down to wait for the others.

The sun was getting low and Joe knew darkness would soon follow. He reluctantly faced the fact that the Jeep must have already left and was not coming back. They had left without him. He had no choice but to walk back on his own. He didn't know if they had called to him or beeped the horn or just said fuck it, he's not here, so let's go. He felt that's exactly what they had done. He was learning fast that they would not wait long for anyone. You were on your own with this bunch. He decided that when he got back, he wouldn't bitch or say anything about being left on the mountain many miles away from the cabin. It wouldn't do any good anyway. They would just ridicule him and call him a pussy or some such thing. No, sir, he wouldn't give them the satisfaction.

He held his rifle at the ready as he began the long walk down the trail to the road. He thought about the scream they had all heard that morning and half-expected to see Bigfoot come out from behind a tree. He quickened his pace and kept alert as he followed the trail in the diminishing daylight. Soon he was no longer able to follow the narrow trail. It was lost in the darkness. He realized that when he found himself tangled up in a patch of saw briars. He knew the general direction of the cabin from where he was, so he decided to travel in a straight line and cut through the woods to the county road. Once on the road, it would be an easy walk back. As he slowly picked his way through underbrush, over fallen trees, and down rock ledges, he was getting madder and madder at that bunch of inconsiderate assholes for leaving him. What if he had gotten hurt, or broke his leg or something? He would be on the mountain all night and who knows when they would come back tomorrow, if they did at all. He had visions of walking into the cabin and opening fire on the lot of them and seeing if they would laugh then as they flopped around on the floor with .44 Magnum bullets in their guts.

Just as he was grinning at the thought, he walked into a fast-running stream of icy cold water. The shock brought him back to reality, and he jumped out of the water onto a large rock. The stream was fast and wide. He knew he would have to cross it and would get good and wet when he did. He damned himself for daydreaming and not paying better attention to his surroundings. Instead of getting even madder, he started to laugh at his situation. He stepped off the rock into water above his knees and slowly walked across the stream. After crossing, he briskly walked through the underbrush and a few additional smaller streams, more determined than ever to reach the road. He knew he finally made it when through the trees, he saw the headlights of a car driving past about fifty yards ahead. He couldn't see the road until he was almost on it, but by God, he made it. He shouldered his rifle and briskly walked the remaining few miles to the cabin.

He entered the warm, crowded cabin without a word being said by anyone except Rizzo, who asked, "Where you been? We thought you got a deer and was dragging it back."

Joe looked him in the eye and asked, "Where have I been? Where the hell were you? I thought we were all supposed to ride back together."

Naz laughed and said, "Ride back together with who? That pussy Rizzo left as soon as we were all out of sight. He spent the day at the restaurant with these other great American sportsmen."

Rizzo said in his defense, "Fuck you, I was startin' to get sick and I ain't gonna sit my ass down on some cold rock and get worse."

Naz laughingly answered, "Sick, my ass. You never spent more than ten minutes in the woods in your life. How many deer have you ever shot up here? Look around, I don't see none."

It was true, thought Joe. None of the deer trophies had Rizzo's name on them. Some of the others laughed along with Naz while Rizzo tried to change the subject. Joe decided to drop the whole thing and say nothing more. That episode should have prevented Joe from going back to the cabin for another deer season. But it didn't matter. He wasn't going to let them beat him.

***

The state trooper was still following behind Joe, which gave him the sickening feeling that this wasn't over yet. He expected to see the flashing lights come back on at any moment. Janet kept asking, "Is he still there? Is he still there?"

"Fuck yeah, he's still there," answered Joe with his eyes glued to the rearview mirror. "Don't turn around, just keep looking straight ahead."

Careful not to exceed the speed limit, Joe drove on, with the trooper following about fifty yards behind. His anxiety level rose higher when they passed a sign stating that Woodstock was only a few miles ahead. He knew he would have to take the exit and drive into the town. He wondered if the trooper was going to follow him to his supposed friend's house to drop off the scrap iron he was hauling. Joe thought for sure that's what the cop was doing. He was going to verify Joe's story, and only then would he be satisfied. Joe racked his brain feverishly, trying to remember if he knew anyone in that town, but came up empty. He didn't know a single soul there. He thought maybe he should just pick a house, go to the door, and ask whoever answered some bullshit question just to buy time. He could act like his friend was not there at the moment and he would have to come back later. He could say they had to get a motel room for the night and meet with the friend tomorrow. Would that satisfy the cop, maybe? But what if it didn't?

Joe's panicked planning came to an abrupt end when he saw the trooper's car slow down and begin to turn around.

"Okay, okay, he's turning around," he said. "Yeah, he's turning around."

"Is he really?" asked Janet as she turned to see.

The trooper's car was indeed driving back the way they had come. Joe continued to watch it until it disappeared around a curve. As they drove past the Woodstock exit, they let out a sigh of relief for their good fortune.

It was almost dark when they arrived at the little town of Mount Tremper. The cabin was a few miles from town on a narrow, winding road leading up the mountain. The snow had been cleared off the mountain road, but it was still somewhat slippery. Joe was relieved to see the cabins they passed were dark and appeared to be unoccupied. As he suspected, the steep driveway leading up to the family cabin had not been plowed, which forced him to stop on the road below. He would have to climb up a steep bank through deep snow to reach the cabin, but that was the only way. Joe told Janet to stay in the car while he climbed the bank to check things out. Of course, the cabin was locked up tight, so Joe looked around to see if there was a good place to hide the guns. There was a small, three-sided shed where firewood was stored, but that wouldn't do. He next looked at the crawl space under the cabin. It was free of snow and he thought that might be a good spot. He descended the hill back to the car and told Janet what he was going to do.

She asked, "What do you want me to do?"

Joe answered, "Nothing, just stay in here with Marie. I'll be as fast as I can so we can get the hell out of here."

Joe shut off the headlights, but kept the engine running to keep the heat on. It was bitterly cold and very dark. He opened the trunk and picked up four rifles, then began to climb the hill. He immediately realized that it was going to be a lot harder than he thought, as he kept slipping and falling carrying the awkward load. Already out of breath, he reached the top with the first load. Cursing to himself, he walked to the side wall of the cabin and dropped the guns in the snow. He picked up one of the guns, a very nice old Winchester, and threw it under the cabin. It caught on a rock and dropped only a few feet away from him. He realized it would be near impossible to hide the rest under there, so there was only one thing left to do.

Joe walked around to the front of the cabin with one of the guns and smashed the window near the front door. He picked away the broken glass from the window frame, then climbed inside. It was colder in there than it was outside, and pitch black. He dared not turn on a light, but fumbled to unlock the door and push it open against the snow. He went outside, picked up the other three rifles, threw them inside, then slid back down the hill.

He picked up four more guns and began his climb once again. Oh, how he wished he had some help; this was going to kill him. Breathing heavily, he reached the cabin door and dropped the guns inside. He knew he couldn't just pile them all by the door, so he planned to bring his flashlight on his return trip and look for places to hide them. Back with another load, he went inside with the flashlight and walked over to the pullout bed. He pulled it away from the wall enough to fit what he had already brought up, then looked around for other hiding places. The only suitable place he found were the bunk beds in the back room. Some of the beds had foam pads, but most of them were bare wood. No matter, the guns would be safe back there and at this point, he really didn't care what happened to them.

He made many more trips up that hill, taking frequent rest stops to catch his breath. He felt his heart pounding in his chest and his legs burned with exhaustion, but he had to keep going. He didn't ask Janet for help, because she was pregnant and anyway, she would probably just bitch at him some more. He didn't want to hear it. When he carried up the last load, he was near collapse. He dropped the guns in the back room, shut the front door, and lay in the snow on his back for a few minutes, staring up at the night sky. They were gone, out of his hands. He didn't even keep the ones he had wanted so badly. He never wanted to see any of them again. All he wanted to do now was go home.

They left the area as quickly as possible, driving back the way they came. Joe hoped the trooper would be gone as they approached the spot where he had been pulled over a few hours before. To Joe's relief, there was no sign of him as they entered the ramp to the southbound Thruway. They drove in silence to the next exit, where Joe decided to get off and stop somewhere for something to eat. They ate quickly, not saying much to each other. Marie was getting tired and cranky, so they hurried back to the car and continued heading south toward home.

After a while, Joe smiled and turned to look at Janet. Trying to lighten the mood, he said, "Oh, by the way, happy Valentine's Day."

Silence.

***

Joe decided to stop by his sister's house before going back to his apartment. He wanted some answers about all that had happened, and he also wanted to tell Sandy where he took the guns.

When Sandy answered the door, the first words out of her mouth were, "Where've you been? I've been trying to call you for hours. Where did you go?"

Joe answered, "I had to get rid of the guns, remember? I didn't know what to do with them, so I brought them up to the cabin and hid them there."

Sandy's face turned as white as the snow outside. She stared at him for a long moment, then yelled, "Why the hell did you take them there?"

"Why not?" answered Joe. "It was the safest place I could think of."

"Didn't Rizzo tell you where he got them?" Sandy said, still shouting.

Joe said, "All he told me was that they came from someplace far away, and not to worry about it."

Sandy shot back, "Yeah, that place is Mount Tremper. Mount Tremper is where the gun store they robbed is. I can't believe you took them back there. Oh, my God, I can't wait to hear what Rizzo is going to say when he finds out where you took them."

The anger was building in Joe as he thought about all the crap he went through that day, and he was in no mood to be yelled at by anyone, especially his younger sister.

Joe hissed, "Do you have any idea what I went through today ever since I got that fuckin' phone call about Rizzo getting arrested? I had to lie to my boss about leaving work, load all those fuckin' guns in my car, drive around looking for a place to dump 'em, drive upstate, almost get busted by the cops, and then almost get a heart attack getting them into the cabin! Rizzo didn't tell me they were from up there. How the hell was I supposed to know that's where he robbed 'em!"

Sandy sat down at the kitchen table with her head in her hands and said, "You know, that's not even what the cops were looking for. They don't know shit about those guns. They were looking for the murder weapon used to kill that bastard Santoro."

"You got to be shittin' me," Joe said. "They didn't know about those guns. I did all that for nothing. I almost got arrested. All of us almost got arrested. Shit, it was just pure luck that I'm not in jail right now."

Janet added, "I would be there with you, don't forget, and Marie too. Oh, my God."

Janet relayed to Sandy what had happened on their little trip upstate while Joe just sat there staring at the wall.

It was getting late and they all were pretty upset and very tired. Joe's clothes were still damp from sliding up and down in the snow, Janet and Marie were exhausted, and Sandy's apartment was still a wreck from the police search that morning. They decided that enough was enough for one day. Joe took his family home.

The next morning, he felt like the previous day had been only a bad dream, a very bad dream. He was actually eager to get back to his normal, dull routine. It was Joe's turn to drive to work, so he picked up his boss for their commute to New Jersey. He wanted to forget yesterday and put the whole episode out of his mind. Somehow, he had gotten through it, he was safe, everything was now back to normal. He didn't even want to think about Rizzo being locked up in jail. He had been so scared yesterday that the nervousness still hadn't left him, and he wasn't sure it ever would. Against his will, he kept playing it back in

136

his mind over and over. How did he escape that cop who pulled him over? How did the cop not see what was in the car? Joe could not believe his luck. As they crossed the George Washington Bridge, he looked around and thought what a beautiful day it was.

Jim kept asking him about Rizzo's arrest. It had made the headlines in yesterday's paper and Jim was curious to hear what Joe thought about his brother-in-law. Joe said he didn't really know anything, but his sister had assured him that they were completely innocent. He added that he had been at the doctor's office with Janet after he got home and didn't hear about the arrest until later that night.

Jim said, "Man, they were arrested for murder, that's serious stuff. Would they do anything like that?"

Joe answered, "Naw, they're not like that. I don't know why they're being accused of murder. It has to be some kind of mix-up. It'll get straightened out."

Joe hoped that would be the end of it and changed the subject, talking about Janet's fictitious doctor visit.

***

After an uneventful day at work, Joe returned home to learn that they were invited to Janet's parents' house for supper. That was the last place Joe wanted to go, but after yesterday's events, he knew he'd better not refuse. Joe asked his wife if her father would be there, saying that it might be a little uncomfortable after Rizzo's arrest the day before.

Janet answered, "We're going to have to face him sooner or later about this, so it might as well be now. Besides, he'll probably be in a good mood. He finally got what he wanted."

"Yeah, he got what he wanted, but that doesn't mean he'll be in a good mood," Joe said.

Joe always hated being in the middle of this cops-and-robbers situation, and now that it was coming to a head, he knew it would only get worse.

Detective Marino was indeed in rare form. At the supper table, Dominic went on and on about how the Buccelli brothers were finished and would be spending the next twenty years or longer in prison.

"Those assholes are up against professionals now," he ranted on. "They won't get away this time. We have eyewitnesses, wiretaps, the car they used, everything we need to send them away. This time they went too far. Nobody gives a shit about that scumbag they shot, and I don't care either, only that they get convicted for it. You hear that? Your little pal is going away for good."

Joe sat there in silence, slowly eating his supper. Janet left the table and took Marie into the other room.

"Dominic, why don't you be quiet and let them eat in peace?" her mother said.

Janet's mother, Fran, was the only one who could speak to Marino like that. She was barely over five feet tall, but she was feisty and wouldn't back down from anyone. But when Marino looked Joe in the eye and asked him if he knew anything about the murder, Fran got up and left the room as well.

Now Joe was facing his father-in-law's stare across the kitchen table.

He answered, "I didn't know anything about it until yesterday. Rizzo never said anything, neither did anyone else. You have eyewitnesses that saw them do it?"

Marino smiled as he said, "That's right—we have three people that saw them. Three people that will testify in court they killed that guy. We're gonna nail them for murder, conspiracy to commit murder, possession of illegal guns, grand theft auto, and anything else we can throw at them."

Chuckling under his breath, Marino got up and left the room, leaving Joe sitting there alone. He took another bite of his stuffed pepper and thought, wow, I guess they did it.

***

The next day at work, all Joe could think about was that Rizzo and the brothers he had gotten to know and like had indeed committed murder. He couldn't wait to talk to his sister to hear what she knew about it, or if she knew anything at all. Thinking back over the past few months, he began to realize that clues had been dropped and comments made that should have raised his suspicions. Rizzo had been acting differently in some ways, somewhat subdued, except for the night he brought over the guns. Then he seemed like his old self. Maybe the thought of making a quick ten grand had lifted his spirits. But now he was in jail, awaiting trial for murder, among other things. That money, when he gets it, surely will have to go to paying a lawyer.

When the telephone rang, Joe paid it no mind until Jim reached over and handed him the receiver.

"Here, Joe, it's your wife," he said.

Joe thought, oh, wow, déjà vu. He hoped not.

This time, Janet was calm and not screaming for him to come home, but the call was bad news all the same.

She said, "Sandy just called me and said Rizzo's father was arrested today and taken to jail."

Surprised, Joe asked in a low voice, "Why did they arrest him? He's just an old man. He couldn't have been involved with that other thing."

"Yeah, well, you'd better sit down," Janet said. "The state police found those things we brought up to you-know-where. They found them this morning, then sent word down here and had him arrested, since the cabin is in his name. I hope you're satisfied. That was a stupid place to take them."

"Oh, man, you gotta be shittin' me. What else did Sandy say?" Joe asked, his voice getting lower.

"That's all she knows for now. She's been trying to find a lawyer with Bette and Donna all day. Rizzo's mother just called her with the news. So far, Sandy hasn't said anything about us being involved, but I'm sure they're gonna find out sooner or later. I'm so embarrassed I don't think I could ever face them again."

Joe wasn't worried about facing Naz's or Pete's wife, or their mother, for that matter. It was Naz and Pete he was worried about. How would the brothers take it when they learned Joe was responsible for their father being locked up? Just the thought of the state police being in the cabin just days after Joe broke in gave him the creeps. Now he wondered if he had done a good enough job wiping off any fingerprints he might have left on those damn guns. The area had looked deserted, but could he be sure no one saw him break in, and maybe get his license plate number? He knew only time would tell. It seemed the nightmare was not over yet.

140

After work, Joe wasted no time packing up Janet and Marie and heading for his sister's house. Sandy was on the phone with Pete's wife, Donna, when they arrived. Hanging up, she announced that they had an appointment with an attorney the next day. Donna said he was a good lawyer, and he seemed very interested in trying the case.

For the past several days, the story about the crime-family murder had made headlines and was well known citywide. Now, added to that was the breaking story of the seventy-three-year-old family patriarch being arrested for gunrunning. This was turning out to be the major news story of the year and Joe was right in the middle of it.

Joe sat down at the table. Looking directly at Sandy, he asked, "So they found the guns. Why were the cops looking up there, anyway?"

"They were looking for the murder weapon," Sandy said. "They were searching everywhere they could think of, any property the family owned. They found out that the family owned the cabin, so they contacted the state police up there to have a look. And guess what? They find all the guns robbed from a local store last week. The cops down here thought that was hysterical and couldn't wait to arrest Rizzo's father. The poor old man didn't have a clue what they were talking about. He looked totally lost when they took him away in handcuffs. They also added the theft charges to Rizzo and the others. I sure wish to hell you didn't bring them up there."

Joe wished the same thing, but it was too late now. He said, "You know, if I knew where Rizzo got them, I never would have taken them back there. I thought that would be the safest place. So what happens now? Am I going to be connected to this?"

Sandy, looking somewhat annoyed, said, "Oh, don't worry. Your name will not be mentioned, unless Rizzo says something. He was

141

pretty pissed off when he found out where you took them. We were going to need that money, and now it's gone."

Joe sat there silently for a minute, then said, "Janet's father says they have eyewitnesses who saw them shoot that guy. Did they really do it?"

Smiling, Sandy asked, "Do you think they did?"

Joe smiled back and said, "At first, I didn't think so, but now I kinda think they did. I heard them talking about it a lot at the cabin during deer season. Now that I look back, it all makes sense. I'll bet I even know how it happened. One of them was talking to Max when the car pulled up, and then when Max looked to see who it was, they shot him."

Sandy looked at him in disbelief, then asked, "Did Rizzo tell you that?"

"No, he never said anything like that."

"Then how did you know? Did Janet's father tell you anything?" Sandy asked nervously.

"No one told me anything. I just got a feeling that's what happened, and I guess I'm right, ain't I?"

"You can't say that to anybody," she said loudly. Then looking over to Janet, Sandy said, "Oh, my God, neither of you can say anything about this. No really, I'm not kidding. You can't say a word."

Joe could see she was about to get hysterical and said, "Hey, don't worry. We want to stay as far away from all this as possible. But since it's all out in the open now, you might as well tell us the whole story."

142

Sandy sat there for a moment staring at them both. Then she said, "You know, it will feel good to tell someone and talk about it with somebody besides those dumb bitches Donna and Bette. Donna, that stupid ass, is the reason they got arrested in the first place. Her and her stupid big mouth started telling people when she was getting her hair done about the murder, almost bragging about it. Before you know it, word gets back to the cops and they start an investigation."

Joe interrupted, asking, "How did she find out in the first place?"

Sandy angrily answered, "She overheard them planning the whole thing in Pete's kitchen the night before. All of them used to meet there to plan their jobs or whatever and sit around for hours. That stupid bitch couldn't keep her mouth shut, and now look what happened."

Joe mentioned that Janet's father had said something about wiretaps and conspiracy to commit murder.

Sandy's eyes widened. "Oh, my God, I wonder if they had a bug in Pete's house," she said. "If they did, they could have heard everything they were saying about the murder. They were being picked up and questioned a lot, and you know they talked about it when they were together. Oh, my God. Oh, my God." Then she started to cry.

CHAPTER EIGHT—A SIMPLE SCORE

Naz sat behind the wheel of the parked van, shivering in the cold, while his three brothers loaded the merchandise as quickly as they could. They had received a tip a few days ago about a supply of new clothing being stored in this warehouse in preparation for the upcoming Christmas season. The place was easily broken into and they were anticipating a very lucrative haul.

Naz turned in his seat, but he was unable to see out the back of the van due to the stacks of clothing. "You guys almost done?" he called out. "I'm freezing my ass off in here."

Rizzo answered, "We still got some room, might as well fill up. One or two more loads should do it. Here comes Pete now."

Pete dropped his load in the van, then sat down on the bumper, saying, "That's it for me. We got enough."

"Where's Bugsy? We gotta leave some room for us to sit," Rizzo said.

"He was loading up on Calvin Klein jeans when I passed him," Pete said.

"I hope he was checking on the sizes," Rizzo said. "Getting smalls ain't gonna mean shit. We can't sell smalls. Hell, we can't even give 'em away."

Pete answered, "I got all larges and extra larges for all the fat-asses we know. I even got some double-X large for that tube-of-shit Rocky." Then he shouted out to Naz, "Hey, man, start the van and get some heat in here!"

Just then, Bugsy came out, carrying a huge pile of jeans that towered over his head.

Rizzo said, "Where the hell are we supposed to sit now, asshole?"

"Just shove them in," Bugsy said. "These are worth a lot. Might as well get all we can, while we can."

Pete and Rizzo squeezed into the front seat while Bugsy climbed up onto the pile of clothing, his back pressing against the roof of the van. They drove off feeling pretty good about this score. They had no idea how it was going to change all their lives.

Over the next few days, the brothers tried to find buyers for their hoard of merchandise. As word spread around the neighborhood about the huge clothing sale the Buccellis were running, the information found its way to a friend of the owner of the stolen goods. Once the owner realized who the thieves were, he knew he couldn't go to the cops because that would most likely be a waste of time and he would never see his merchandise again. He also knew he couldn't confront the Buccelli family directly. However, he did know someone he could talk to who could try to get his stolen property back.

He had known the Santoro family for many years, and thought Max might be able to help him out. He explained to Max that word was out that the Buccelli brothers were behind the burglary of his warehouse and were now quietly selling his merchandise all over the city. The clothing was part of his Christmas inventory and would directly affect his family's income during the holiday season. Max knew the Buccelli brothers well, but that didn't mean anything to him. They had insulted a friend of his, and that's all that mattered, fellow thieves or not.

The Santoros and Buccellis had independently worked the city for years, never before infringing on each other. They weren't rivals, as there was always plenty to go around, but they were well aware of each other's activities.

After making his own inquiries, Max found out the Buccellis were indeed responsible for the theft from his friend. He knew what he had to do as a point of honor. He would demand all the unsold merchandise be returned immediately, along with all money made from the sales. He also would demand five thousand dollars in payment for the insult his friend had suffered. Max felt strongly that an insult to a friend of his was an insult to himself as well. He would get all of it back, or he would track them down and make them pay dearly for daring to defy him. He didn't care how many of them there were. Max didn't have a family of brothers behind him, but that wouldn't stop him. In fact, he never gave it a second thought.

***

After meeting with several attorneys, Sandy finally settled on one. She rejected the lawyer Donna and Bette chose to represent their husbands. She didn't like him at all, even though he said he would represent all four brothers at a relatively decent price. She wanted the best she could afford for her husband's defense, even if it took all the money they had stashed away. Since Bugsy wasn't married, she took it upon herself to include him in her search. She felt reassured in her choice when her attorney insisted that Rizzo and Bugsy would have separate trials, while Naz and Pete's attorney wanted to try them together. Sandy's attorney was surprised with that decision, as it automatically implied a conspiracy, which makes a defense much more difficult. Sandy was pleased and hopeful with her choice of David Kaplin to handle Rizzo's defense.

Kaplin's offices were in a Manhattan high-rise, which told Joe that his rates were going to be exorbitant. He expressed this to Sandy, but she was adamant about using him.

"Look, he's a very good lawyer and he really wants to try this case," Sandy said. "He's read about it and finds it kinda fascinating—a whole family involved in a murder. I know he's expensive, but he's willing to work with us. Oh, by the way, he wants to meet with you and Ma sometime soon."

***

When Naz heard that Max Santoro was looking for him to discuss the job they recently pulled, he quickly called a meeting at Pete's home. The brothers met there often to discuss future and past jobs, or to talk about upcoming hunting and fishing trips. This meeting was different, very different. Naz relayed what he had heard on the street about their recent victim being a longtime friend of Max's. They all knew this could develop into a very bad situation. They didn't really fear the cops being informed that they were the thieves, although they knew the police probably surmised it anyway. They were always careful not to leave any physical evidence behind that could incriminate them. It was Max they were worried about.

Naz told them he was going to meet with Max and find out what he had in mind. "I don't know what he's thinking," he said. "I mean, shit, so we robbed some *facha di gots* friend of his. So what? What are we supposed to do about it now? We never bitch about who he robs."

Pete said, "What if he wants us to give back the stuff we took?"

"Well the fuck with that. That ain't gonna happen, no way," answered Naz.

147

Rizzo, sipping from his teacup, added, "You know that guy's a crazy son of a bitch. You can't trust him. Are you gonna meet with him alone?"

Naz thought for a moment, then said, "Yeah, he won't do nothing yet. Right now, he just wants to scare us into doing what he wants, whatever the fuck that is. I'll meet with him tomorrow and find out what's what."

The next afternoon, Naz called his brothers and left messages for them to be at Pete's house at 8:00 p.m., sharp. They all arrived on time, except for Bugsy. They sat around the kitchen table while Pete poured hot water into their teacups.

Naz asked, "Where's our goof-off brother? I left a message for him to be here. This affects all of us."

"He's probably out with that broad he's been banging. You know, the one who looks like Cher," Pete said.

"Cher, my ass, this is important," Naz said angrily. "He needs to hear this and not be fuckin' around with some twat."

Rizzo said, "Look, tell us what happened and don't worry about Bugsy. We'll fill him in later when he comes in. He never misses a meeting."

Naz took a sip of tea and said, "Well, it's worse than I thought it would be. That fuckin' wackadoo wants all the shit we took given back, plus all the money we made selling any of it, and to top it off, he wants an extra five grand for his shithead friend for his hurt feelings. How about that?"

"You gotta be shittin' me," Rizzo said.

"I wish I was, but that's what he said. And he wants it all by the weekend. We got a real problem here."

Pete asked, "What did you tell him?"

"I said I would have to talk it over with you guys, but there's not much more to say. That's the deal. If we don't pay, he said he'll not only come after us, but he'll come for our kids, too. And that crazy fuck will do it."

Just then, the front door of the apartment opened and Donna walked into the kitchen, looking surprised to see them all there.

Pete said, "I thought you were going shopping with your friends tonight. What happened?"

She answered, "Everybody got tired and wanted to go home, so that's what I did. Are you guys planning another trip?"

Pete answered, "Yeah, deer season is coming up and we're planning on what to bring."

"Can I get you anything?' she asked.

"Naw, I made the tea, we don't need nothing else," Pete said.

"Okay then, I'm going to read in bed. Good night, you guys," Donna said as she left the room.

Naz quietly asked, "Can she hear us in there? Why did she have to come home now? We got to work this thing out."

The front door opened again. Bugsy entered the kitchen, asking, "Am I late?"

"Yeah, you're fuckin' late. Sit down and be quiet, Donna's in the other room," answered Naz in a low voice.

Bugsy asked quietly, "Well, did you talk to the maniac?"

Rizzo answered, "Yeah, and we got a real problem. He wants all the shit back, plus any money we made, and then get this—an extra five grand for his friend's trouble."

In a harsh whisper, Naz said, "Hey, remember to keep your voice down, numbnuts, she's in the other room. Well, okay, now we all know. The question is, what are we gonna do about it? We can't give in to that prick or it will never end. We'll have to start paying him tribute every time he thinks we fucked him over. Everyone knows he's a little *oobatz*, not right in the head, which makes him real dangerous. I'm not going to wait around for him to bash my head open with that fuckin' bat of his. So what do we do?"

Pete softly said, "Of all the places we could have hit, why the hell did we pick that one?"

Rizzo, forgetting to lower his voice, added, "Well we did, and besides, that was a pretty damn good score. I already made almost a thou from selling that crap, and I sure as shit ain't gonna give it back."

Naz, holding his hands as if to pray, said quietly, "Will you please keep your fuckin' voice down. Are you stupid, or what?"

Rizzo leaned over to him and whispered softly, "Fuck you. How's that?"

Pete softly said, "Alright, damn it, cut the shit. What are we gonna do?"

A few seconds later, Bugsy softly whispered, "We gotta blow him away."

Everyone looked at Bugsy without saying a word for a few moments.

Then Naz said, "What do you mean, we gotta blow him away?"

Bugsy, staring off as if in a trance, said, "What else can we do? I'll do it. It'll be like 'Nam."

The brothers sat there in silence, each one with his own thoughts about the dire situation they faced, and Bugsy's equally dire proposed solution.

Finally, Pete said, "We can't do that. We can't murder somebody, no way. There has to be another way. Look, something like that has got to be the last resort, that's not something we should even be talking about yet. Maybe we could bide our time, let some time go by, and maybe the crazy fuck will forget about it."

Rizzo said, "You know this guy, that's not gonna happen. He's gonna come after us if he doesn't get what he wants. Damn it, you know that. I don't like the idea of killing anybody either, but I think Bugsy's right, what else can we do?"

Naz added, "I think Pete has a good point. We should try to talk to him some more. He's in the same business we are, right? He's got to understand that sometimes we might step on each other's toes, it can't be helped. Wanting us to pay it back is not the solution. That's not going to happen. You know if it was the other way around, he wouldn't pay us a goddamn cent. That's the truth and yous know it."

151

After a pause, Naz continued, "I'll go see him again tomorrow, but we all know that more talk is probably a waste of time. I think we need to come up with a plan in case more talk doesn't work."

***

Joe, his mother, wife, and sister took the elevator up to the thirty-fourth floor of the glass-sided high-rise office building in midtown Manhattan. They had an appointment with the Kaplin, Cohen, and Gross law firm to discuss Rizzo's legal defense. Four months had passed since Rizzo and his brothers were arrested for the Max Santoro murder. They all were denied bail, which created a hardship for Sandy and the other wives while their husbands were incarcerated.

During that time, Sandy had told Joe about her conversations with the attorney on how the case was progressing, but now Kaplin wanted to see him. At first, Joe refused to go, unsure and a little uneasy about why the lawyer had requested him to come to his office. He was concerned that he would be urged to testify on Rizzo's behalf, which would just add more stress to his family situation. He could picture Dominic Marino's face when he heard that Joe was testifying as to what an upstanding citizen Rizzo was and therefore incapable of committing any murder. He figured the reason for including his mother and sister in this meeting was to soften his resistance. In that, he was partly right. After his sister and mother's urgent pleading, he reluctantly decided to take the meeting.

After a few minutes in the waiting room, they were escorted into a spacious office, where Kaplin sat behind a large, ornate desk. A younger male assistant stood at his side. After the greetings were made, they were invited to sit in a semicircle facing the large desk. Kaplin wasted no time explaining the seriousness of the charges and the difficulty and expense of preparing a defense. He explained that three

152

eyewitnesses had already testified before a grand jury, identifying Rizzo as the driver of the car. They also had taped conversations and phone recordings that implicated him in a conspiracy to commit murder and then attempting to cover it up, as well as charges for illegal possession of firearms and unauthorized use of a vehicle.

The lawyer then said, "Added to that are the new charges for the possession of stolen property, namely the seventy-plus rifles found in their hunting cabin upstate, which were stolen from a nearby gun shop. If found guilty of these charges, he could easily spend the next forty years in prison."

Joe could feel Sandy's eyes bearing down on him when the lawyer mentioned the rifles. It would be a long time before he lived that down.

Kaplin next took a different approach, saying how families should stick together in times of trouble and should always be ready to help out where they can. He told a moving story about how his family stood by his brother when he needed money to start a business, how they all came together and gave what they could. He said that's what strong, caring families do in times of need.

Joe at first felt relieved, then annoyed as he realized what the purpose of this meeting truly was. This was just a ploy to get money. This lawyer wanted Joe and his mother to help pay for Rizzo's legal expenses. Knowing that wasn't going to happen, Joe decided to have a little fun.

"Mr. Kaplin, let's get to the point. How much is this trial going to cost?"

The lawyer began to explain how the expenses mount up with all the paperwork, the investigations that are needed to try and discredit the witnesses and counter any hard evidence presented, plus travel expenses, office staff, et cetera, et cetera. He then added that the quality of the defense is directly related to the amount of money available to pursue it. Simply put, the more money at his disposal, the better the defense. To make his point, he said bluntly, "You can kill the president and give me half a million dollars, and I will get you off."

Joe let that comment sink in a little while, thinking this lawyer didn't seem to care if Rizzo was guilty or not. It was all about the money and a chance to show off his skills.

Joe said, "Okay, I understand, but we need to know, how much are we talking about here?"

Looking Joe right in the eye, Kaplin said, "For this defense to be effective, we will need close to one hundred thousand dollars. Even though I'm only defending two of them, there are four brothers involved here, a whole family. That already looks like a conspiracy, and to be totally frank, these guys all look like criminals. They are going to be hard to defend. I'm sorry, Sandy, but I'm afraid it's true."

Joe looked over to his sister, noticing a slight smile on her face.

The lawyer continued, "Your sister has already given all she can, plus we are taking possession of the property upstate, the small house or cabin. Rizzo's parents are giving what they can as well, but they also are having to help the rest of the family with the other defense team. So, we are calling on all other family members to contribute whatever they can so we can get Rizzo back home with his family."

Joe asked, "Do you think they're innocent?"

"That's not my job. I don't care if they're innocent or not. My job is to win this case, and with enough funds at my disposal, I will do just that," Kaplin answered curtly.

Joe glanced over at Janet, his mother, and sister, who all sat with their eyes downcast, saying nothing. He then looked back at the lawyer and said, "Mr. Kaplin, there is no way we can contribute a large sum of money like you're talking about. We just don't have it. Did my sister know what your fee was going to be when she hired you? I don't think she did, she would know she couldn't afford it. If we all knew what the cost was going to be, we would have said, 'Thank you, Mr. Kaplin, but we cannot afford your services' and found someone else."

With that, the lawyer's young assistant began to berate them about not being willing to help and not sticking together as a decent family should. Kaplin quickly recognized the anger rising in Joe and advised his assistant to leave the room, realizing he was not helping the situation. The lawyer went on to say they wouldn't be required to pay the entire balance, but if they didn't have the funds they could each take out a loan for, say, ten thousand dollars, which would be a tremendous help. Other members of Rizzo's family also were being called in to do the same. Finally, Joe said that he would be unable to secure a loan for that amount, or really any amount. He was not going to put himself into debt on the remote possibility of Rizzo being released from jail. He asked the lawyer if there would be a guarantee of Rizzo's acquittal, or as Joe put it, would the money be wasted on a lost cause?

Then Joe added, "After all, we aren't talking about him starting a business here, are we?"

The lawyer replied, "Of course there can be no guarantee, but as I said before, I will do my best to secure his release, if I have the funds to do so. Look at your sister, she's crying."

Joe looked over at Sandy, then back at Kaplin and said, "She's been crying ever since she married the guy. If what you said about the

155

evidence they have against him is true, chances are he's not going to beat it anyway. Then she's the one who is going to need money."

Kaplin looked over to his assistant, who had just reentered the room and said, "I guess we have the wrong people in here. Let's call in the other family members. Maybe they will be willing to help out."

***

As the night wore on, the brothers all sat around the kitchen table staring into their empty teacups. They sat there as they had done so many times before, only this time, it was different. This time, there was no laughing or lighthearted jokes, no excitement over an upcoming job. This time, they were deadly serious and a little scared. They agreed that Naz would speak to Max the following night at a diner Naz frequented. It was a place where he would feel somewhat safe against a vicious attack from Max, if that should happen.

Naz softly said, "I'll try and talk some sense into the fucker, but if it goes bad, we got to have a plan and it's got to be a good one. We won't get a second chance at this bastard. If we fuck it up, he will come after all of us for sure.

"If we have to kill him, it will have to happen right away, right at the diner. We can't afford to let him leave. If we're going to do this, we do it together, all of us. That's the only time we'll have the chance to face him on our terms. So I think maybe this is how we should handle it. Let me know what you think. I'll be inside the diner with him, the rest of you will wait outside, out of sight in a car down the street a little. If it goes bad and we have no other choice, I'll come out and light a cigarette. I'll stand by the curb, so be sure you guys don't park too far away—make sure you can see the street in front of the diner. If you see me light up, then you know it's on. Start the car and drive up slowly. How does that sound so far?"

Rizzo said, "It might be better to leave the car running. We don't want him to hear a car start up, that might put him on edge. He might be carrying, so I don't want him to suspect nothing."

Naz nodded agreement, then said, "We need to boost a car, one that runs good and won't stall, and also one that doesn't stand out."

Rizzo said, "I know where we can get one. You know that Persian *gavone* who got the car lot on Locust Avenue? He's got some good cars, and I know where he keeps the keys. I'll check it out tomorrow."

"That guy's no Persian, he's Iranian. There's no such country as Persia," Naz said.

"I don't give a fuck who he says he is," Rizzo said. "He's got good cars, that's all I know."

"Yeah, well, don't act too interested in one, because when it turns up missing, he'll think of you," Naz said.

"I know what to do. I'll bullshit with him while I'm looking around. That *stunad* won't pay me no mind. All he ever does is pop aspirins and bitch about how fast everything happens here. 'Everything in America is fast, fast, fast,' that's all he ever says," Rizzo said, trying to lighten the mood.

"What about a weapon? If I'm going to do this, I want a 12-gauge pump that we can get rid of, a throwaway," Bugsy said in a low voice.

Pete spoke up and asked, "So you're really going to do this? You're really going to kill him?"

157

Bugsy replied, "I thought we got past this. If the meeting goes bad, then yeah, I'm going to kill him. What else are we supposed to do? I don't mind—not at all."

Everyone was quiet for a while, letting the realization of the situation sink in.

Rizzo finally spoke in a low voice, "I got just the gun. It's an old piece of shit that I cut the barrel down real short. A 12-gauge pump, it's not worth nothing. I'll take it apart tonight and wipe it off good, the shells too. Make sure anyone who touches it wears gloves."

Pete got up from the table and walked over to the bedroom, putting his ear up against the closed door. Not hearing anything, he walked over to the stove to put on the teakettle. When he sat back down, the discussion continued.

Naz said, "Okay, after I light the cigarette, you guys drive up alongside us, then call out to Max to come over. When he does, you let him have it, and be sure he's dead. I don't care if you have to pump five shots into him, you got to be sure. I'll run back inside the diner like I don't know what happened. You guys take off. Don't speed or go through any red lights, just drive away normal."

Rizzo said, "We should have another car nearby to switch into in case somebody tells the cops what kind of car they saw. Say we ditch it near the entrance to the parkway, then switch cars there, then take off."

Naz said, "Yeah, that's a good idea. I'll park my van on the street near the parkway entrance. You guys take the keys, then drop me off at the diner about an hour before I have to meet that prick. Maybe the cops will think the guys who shot him left town in a hurry on the parkway. One of you will have to pick me up later on. I'm sure the cops will want a statement from everybody who was in the diner. I'm not going to be

158

able to get out of that. People know me there, and anyway, it will look suspicious if I took off. So, who's going to pick me up?"

Bugsy slowly shook his head, not saying a word. Pete said he wasn't going anywhere near that diner, probably ever again.

Rizzo sat there, shaking his head, then said, "You bunch of pussies, what are you afraid of? I'll pick you up. After all, we didn't do nothing, right?"

***

Sandy really wasn't that upset with Joe about not wanting to contribute to Rizzo's defense fund. She knew he didn't have any money to spare and it would be difficult to secure a large loan without suitable collateral. Joe was glad the issue was dropped and forgotten. She was, however, keeping Joe informed about the investigations and other aspects of Rizzo's upcoming trial.

Naz and Pete were the first ones to be tried. For reasons unknown to the family, some sort of jury misconduct caused their case to quickly end in a mistrial. They both were returned to jail to await a new trial date.

This raised everyone's spirits and Sandy was beginning to feel hopeful for the first time since this all began well over a year ago. Kaplin cautioned her that the evidence against Rizzo was strong, and although he felt sure about his ability to get an acquittal, she should not be overconfident. She learned from him that the police, posing as telephone repairmen, had installed a bug and a phone tap in Pete's kitchen back in January of last year. They had reels of taped conversations from up to a week before the brothers were arrested. The tapes had them discussing ways to answer questions to deflect and

159

conceal their involvement in the murder. They were heard coaching one another on what to say when they were being picked up almost daily for questioning. However, to be used as evidence in court, the voices on the tapes had to be identified. Rizzo was mostly silent during those conversations, and when he did speak, his voice was often inaudible, which would help him greatly. Kaplin also told her that he had found ways to discredit the eyewitnesses in court and along with the lack of any physical evidence, such as fingerprints or the long-sought-after murder weapon, the outcome wasn't looking that bad.

Another piece of good news was that the owner of the gun shop Rizzo robbed last year had dropped all the charges against him for the theft. Kaplin had convinced the shop owner to do it, telling him that he really shouldn't get involved in a court case with a family currently on trial for murder, adding that they were a very close family and the other brothers not on trial might seek revenge in some way. It didn't hurt that the shop owner had recovered his guns, along with a $10,000 "gift" that Sandy had to put up. The case against Rizzo's father for harboring the guns in the cabin also was dismissed. That was mostly due to a lack of evidence, but also the fact that the cabin had been broken into, obviously by someone who couldn't unlock the door. The police surmised the culprits were probably local thieves who used the empty cabin to store their stolen goods. Joe had to smile when he heard that. They later learned that the shop owner closed his store and moved away.

Joe decided to take a week's vacation from work to attend Rizzo's trial. He had never attended a trial of any sort, and this was the big league. With all the continuing newspaper coverage over the past year, everyone was anticipating the trial to begin. Plus, he knew all the players as well as the entire true story, things that even Sandy's attorney didn't know. He was interested to see how it would all play out.

Besides, Kaplin had advised them that it would benefit Rizzo if the courtroom was filled with family members showing their support. It might help the jury believe in his innocence if they saw a number of family members coming to his aid. He told them all to dress well and to be quiet and respectful.

One evening, days before the trial was set to begin, Sandy played for Joe some of the recorded conversations the police had taped from Pete's kitchen. Joe listened with amusement to the comments uttered by the brothers as they tried to help each other with how to respond to the detectives' persistent questioning. One of the few times Rizzo's voice was heard clearly, he was responding to the question of where he was on the evening of November 5. "How the hell am I supposed to know that?" he said. "Do you think I remember every time I sit down to take a shit?" Naz told him that was the right way to deal with it. That day shouldn't stand out any more than any other day. Naz and Pete were heard speaking most often, Rizzo not so much, and Bugsy hardly at all, which Kaplin said would greatly help them in court.

Joe was surprised that the lawyer also had said that he admired how the brothers had left behind no physical evidence whatsoever. No fingerprints were left in the car, or even on the empty shotgun shells found in the street. The shotgun itself had disappeared without a trace, despite the intensive search to find it. Joe was just relieved that he would not be called to testify by either side. There was no evidence that he was connected to the murder, and anything he had heard about it would be considered hearsay and therefore not admissible in court. He was just going to sit back and enjoy the spectacle.

CHAPTER NINE—A COLD NOVEMBER NIGHT

"Hey, Bugsy, why don't you put that damn cigarette out. I can't breathe in here," Rizzo said. When he got no response, he called out, "Hello! Are you still back there?"

Bugsy, not saying a word, took another puff and blew the smoke toward the front seat.

Rizzo, almost yelling, said, "Jesus Christ! Then open a fuckin' window, will ya? Damn, I hate those fuckin' cigarettes."

Pete chimed in, "Will you guys shut the fuck up! I'm trying not to puke in here. I still can't believe we're doing this. Why don't we just fuck it and go home."

Rizzo answered, "Yeah, are you gonna deal with Max and try to make peace? Are ya? I don't think so. We came this far, and we'll go all the way if we have to. Damn it, Bugsy, will you crack the window at least?"

"It's cold outside and the heater in here ain't worth shit," Bugsy said.

"Yeah, but this shitbox runs good, and that's all we need. We dropped Naz off almost two hours ago. We should know something soon."

Pete asked, "How do we know if Max even showed up? None of us saw him go in. What if he's not even in there? How long do we have to wait out here?"

Rizzo answered, "Naz will come out eventually if Max don't show, but don't worry, that bastard will show up. It's a matter of pride with him, a chance to show off to his friend what a big man he is, how he controls everything in the city, the fuckin' asshole."

Rizzo stopped talking suddenly and turned to face Bugsy. "Jesus Christ, did you shit in your pants now?" he said, reacting to a sudden stench. "What the hell are you doing back there?"

Bugsy laughed and continued puffing on his cigarette.

Rizzo opened his window and stuck his head out, taking in deep breaths. "I don't know what's worse, the air in the car or the exhaust fumes out here."

Rizzo let the car air out, then cranked the window shut. The three of them sat in silence, waiting, each with their own thoughts.

After a while, Rizzo said, "You know, we got to be smart about this. The cops might question us if they think we did it, but I don't think they will. They won't know about why we did it and Max has lots of enemies who got reasons to kill him. If we have to do it, I think it will be okay. But we can never talk about this to nobody, not even our wives. We can't trust nobody to keep their mouths shut."

Pete said, "I'm sure as hell not going to talk about it ever. This is one night I want to forget."

Bugsy said, "I got nobody to tell. There's a lot of shit I did that I keep quiet about."

Pete saw him first, but it was Rizzo who said, "There's Naz, He just walked to the curb, and he just lit a cigarette."

"Oh, fuck," whispered Pete.

Rizzo said, "Yeah, well, we all knew this was gonna happen. Okay, here we go. Bugsy, did you rack the shotgun?"

"Yeah, I'm ready," he answered.

Rizzo slowly pulled away from the curb and began to drive down the street toward the diner. No one said anything except for Pete, who kept muttering "fuck … fuck … fuck" under his breath. As they approached the diner where Naz and Max were standing outside, Bugsy slowly cranked down the rear window. He held the shotgun below the window, out of sight. As Rizzo stopped the car next to the two men, Bugsy called out, "Hey, Max!"

Max turned to see who was in the car calling his name. When he recognized who it was, he began to say, "What the fuck do you want?" but didn't get out more than a few syllables before his world went black. He never heard the shot that almost blew out the ears of the three occupants of the car. He never heard the shot that took off his face and sent half his skull splattering to the curb. He never heard the shot as his huge dead body slammed to the ground.

The car began to drive away, but stopped when Bugsy said, "Wait, he's still breathing."

Thinking that the vapor coming from Max's shattered face was breath, he told Rizzo to back up. As the car pulled alongside Max, Bugsy reached out to put the muzzle of the barrel inches away from what was left of Max's head, and blasted again. He calmly said, "That should finish it. Let's go."

***

Joe had finally convinced Janet to accompany him to Rizzo's trial. After all, they had been told the more family members present in the courtroom, the better. Janet wasn't too thrilled to be there, but came anyway, bringing along their daughter, Marie, and their infant son, Zachary. Janet also resented that her husband had decided to use one of his vacation weeks to attend a murder trial instead of saving it for the upcoming Christmas holiday season. By this time, she had had quite enough of Rizzo and his family's bullshit, and wanted no more of it in any way. Her father was always coming down on her for still associating with a pack of murderers, and she was tired of the whole thing. Joe couldn't blame her for feeling that way, but he wasn't going to miss this trial, no matter what. He would attend with her or without her.

As they were seated on the first day, Joe looked over at the jury that would decide Rizzo's fate. It was a mix of middle-aged men and women, and all but two were white. Just by looking at them, Joe couldn't tell how they would react to the gruesome murder Rizzo was accused of, or how they would judge him.

The judge entered the courtroom, and everyone stood as the clerk introduced him and declared the court in session. The judge was a slightly overweight man with a pleasant-looking face. Joe guessed him to be in his sixties. Rizzo's trial was underway.

Richard Dunaway, the district attorney prosecuting the case, was a skinny, nervous-looking fellow in his late thirties. He began his opening statement, laying out the evidence obtained from the wiretaps and the bug in Pete's kitchen as proof of a conspiracy to commit murder, and explaining Rizzo's part in carrying it out. He added how he would go on to prove guilt through three eyewitness accounts placing Rizzo in the driver's seat of the car used in the murder. He described the brutality of the murder itself and the utter callousness of backing up the car to shoot

Max again after it was obvious he was already dead. His opening statement went on for about forty minutes, and Joe thought the case seemed strong at this point. During the presentation, Joe occasionally looked over at the jury and back at Rizzo to see if he could detect any responses. The jurors sat stone-faced. All Rizzo did was lean over occasionally to talk to his attorney or play with his tie.

Next, the judge called for Rizzo's attorney to deliver his opening statement. Kaplin rose, and approaching the jury, said how the evidence presented by the prosecution will be proven to be false and circumstantial, adding that not a shred of physical evidence will be presented to connect Rizzo to what was, indeed, a horrific crime. He said that any close-knit family that was always getting together to discuss hunting and fishing trips, and were being picked up by detectives almost daily and grilled about a murder, would, of course, talk about it in the privacy of their homes. That alone would not and could not prove that Rizzo was guilty. He went on to say that the eyewitnesses the prosecution was so proud of would be proven to be unreliable, and that was the full extent of their evidence. He closed by telling the jury they must remember that just because someone is indicted for a crime doesn't mean he is guilty. After hearing that, Joe was beginning to think Rizzo might have a chance after all.

***

As they drove quickly toward the parkway rendezvous with Naz's van, they each let out fits of nervous laughter.

After a few minutes, Rizzo asked Bugsy, "Why did you tell me to back up and then shoot him again?"

"I saw that he was still breathing and might not be dead," Bugsy said.

"What are you, *stunad*? Of course he was dead," Rizzo said. "How could he not be dead? I saw his fuckin' head explode. What you saw was steam from the cold air, not him breathing, dumbass."

"Naz said to be sure he was dead, so that's what I did. Now I'm sure," answered Bugsy.

"Yeah, well, me backing up would give somebody more time to look us over and ID the car, in case you didn't think of that," Rizzo said.

Half-laughing, Bugsy said, "Anybody who saw what happened back there would shit in their pants and not give a fuck about the car, I guarantee."

Pete sat in silence, looking out the window and wishing he were somewhere else.

When they arrived at the parked van, Rizzo shut off the car and doused the headlights. They sat there for a minute or two, looking around to see if anyone was nearby. Satisfied they were alone, they exited the car. Even though they all wore gloves, they wiped the inside surfaces with a rag they had brought with them. That's when Rizzo noticed that Bugsy's face and shirt were covered in bloody spots, hundreds of them. He also saw that the side of the car that had been facing Max was covered in blood. There was no time to clean the car, but Rizzo said they all would have to strip off their clothes as soon as possible. He started the van and drove off.

"We'll go to my apartment. It's the closest. Bugsy, you need to strip down now and wipe off your face."

"I don't want to ride around in the back of a van naked with two guys in the front!" Bugsy protested.

Rizzo said with a laugh, "If we get stopped, I'll tell the cop we just picked up a *fanook*. It's better than him seeing you covered in blood."

No one except Rizzo thought that was funny.

***

On the second day of the trial, the judge ordered that from now on, extended family members would not be allowed in the courtroom. The prosecution believed it would be a distraction for the jury. Joe thought an incident in the hallway during a recess the day before might have played a part. As they were all being called back into the courtroom, Marie rolled a small rubber ball she was playing with down the hallway.

As the D.A. was entering the courtroom using another doorway, he tripped and almost fell over the rolling ball. Rizzo's family saw what had happened and they all busted out laughing, loudly. The D.A.'s face turned red with embarrassment, which made Joe sure that he immediately filed a complaint with the judge. Janet was relieved that she could stay home with the kids, but Joe decided he would continue to attend the trial.

The prosecutor called his first witness, who was one of the waitresses working in the diner on the night of the murder. Of course, Rizzo was not present in the diner that night, but he asked her if she had ever seen him before. She said that she had, that he was driving the car that backed up to the fallen victim when he was shot again. She went on to describe what she saw and the reactions of the people in the diner and the man who ran inside just after the first gunshot. She wasn't questioned further about that man because it was considered irrelevant to Rizzo's case. After more testimony about what she saw and when she called the police, the prosecutor ended his questioning.

168

It seemed to Joe that Kaplin had an easy time with this witness during his cross-examination.

He asked the woman again, "Are you sure it was the defendant you saw driving the car?"

"Yes, I'm sure, she said.

"On which side of the car was the steering wheel? On the right or the left?

She thought about it for a moment, then answered, "The steering wheel was on the left side."

Kaplin then brought up the fact that the angle of sight from the diner window simply would not allow anyone to see that far into a car that was at least fifty feet away.

He asked her, "At what time did the shooting take place?"

"I believe it was about midnight," she answered.

"Was there a streetlight or any other kind of light directly outside the front of the diner?

"No, there wasn't."

He asked, "Were the interior lights of the car on, where you could see the occupants with any certainty? And can you even tell us how many people were in the car?"

She lowered her head and answered, "The car was dark and I couldn't tell how many people were in there."

"Did the driver of the car have a beard?"

"I don't know."

"You don't know because you really couldn't see anything in there, could you?" he asked.

With that, the prosecutor objected, so Kaplin said he had no more questions.

The next witness the prosecutor called was a postal worker, who on that night was on his way to work a night shift nearby. He had been walking on the side of the street opposite the diner when the murder took place. The prosecutor asked if he saw the driver of the car in question. He said yes, he did, and pointed to Rizzo at the prosecutor's request. The prosecutor asked him to describe what he saw.

"As I was walking down the street on my way to work, a dark-colored car stopped opposite of me," the witness said. "I didn't take any notice of the car until I heard a loud gunshot and saw the car drive away, then stop and back up. I heard another gunshot, so I pressed myself against the wall of a building in the shadows to stay out of sight. As the car sped away, I saw a body lying in the street, covered in blood."

He went on to explain how he ran inside the diner, shaking in fear, and saw the other people in there either in shock or crying.

"What did you do then?" the prosecutor asked.

"I told one of the waitresses what just happened outside, then I asked her for a cup of coffee. She told me she also witnessed the whole thing from the window. After she quickly served me, she reached for the phone to call the police. I sat at the counter having more coffee until the police arrived and took my statement."

Again, the prosecutor asked if the man driving the car was the defendant in the courtroom, and again, the witness said yes. Joe thought this witness sounded credible.

Kaplin rose to cross-examine. He started by asking the witness, "Can you describe the physical appearance of the driver of the car you saw on the night in question?"

The witness stated, "Yes, I can. The man I saw driving the car had a large nose and what appeared to be a heavy black beard."

When Rizzo heard the comment about a large nose, he reached up and felt his nose, which caused some of the jurors to chuckle.

Kaplin asked the witness, "Are you absolutely sure it was the defendant you saw driving the car?

"Yes, it was him."

"How can you be so sure, when Mr. Buccelli was never known to have a beard of any kind?"

"I know that's the man I saw in the driver's seat."

Kaplin moved along to when the witness entered the diner and ordered something to drink. "What was it?" he asked. "Was it a cup of coffee?"

"Yes, it was coffee."

"How many cups of coffee did you have?" asked the lawyer.

"I had three cups before the police arrived."

Kaplin looked over at the jury for a moment, then said he had no more questions.

At this point, both legal teams approached the bench and engaged in conversation with the judge that Joe was unable to hear. The judge instructed the jury to leave the room, and the jurors were escorted out. The private conversation between the lawyers and the judge continued. Shortly thereafter, court was recessed for the day. Joe left not knowing what had transpired, but he began to believe Rizzo's case wasn't looking too good.

On the next day, the third eyewitness for the prosecution was called to the stand. She was an elderly woman who lived in one of the buildings across the street from the diner. Her third-floor apartment faced the street, and by happenstance, she had been sitting by the window when Max was shot on the street below. She described the car she saw when she heard the gunfire and how it pulled away, then backed up. That's when she heard another gunshot before the car sped away. The lawyer asked her if she saw the driver of the car and she said yes, she had. When asked to point him out, she pointed a shaky finger at Rizzo.

"Did the driver look like he had a beard?" Kaplin asked her.

"Yes," she answered. "I believe he did have a large, black beard."

Kaplin didn't spend too much time with this witness. He asked her some questions about her eyesight, then asked her to confirm that she thought the driver had a beard. He asked her if the car she saw was a convertible or a hardtop. She answered that it was a hardtop.

Kaplin smiled. "How then," he asked, "could you describe the driver of the car with certainty from your third-floor window's vantage point, through the car's metal roof?"

She didn't have an answer, but looked over to the D.A., who sat there stone-faced, saying nothing. There were no more questions.

***

Rizzo drove the van into the driveway of the two-family house where he and Sandy lived in the second-floor apartment. Rizzo and Pete decided they didn't need to change clothes yet, since neither of them was near an open window when the blood went flying. Rizzo told the others to stay put while he went up to get some clothes for Bugsy and a large, plastic garbage bag. Sandy was still awake, and seeing him so hurried, asked what was going on. He mumbled some inaudible explanation as he ran back out, leaving her standing in the doorway, very concerned. Back in the van, he threw the clothes to Bugsy and told him to put his bloody clothes into the bag. Sandy watched from the window as the van backed out of the driveway and quickly drove away.

On the way to Pete's house, they discussed how to handle themselves over the next couple of days. They knew everyone would be talking about Max's murder and trying to figure out who was responsible. They would have to be convincing in their ignorance of the whole affair. Once word got out that Naz was with Max when he was killed, suspicions would be thrown their way. But if they were all smart and had their stories straight and stuck by them, they were confident they could ride out the storm.

Rizzo said to Bugsy, "You need to burn your clothes right away, and get rid of that shotgun, pronto."

Bugsy answered, "I know what to do, don't worry. Nobody will ever find the gun, believe me. I can't wait to get home and take a shower. I still feel like I got that bastard's blood all over me."

173

Rizzo said, "You sure as hell do—it was all over you like spray paint. Naz is gonna have to clean out his van, there might be some blood in here, and I'm gonna burn my clothes too, just in case. Pete, you better burn yours too."

Pete answered in a low voice, "Yeah."

When they arrived at Pete's house, he got out of the van and went inside without saying a word. Bugsy went over to his car, toting the bag with his bloody clothes and the shotgun. He stuffed them in the car and drove off without saying anything. Rizzo walked over to his car, got in and sat there for a while. He let out a large puff of air, already noticing how things were different. His relationship with his brothers had already changed. He couldn't quite put his finger on it, but the feeling was there. He was afraid they might have lost something, something they had always had in the past. The bond that held them together all these years, through all their experiences, might not be there anymore. He was afraid that resentment would build up between them, each one blaming another for what they had done. Maybe they had gone too far. But the fact remained, it was done, and nothing could change that. He said to himself, "Fuck it," and drove off to pick up Naz at the diner.

***

After the witness testimonies were completed, the D.A. played for the jury the portions of the taped conversations where Rizzo could be heard speaking, but the recordings were few and inconclusive. Rizzo, while surely unaware of it at the time, did not incriminate himself in the murder. All he ever discussed was the harassment of constantly being picked up by the police and questioned. He never mentioned taking part in the murder itself.

He was heard saying on the tape, "They want to know what I was doing on this day and on that day. How the hell am I supposed to know that? Do I write down every time I take a shit?"

Many in the courtroom laughed upon hearing that, and Joe enjoyed hearing it again himself. At that point, the prosecution rested its case.

Now Joe thought the prosecution's case looked weak. There was no physical evidence presented, nothing at all that would prove Rizzo's guilt beyond a reasonable doubt. Rizzo's fingerprints were not found in the car, even though he was accused of being the driver. The conspiracy charges were tenuous and had almost been dismissed at the outset of the trial due to a lack of evidence. The brothers all denied meeting at Pete's house just before the murder. All, that is, except Pete, who at first admitted they all met there, but later said he was confused and recanted. There wasn't even a plausible motive the prosecution could point to, calling it just a falling-out among thieves. The only real problems that remained were the eyewitness testimonies that fingered Rizzo as the driver, even though Kaplin had already chipped away at their credibility.

Rizzo's attorney issued a motion to dismiss all charges for lack of evidence. The motion was denied, and so the trial continued.

The following day, it was Kaplin's turn to call witnesses. The postal worker was called back to the stand and was asked again to recall what he saw and what actions he took. The lawyer asked him again about what he did before the police arrived, and again, he said he was very scared and ordered coffee.

Kaplin asked, "More than one cup?"

"Yes," the witness answered.

The next witness he called was the waitress who had previously testified. Kaplin brought her to the point where the postal worker had rushed into the diner and told her what he had just seen outside. She said he was very upset and wanted a drink to calm him down.

"Is coffee something people normally drink to calm their nerves?" Kaplin asked her.

The waitress smiled. "No," she said.

"What did he order to drink?"

"Scotch," she said. "He ordered scotch."

Joe heard a distinct gasp coming from the jury.

Kaplin asked her, "Does the diner usually serve alcohol?"

"Yes, we do," she answered. "We have a fully stocked bar."

"How many scotches did he order?"

"Three or four, I think."

Joe remembered something the judge had said when he was giving instructions to the jury at the beginning of the trial. One of the things he emphasized was that if any witness was caught giving false testimony, then their entire testimony could be discounted. Joe wondered why the man would lie about what he ordered to drink. He found out later that the postal worker feared he could lose his job if it became known that he was drinking alcohol while on duty. Joe thought that was a pivotal moment in the trial, that one little lie might cause the jury not to believe anything the witness said.

Kaplin called some other witnesses to testify if they had ever known Rizzo to have a beard, including the two detectives who had worked on the case from the beginning. They all answered no, they never saw Rizzo with a beard. The meaning of the term "clean-shaven" became an issue. Did it mean just-shaven, or simply without a beard? Joe couldn't understand why the beard issue was even being discussed. In all the years he had known Rizzo, he never once saw him with a beard.

***

On the way to the diner to pick up Naz, Rizzo suddenly remembered that he was still wearing the clothes he had on during the shooting. He thought it would be a good idea to go home to change. He couldn't believe he was about to make such a stupid mistake. He wasn't thinking clearly. That was dangerous and would have to stop. When he arrived back home, he was surprised to see that Sandy was still awake. She knew he was up to something and wanted to know what it was. He began removing his clothes, telling her he was hawking a score and needed to go out again. He began to pack the clothes into a garbage bag, including his new heavy jacket with the thick, black fur collar, when Sandy stopped him cold.

"Why are you putting your new jacket into a garbage bag? It's brand new!" she exclaimed.

"Don't worry about it. I ain't got time to talk about it now. Go to bed. I'll be back later," he said as he got dressed in fresh clothes.

Sandy mumbled something under her breath as she stormed off, slamming the bedroom door behind her. Rizzo was in no mood to put up with her bullshit, so he just grabbed the bag of clothes and left. He stuffed the bag into a garbage can for now. He would burn everything tomorrow.

When he turned the corner toward the diner, he couldn't believe his eyes. The whole street was lit up like a carnival. Dozens of police cars were there, parked every which way, with their lights flashing. A fire truck was parked in the middle of them. A hoard of people was standing behind a taped-off area around the diner's front door and sidewalk, while a cop was telling people driving by to keep moving. Rizzo drove on past, found a parking spot a few blocks away, and then walked back to the crazy scene.

When he got there, he approached a random man in the crowd.

"What's going on?" he asked.

"Someone was murdered here in the street a little over an hour ago," the man said.

"Who was it?" Rizzo asked.

"I don't know, but whoever it was, he really got blasted. The fire department is over there now hosing down the sidewalk and street to wash away the blood, brains, and bits of bone."

Rizzo couldn't help but smile at the thought that he was responsible for this whole scene. Out of this whole crowd, he was the only one who knew what had happened here, and that gave him a sense of pride.

That feeling was amplified when he overheard a cop saying, "I don't know who did this, but I would like to shake his hand. That guy was one mean and hated son of a bitch who got what he deserved. The world isn't going to miss him."

It took every ounce of restraint in Rizzo not to jump on top of a police car and shout out, "I'm the one! I'm the one who did it!"

For the first time that night, Rizzo started to feel good about what they had done.

***

Before Rizzo's lawyer concluded the defense, he introduced another witness, who testified that Max was known to be involved in the drug trade and had been dealing in it for some time. The D.A. objected, but was overruled. So, Kaplin had introduced another possibility and motive for the jury to contemplate. Joe had one more day available to him to attend the trial and was hoping he would be there when the verdict came in, but it looked as if that wasn't going to happen.

He did get to hear the closing statements from both sides. After the judge gave the jurors their final instructions, the prosecutor began his final arguments. He reiterated the brutality of the murder and relished in stating that after they shot Max, they made the cold decision to back up and shoot him again. He comically said, "They didn't back up to give him first aid ... they backed up to shoot him again at close range."

He asked the jury to overlook the minor discrepancies in the witness accounts and focus on the fact that Rizzo was identified as the driver of the car, and that he knew the victim. He stated that all the pieces of the puzzle were there, and the jury should bring justice and closure to the victim's family by reaching the decision of finding Rizzo guilty of murder in the first degree.

When Kaplin's turn came, he reminded the jury that the prosecution had not presented one single piece of hard evidence. Their witnesses had proved to be unreliable, he said, including one who lied under oath. He went on about "all that nonsense about the phantom beard testimony," to which some of the jurors cracked a smile. He mentioned how testimony had showed that Max was involved in drug-related

179

criminal activities and could have been the victim of a drug deal gone bad. He added that the car used in the murder was found by an entrance to the parkway, suggesting that after changing vehicles, it would afford the killers a fast and easy escape route out of the city.

And then he offered the *coup de grace*, asking the jury not to let the police close this case. They needed to continue their investigations to catch the real killers.

The prosecutor made his final rebuttal, trying to turn the tide, but from where Joe was sitting, he felt that Rizzo had a good chance of being acquitted. He was impressed with the way Kaplin had handled the case, but he was still glad he hadn't given him any money.

The judge gave the jurors their final instructions, and they went off to start deliberations. The trial was over. Now everyone had to wait for the verdict.

***

Rizzo spotted Naz standing with a group of people who had gathered beside the cordoned-off area in front of the diner. He stood casually with his hands in his pockets while he spoke to one of the officers. Rizzo watched for a while, not knowing whether he should approach them or not. Even though he thought of himself as a hero of sorts, he still was reluctant to expose himself to a cop. He decided to wait around until Naz could break away from the cop before he would try to signal him. Rizzo learned from one of the spectators that an ambulance had taken Max's body away about ten minutes ago, shortly before he arrived. He was sorry he missed that.

After nearly an hour, the crowd started to dissipate, and Rizzo stood there trying to spot Naz again, feeling like an idiot. He was getting tired standing there in the cold, and thought he would appear suspicious if he hung around much longer. He was about to say fuck it and leave, when he heard Naz call to him from across the street. Naz had been trying to get his attention without calling out, but Rizzo kept looking the other way. Rizzo pointed to where the car was, and keeping apart, they both started off in that direction.

Once in the car, Naz spoke with a nervous energy, asking about how it all went. He asked one question after another, wanting to know every detail. Did they wipe the car? Where was the shotgun? Did they think anybody saw them or could identify them?

"Jesus Christ, enough already," Rizzo said. "Everything went fine, just like we planned. Bugsy has the gun and he'll get rid of it for sure. He was covered in blood, though. So was the car. I had him change clothes and told him to burn the ones he was wearing. Pete was sort of out of it. He'll probably stay in the house for a month. How about you? What did the cops say?"

Naz answered, "They think it was a bad drug deal or some kind of Mafia hit. You believe that shit? A Mafia hit. They all seemed to be happy about it, though. Nobody liked that fucker—they were all glad to see him dead. You know, I think we'll be okay. I don't think anybody is gonna think we had anything to do with it. I just told the cops I was standing outside smoking a cigarette when Max came out and this car pulled up and shot him. That's what happened, right? They asked me if I recognized anybody in the car and I said, 'Fuck no, I just got the hell out of there.' You know, I almost puked in the diner."

Rizzo drove to Pete's house, where they had earlier parked Naz's van. They parted, then Rizzo drove home. Tomorrow, he would face his wife.

***

Joe was disappointed he could not be in the courtroom when the verdict came in, but his vacation week was over, so he was back at work. Jim was full of questions about the trial and Joe was happy to talk about it, saying how it was truly a learning experience. Jim, of course, wanted to know if Rizzo was guilty. Joe dodged the question by saying he really didn't know. He did say that, judging from the lack of evidence, it seemed that Rizzo was innocent, but they would have to wait for the jury's decision.

That decision came two days later. Joe was sitting at his desk when the telephone rang. Jim answered it and handed it to Joe. Jim started to walk away, but realizing what the call might be about, he turned around to watch. Even Louie stopped working and looked over at Joe. The call was from Janet. Sandy had just called her to say the verdict had come in. Not guilty on all counts. Joe couldn't believe it. He thought it might happen, but of course, he had his doubts. Rizzo got away with it. He got away with murder.

However, Rizzo still was not a free man. Joe learned that he had pleaded guilty on the gun charge before the trial, on the advice of his lawyer. After all, the police had found the unlicensed weapon in Rizzo's apartment during his arrest, so there was no getting around the fact. For that, he would have to serve nine months in prison. It was a bittersweet ending, but it could have been a lot worse.

There was little celebration after the trial, as Sandy would have to make do without her husband for a while longer. She still had some money hidden away, along with quite a lot of items she could sell. Joe and Janet helped out as much as they could, as did Joe and Sandy's mother.

On one occasion, Joe took a ride with Sandy and Rizzo's parents to visit Rizzo in prison. Joe felt uneasy riding in a car with Rizzo's father after causing his arrest for hoarding stolen guns. No one mentioned anything about it, and Joe was surely not going to bring it up. The conversation centered on Bugsy's upcoming trial. Wisely, he also had retained David Kaplin as his attorney. The trial was due to begin in a week, which made his parents apprehensive. Joe and Sandy didn't have any feelings about it either way. Rizzo had been acquitted of the murder, and that was all they were concerned about. Joe did wonder if Kaplin would again prove his worth and get Bugsy off as well. Only time would tell.

During the visit, Joe was forced to speak with Rizzo on a phone receiver and only see him through thick, dirty plate glass. Rizzo was upbeat, knowing that he would be released in a few months.

***

It didn't take Sandy long to figure out what had happened the previous night. The news of the shooting was all over television and the front page of the newspaper. That, along with Rizzo's suspicious behavior, had convinced her he was somehow involved. At first, he tried his usual defense of complete denial and ignorance of the whole thing. Being adamant in his denial had served him well in the past, but not this time. His smile gave him away. He couldn't help but smile as he was denying his involvement. He knew Sandy wasn't buying it, so against his better judgment, he decided to swear her to secrecy and tell all. She sat there staring at him in total disbelief and shock. She knew very well of his exploits, capers, and scores, but this was something new, and she didn't want to believe it was true.

"Why did you have to kill him? What if you get caught?" she said, almost yelling at him.

Rizzo was relieved that the murder itself didn't seem to bother her as much as the thought of him being caught.

"Look, we had to do it and we were very careful, very careful," he said. "No one will suspect us. They already think it was some Mafia drug deal gone bad, that's what the cops are already saying. Nobody knows about this, so you can't tell nobody, and I mean nobody."

Rizzo didn't want to tell her, but once he started, he blurted out the whole thing. He was still feeling a sense of pride about what they did and really wanted to talk about it with somebody, but he knew that would be extremely dangerous. Not everyone would understand and pat him on the back for a job well done. Then he wondered if his brothers were going to tell their wives. He surely hoped not. He knew one in particular couldn't be trusted not to tell the whole world. He decided to stop by Pete's house and tell him to be sure not to tell his wife anything about what they had done. Everyone knew that bitch had a big mouth. He didn't want to insult his brother, but felt he had to make sure. Of course, he would never admit to anyone that he had just told his own wife the whole story.

***

Dominic Marino flew into a rage when the verdict of not guilty was announced. How could this be? Everyone knew the bastards were guilty. Even the fact that Rizzo would spend the next nine months in jail on some bullshit gun charge didn't ease his anger and disgust. He could not understand how the system had failed, how that bastard had escaped justice. He blamed that idiot of a prosecutor for this travesty. He was too young and inexperienced to handle a trial of this magnitude; that trial should have been won easily. Marino was even more exasperated when he learned that the same prosecutor would be working on the next trial as well, and that Bugsy would be in court with the same attorney Rizzo had used. This time, the result had better be a guilty verdict, or heads would roll.

Joe and Janet decided it would be prudent to stay away from her father for a while. A few months later, when Bugsy's trial ended with a verdict of not guilty on all counts, Dominic Marino was surprisingly quiet. There was no explosion of temper or savage ranting. Janet was afraid he would have a heart attack from the pent-up anger he must be feeling. She asked her mother what he was doing at home, how he was handling the disappointing result for a second time. Fran said he walked around the house as if in deep thought and wouldn't say much. After all the bragging he had done before the trials about how Rizzo and his brothers would surely be sent to prison, this was indeed a major embarrassment for him.

All he could do was look forward to the next trial, when Naz and Pete would be tried together with new attorneys and facing a new prosecutor. He felt in his gut that the Buccelli luck would run out this time.

***

After Bugsy's acquittal, the two remaining brothers in custody were joyously optimistic. Rizzo and Bugsy found not guilty, along with the mistrial at their first appearance in court, led Naz and Pete to believe their freedom was assured. They couldn't wait to put all this behind them. Even their wives declining to use David Kaplin's services, saying he was much too expensive, didn't dampen their enthusiasm.

A new, more experienced prosecutor was named, signaling that this time things may be different. Joe had no desire to be at this trial, but his sister decided to attend occasionally to lend her support. At once, Sandy was amazed at the difference in tactics the defense attorneys used

185

compared to Rizzo's case. Although there was again a total lack of physical evidence, this time the defense wasn't helped by the recordings, on which both brothers were clearly heard implicating themselves in the murder. Unlike Rizzo and Bugsy, these two talked constantly and said plenty, which would be hard for the defense to counter. Also, Naz was without a doubt placed at the scene by many witnesses. They saw him arguing and fighting with the victim moments before he was killed. The attorneys realized this and made, it seemed to Sandy, a half-hearted effort. So, it was no great surprise when after only one day of deliberations, the jury found Naz and Pete guilty of first-degree murder. They later were sentenced to twenty years to life in a maximum-security prison for the murder of Max Santoro.

Joe felt sorry for them. Even though they had brutally killed a man in cold blood, he had gotten to know them well over the years and had seen other sides to them. The fun-loving, adventurous parts of their personalities could not be forgotten and would be missed. Already things had changed drastically. Gone was the hunting cabin, gone were the fishing trips, and gone were any future good times they would have all spent together. The brothers who were not involved in the burglaries or the murder turned their backs on those who were, blaming them for their family's misfortunes.

***

Dominic Marino got a little bit of satisfaction when two of the four were convicted and sentenced. Two was better than nothing, but he was not about to give up so easily. He knew Rizzo was a career criminal, meaning that he could not stay away from illegal activities for long. His only wish was that he would get another chance at him before he retired from the force.

One night after supper with Janet's parents, Dominic Marino asked Joe to follow him into the living room. They both sat down in silence for a few moments. Joe became uneasy and began to wonder what his father-in-law was up to.

Marino stared into Joe's eyes and said in a low and serious voice, "I want you to do something for me."

Joe said nothing as he slightly nodded his head.

Marino continued, "I want you to tell your brother-in-law that me and Fran are going to visit her sister on Long Island next weekend. Tell him we're leaving Saturday morning and won't be back until Sunday night. Then I want you to tell him that you found out I have money hidden in the basement. Tell him that I put away fifty thousand dollars in a box behind a file cabinet by the furnace."

Joe sat there not believing what he just heard. Was Marino attempting to set up an ambush for Rizzo? He soon had his answer.

"I'm going to be waiting down there, and when he shows up, I'm going to kill the bastard," Marino said with a smile on his face.

Joe sat there for a moment then slowly answered, "You know, I don't think I want to be involved in something like that. But you're only kidding, right? I mean this sounds like a conspiracy to commit murder."

Joe was certain Marino was joking, just living out a fantasy he was having of getting his final revenge. Was he trying to see where Joe's loyalties were, what side he was on? Did he want to know if Joe would easily and freely enter into a conspiracy to commit murder?

Joe was less certain it was all a joke when Marino got up and left the room saying, "It's not murder, I'd just be killing a burglar. Let me know what he says."

At first, Joe had no intention of telling any of this to Rizzo. But then Joe thought he should let Rizzo know just how much hatred Marino harbored toward him. It might make him think twice about committing any crimes locally, where if he were caught, Marino would be in a position to do Rizzo bodily harm. When Joe finally relayed the message to Rizzo, he just laughed, shrugged his shoulders, and asked, "Does he really have money down there?

"What do you mean, does he have money down there? You realize it's a trap—the guy wants to kill you. And no, I don't think he really has any money there. That's just bait so you break in and give him the excuse he wants to kill you. Don't you get it? The guy hates you because you beat the murder rap. He was embarrassed after all the bragging and gloating he did all over the city about finally putting you guys away. Man, you better stay far away from him and his house."

Marino never mentioned any of it again and Joe hoped that maybe he was just drunk.

***

Rizzo needed money. After his release from prison, he had to sell his truck, along with other personal items, and any cash he had hidden away was dwindling fast. With Naz and Pete away serving time, and Bugsy gone for parts unknown, Rizzo needed a new crew. With his brothers, he had had a well-oiled machine; they all knew what to do and they were good at it. They had operated together for years, honing their skills, leaving no trace behind that would incriminate them. They took pride in their ability to sniff out hiding places where people thought

188

their money was safe. Rizzo was especially proud of his ability to open safes, which he called the "iron man." Cracking open the iron man was one of his favorite challenges. Finding people he could trust and who would have the necessary skills would not be easy.

After he was released from prison, he actually tried going straight by looking for a job. He knew many people in the city who had businesses and jobs for someone like him. However, when they asked about his employment history, Rizzo just smiled because he didn't have one. In his entire life, he had never held an actual job. He had never even acquired a Social Security number. The only evidence one could find of his being alive was his rather colorful arrest record, along with some time served in jail. Because of the murder trial, even people he knew well were reluctant to hire him. After a while, he realized that the only way he knew how to make money was to steal it, so he would have to find a way to do that again.

Rizzo still had his informers, and from time to time, they would feed him information about some potentially lucrative score, but without a reliable crew to back him up, he was unable to act on the tips. Desperate, he resorted to stealing a few cars and selling them to a local chop shop to be dismantled for parts. The money wasn't good, and he felt that kind of work was beneath him, considering the skills he had acquired over the years. His search for a new crew went on.

CHAPTER TEN—OLD FRIENDS

Joe was at home one night, working on a small painting he had just started, when he heard a knock on the door. After the birth of their son, he and Janet needed a larger apartment with another bedroom for their growing family. Joe would set up his easel in the kitchen every night after Janet and the kids went to bed, and paint for a few hours. He had been accepted into a prestigious art gallery, where he was building a following for his work. He was beginning to wonder if his lifelong dream of being a professional artist might actually come true.

When Joe answered the knock at the door, he stepped back in surprise. It wasn't Rizzo that Joe was shocked to see, but the man standing beside him.

Snake Lips entered with Rizzo, and then smiling, said, "Joe Shoes, *che ne dici?*"

Joe hadn't seen him since the trip to Canada many years ago, and had forgotten all about him. Now here he was, standing in Joe's home.

Not smiling, Joe nodded at Snake Lips and said, "Yeah, what's up with you?"

Not that he cared in the least. Rizzo and Snake Lips walked into the kitchen, and then sat down at the table.

"Got any tea?" Rizzo asked.

"Tea? Yeah sure, I'll put the water on," answered Joe.

Joe didn't like this one bit. Why did Rizzo bring that asshole here? Joe watched as Snake Lips looked around his apartment like he was making mental notes about what might be worth taking at some later date. Joe knew how these guys operated, always looking for an opportunity.

Rizzo looked over Joe's painting and asked, "So how much is this one going for, two, three grand?"

Joe laughed and said, "I doubt it, maybe eight or nine hundred if I'm lucky. You never know with these things."

Actually, Joe was getting a lot more for his art, but thought it best to downplay what it was worth around these two. Joe wondered if Snake Lips was a part of Rizzo's new crew. That question was soon answered.

Rizzo asked Joe, "You know a lot about art, right? You know about what things are worth if we got something to sell."

Well, there it is, Joe thought. They have some stolen artwork they want to fence. Joe didn't mind giving his opinion on some artwork, as long as Rizzo didn't want to leave any of it here. That wasn't going to happen again.

He asked, "Well what kind of art do you have? A painting?"

"Nah, it's not a painting like what you do. It's like a drawing, pencil or some shit. It's on a piece of paper about yea big," Rizzo said, holding his hands apart. "Vinny says it might be worth a lot of money, so I thought you might know something about it."

Joe then realized that "Vinny" was Snake Lips' actual name. It was the first time he had heard it. Joe didn't care, though. He would always be Snake Lips to him.

Joe asked, "Is there a signature or name on it? And what's it of—is it a landscape or a portrait?"

Rizzo said, "It's a picture of some kid, just the head, and yeah, there's a name on it, but it's hard to read. It looks like 'P. P. Lupins' or 'Pupins' or something like that. It looks pretty old and faded, but I don't know, maybe it's worth something."

Joe sat there thinking for a minute, and then a realization came over him. It couldn't be. Could it?

Joe slowly asked, "Could it be P. P. Rubens? PETER PAUL RUBENS?"

Just then, the teakettle started whistling.

Rizzo said, "Yeah, it could be that, Rubens. Why, is he famous?"

Joe got up to remove the teakettle from the burner, then turned to Rizzo. "You have a Rubens drawing. How the hell did you get that?" he said, still not believing it possible. "Where is it now? Do you have it with you?" Joe didn't care about any consequences; he had to see it.

"It's at Vinny's house with some other shit we got. So, is that guy famous, or what?"

Joe was almost speechless as he reached for the mugs to fill with hot water, then asked, "Sna—. . . uh . . . Vinny, you want some tea?"

"Sure, might as well," Vinny said.

"Yeah, he's famous," Joe said as he served the tea. "He's considered one of the great masters. He's famous, alright. So, what else did you get from the . . . what? Was it a museum?"

192

Vinny answered that it wasn't a museum, just some tip that they got, and there was no need to go into it any further. Joe realized that Vinny wasn't going to be as forthcoming with information as Rizzo generally was. Rizzo said that they came away with some other items that also might be valuable, one of which was a large, white vase that had some Chinese pictures painted on it in blue paint. Vinny said that he was using it as an ashtray at home. An antiques dealer they knew and had worked with before was interested in buying the items, but they didn't want to get ripped off by selling them too cheaply. That guy had always offered them pennies on the dollar in the past, and he was very eager to see what they had this time.

Joe said he would like to see the drawing, but stated that he was not an expert on historic art, and especially not oriental vases. If the items were indeed authentic, they could be worth a fortune. "But that's only if they're authentic and not reproductions," he said.

Rizzo asked, "So can you tell if they're real and about how much they're worth?"

Joe answered, "Not with any certainty. Like I said, I'm not an expert. You have to check out the paper it's on to see if it's the right kind and if it's old enough, then you need to find out what kind of pencil or chalk was used. There are all kinds of tests experts use to determine if something is authentic or not. Maybe the dealer you know can tell. Do you trust him enough to tell you the truth?"

"I don't trust that rat bastard at all, you kiddin' me?" Rizzo said. "I know he's always fuckin' us over, but he's the only one I know who will buy this shit without asking any questions. We got to move it fast before the people we robbed get back. They're well known and are probably gonna be pissed."

"Yeah, I guess they might be," Joe said as Rizzo and Vinny got up to leave. Expert or not, Joe had reaffirmed what they hoped and nothing would wipe the smiles from their faces.

After they left, Joe thought about how Rizzo always seemed to have such incredible luck. After a lifetime of crime and never being caught, beating a murder rap, and now maybe making a ton of money from some stolen art treasures. A thought entered his mind that maybe a reward would be offered on the stolen artwork, but he immediately decided that would be too dangerous to even contemplate. He didn't want to get involved in any way, but he was curious about who the well-known victims were, and eager to see the Rubens drawing if he could. When Rizzo called him the next day, Joe thought that's what the call was about. He was wrong.

Rizzo asked if Janet was home, a sure signal that right away made Joe nervous.

"Why? What are you up to now?" Joe asked. "You want to bring over the drawing?"

"Nah, I got something I want to tell you. Who knows, you might even be interested."

"Janet's at her mother's house with the kids."

"Good, I'll be right there," Rizzo said.

"Is Snake Lips with you?"

Rizzo replied, "No, and I don't want him to know anything about this."

Relieved at hearing that, Joe said, "Sure, come on over."

Joe nervously awaited Rizzo's arrival, convincing himself not to agree to anything Rizzo proposed. Things had calmed down with his father-in-law, and Joe wanted to keep it that way. Even though Captain Marino still on occasion asked Joe about Rizzo's activities, Joe always played dumb and said he didn't know anything. He was just grateful Marino never again brought up the trap scenario he'd been plotting.

Rizzo arrived, and Joe put the kettle on the stove and then sat at the table to hear what Rizzo had to say. After all the years of hearing his incredible stories and offerings, he was not disappointed with this one.

"You know that place me and Vinny robbed last week, where we got that picture? Well, there was something else we saw in there and I can't let it go. It was in a glass case that filled the whole wall, and it had a separate alarm system on it. There was no time to crack it—we had to get out fast. Vinny says forget about it, but I can't. So if that pussy don't want to go back to get it, then fuck him, I'll go myself."

Joe was now intrigued by Rizzo's story, but he was waiting for the other shoe to drop. He knew Rizzo wanted him as an accomplice, and Joe was preparing to decline, no matter what it was. But so far Rizzo hadn't asked that. He just went on about how this was the score of a lifetime, what he called a "retirement score." After this, he said, he wouldn't have to worry about money ever again.

Finally, Joe asked, "Well, what is it? What was in the case?"

"Gold, a whole wall full of gold. There were gold plates—big ones, little ones, cups, goblets, serving dishes, forks, spoons, all kinds of shit. All gold. Big trays, little trays, even salt and pepper shakers, you can't imagine what was in there. It was all shiny, beautiful gold. And if that *stronzo* fuck don't want to get it, then I will, and he ain't getting none of it."

Rizzo added that it had to be done fast, before the people came back. "We got past the main alarm, but the one on the case was different," he said. "I couldn't see how it was wired, and we thought we were out of time. Then I find out the people won't be back until Thursday, so there's still time to get it. I got some help to go with me, and I don't know, but I thought that maybe you would want to come along. I would feel bad not giving you the chance, so think about it. We're going to break the case open, alarm or not. Grab all we can, then get the hell out of there before the cops show up. This is really a big one."

Joe said, "You know you're taking a hell of a chance with this. Once you break the alarm, how do you know how much time you'll have before the cops surround the place? Gold is heavy. How are you going to carry it all?"

"Believe me, I know how heavy gold is, I've been there before. I got plenty of help."

Joe said, "Well, then you don't need me if you got enough guys."

"No, I don't need you. I wanted to give you the chance, that's all. Believe me, you'll be sorry you didn't come along on this one. But if you don't want in, fine. Maybe I'll toss you a cup so you could toast my good fortune."

"What about the Rubens drawing and the vase and all the other stuff you got? Aren't you getting a ton of money from that?" Joe asked.

Rizzo said, "That fuckin' dealer told us he has to contact a guy somewhere in Europe who deals in that kind of shit. He says it may take a while and he can't give us any idea on how much we will get or when. I don't trust that bastard. I know he's gonna rip us off. That's why I'm

196

doing this. This is mine—no dealer, no Vinny, just a couple of *gavones* I can take care of easy enough."

Joe didn't want to know what he meant by that, but it was easy for him not to get involved. He had no interest in any of this and wanted no part of it. He wished Rizzo luck, and then added that it would not be a good idea to bring any of it over to his house. Janet would completely lose it this time. She might even run to her old man.

"Don't worry," Rizzo said. "I already got a place to hide it."

With that, Rizzo left, leaving Joe with the thought that he may never see him again.

CHAPTER ELEVEN—ALL THAT GLITTERS

A few days passed without any word from Rizzo on how it all went. There were no news reports or articles in the paper about his arrest, so Joe figured all went well. He was anxious to see some of this golden treasure, but he did not ask Sandy anything about it.

Later that week, Joe was at his mother's house with Janet and the kids. When he went down to the basement to replace a blown fuse, he couldn't help but notice some boxes piled against the wall that were not there a few days ago. Suspecting what they might contain, he went over and opened the top box. Sure enough, the box held plates, shiny plates. Even to Joe's eye, uneducated about precious metals, he knew right away they were not made of gold. The color was slightly off, there was a distinct metallic smell, and when he tried to scratch the metal with a nail, it was much too hard. His first thought was that all Rizzo had was a pile of brass plates and nothing more, what a blunder.

That's why he hadn't heard anything from Rizzo about his newfound fortune. He surely would want to crow and rub it in Joe's face about missing out on the score of a lifetime. He probably went to his fence right away with a plate and got the bad news. That must have been one of the worst moments of Rizzo's life, maybe even worse than being arrested for murder. To be so high one day, then to have it all vanish the next was so typical of Rizzo that Joe had to smile.

But then Joe got angry as he looked at the boxes piled up in his mother's house, putting her at risk again for hoarding stolen merchandise. He wanted them gone, and gone now. He went upstairs and asked his mother if she knew what Rizzo had brought over in those boxes.

"He never said what was in them, just that he needed to keep them here for a couple of days," she said.

Joe said, "No, they can't stay here. We have to get them out of here now."

His mother asked, "Why? What's in them?"

"They're plates, stolen plates, and they have to go now."

"Ooh, plates! I want to see them."

"You can't see them," Joe said. "If the cops find them here, you'll be arrested for possessing stolen property. You wouldn't like them anyway, they're all brass."

"Who eats off of brass plates? Ugh, get rid of them," she said, waving her hands toward the door.

Joe called Rizzo to set up a meeting, knowing that he never discussed these kinds of things over the phone. He never mentioned anything specific about a job, and if he said anything, he would talk in some kind of code. Joe just wanted Rizzo to get his "treasure" out of his mother's house. Sandy answered the phone, and she seemed upset. Joe figured it was the realization that the plates weren't the golden riches she thought they would be, but it turned out to be worse. She would not talk about it on the phone, but said she was leaving on an errand and would stop by later on that night. She didn't know where Rizzo was at the moment, but asked Joe not to leave their mother's house until she got there. Joe spent the time waiting for his sister by looking over the boxes in the basement.

Many other items were in there besides the plates. Just as Rizzo had described, the boxes contained a whole array of dinnerware, including serving trays, cups and goblets of various sizes, forks and spoons, even little salt and pepper shakers for each place setting. There also was what looked like a tea pitcher with a beautiful, unique design. Joe could understand why Rizzo would, with a quick glance, mistake these items for gold. But upon closer inspection, which he would have had while handling them, he should have known what they really were and left them all behind. Joe didn't know if they had any value at all, but they had been enclosed in an alarmed glass wall unit. They must be worth something.

When Sandy arrived a few hours later, Joe hadn't seen her look this scared since the day of Rizzo's arrest. He asked her what happened.

She nervously answered, "One of the idiots Rizzo took on that job last week was caught trying to sell some of the plates to a pawn shop and got busted. I know he's going to rat Rizzo out, it's only a matter of time. I just spent the last two hours dumping all we had along Old Mill Road. I got rid of all of it. Now we have to get rid of what he stashed here. Is there any of it at your house?"

Janet shot Joe a threatening glance before he answered, "Hell, no, I don't have any of it at my house."

Sandy said, "We better get the rest of it out of here now."

Joe shook his head, thinking even when he doesn't get involved in Rizzo's crap, he still gets pulled into it somehow. Now he again had to load up his car with stolen merchandise and dump it before the police came to arrest everyone. And again, Rizzo was nowhere around. Sandy somehow talked Janet into helping while Joe loaded the boxes into the back seat of his car.

As they prepared to leave, Joe's mother said, "What, are yous leaving? I just made coffee."

"We'll be right back," Joe said. "Watch the kids and save the coffee for us."

Sandy and Janet got in the back seat, one on each side of the boxes, as Joe started the drive across the city to Old Mill Road.

Joe knew Old Mill Road well. He had driven on it many times and knew the sordid reputation it had as a dumping ground for all kinds of things, including an occasional body or two. It was a long, dark, deserted road winding through a heavily wooded area just outside the city limits. When Joe turned onto the road, Sandy and Janet rolled down the rear windows and began tossing out all of Rizzo's treasure into the tall grass. After driving the entire length of the road, Joe turned around to head back. He had driven almost the entire way back before all of it was thrown out. Relieved that he had dodged another crisis, he drove back to his mother's house.

Upon returning, Sandy announced she was going home, got into her car, and left. Joe knew trouble had been brewing between Rizzo and his sister for some time. The lifestyle they were living had to be very stressful. They were nearly always broke, and that, along with the constant worry about the police breaking in the door with guns drawn, caused Sandy to finally reach her limit. Added to that was the guilt over all the ill-gotten gains. Joe knew Rizzo never felt any guilt or shame, but his sister must have, and it was beginning to weigh on her heavily. He thought for sure they were heading for a divorce.

A few minutes after Sandy left, Rizzo entered the house carrying a dozen large, white boxes stacked on top of each other. He placed them on the kitchen table.

"Got any tea?" he asked cheerfully.

Before Joe could ask what was in the boxes, his mother reached over and started to open one.

"They're cheesecakes, different ones. I got a whole truckful outside," Rizzo said.

"Where did you get a truckful of cheesecakes?" Joe asked.

"I was driving home when I saw this delivery truck stop in front of that deli on Pine Street, you know the one where that shithead Elmo works. So I pulled over across the street to see what was in there. You never know what it could be. It might be worth something, so you know, I had to check it out. I look in the truck and there's all these boxes on shelves and it smelled really good in there. Then I see that *stronzo* driver left the keys in the ignition, so I took the truck. Then I'm thinking, where can I go to check out all these boxes? So I drove down to the card room on Chestnut Street."

Joe had heard stories about the card room. It was a private club located in the back-storage area of a small neighborhood bar. It was a hangout where the bar's part-owner, Tony Fats, ran card and dice games, and it was one of Rizzo's favorite haunts when he had nothing else to do. He never gambled there, but it was a good place to get tips on places to rob.

"So I parked the truck out back and took some of the boxes inside," Rizzo continued. "I open them up, cheesecakes—what the fuck am I gonna do with cheesecakes? Everybody came over to see what I had, so I handed some out to the guys. I thought I should try and make up for when I scared the shit out of them last week.

"Ha, you should have seen them all scatter like rabbits when I threw that hand grenade through the front door. They didn't know it was a dummy. They thought one of the assholes who lost money in there got

202

pissed off and tried to kill them. I was outside when they all ran out the door, leaving that tub of shit Tony behind, who's so fat he couldn't get out of his chair. He was in there still screaming for help when they all saw me outside laughing. Some of the guys thought it was a good joke, but a few didn't, especially Tony. He finally came out cursing because he got so scared he pissed his pants. Hey, if they can't take a joke, fuck 'em.

"So, Ma, you like cheesecakes, right?" Rizzo asked as he opened one of the boxes.

"Oh, they look good, but they're so big—where am I supposed the keep them? They gotta be kept cool in a refrigerator, no? They won't fit," she said.

"I don't know, keep some and give the rest away. Who cares? Look, they got 'em already cut," Rizzo said as he scooped out a piece and shoved it into his mouth. He then quickly went to the sink to wash his hands.

"I'll take some home," Joe said, thinking that if he didn't, they would just spoil and have to be thrown away. He then asked, "So what about the truck, what are you going to do with the rest of them?"

"Yeah, I gotta dump the truck fast before the cops start looking for it, but I'll make a few more stops first. You know how I like to spread around some happiness," Rizzo said, grinning.

As he was leaving, Joe had to ask, "So what about all that gold you went after—what happened with that?"

"Ah, that turned out not to be gold, just a bunch of worthless crap. It looked good, all shiny behind glass, but I don't know what the hell it is.

I know it ain't gold and I know it ain't worth shit. I got to get rid of it. It was nothing but a big waste of time."

"Yeah, well, we just got back from dumping all of it on Old Mill Road," Joe said.

"You did? Was Sandy with you? 'Cause we got some of that crap at home."

"Yeah, she was with us and she didn't seem too happy when she left."

Rizzo shrugged his shoulders. "She's always pissed off about something," he said. "But hey, thanks for dumping that crap for me, you really helped me out. Here, have a cheesecake," he said with a big smile.

Rizzo left as Joe reached for a slice of cheesecake and asked his mother if she would pour him a cup of coffee. It was damn good cheesecake.

Rizzo was never questioned about the dinnerware heist. His accomplice must have been too scared to mention his name and took the fall on his own. Rizzo advised him not to admit to the burglary, but to say he found those plates on the side of the road, which again made Joe an accessory to one of Rizzo's crimes. So, with his dreams of a retirement score gone, Rizzo continued on the only path he knew.

***

Over the next year, Joe watched the Buccelli family continue to fall apart. After the murder, the jovial family unit just melted away. The only two brothers who escaped the fall were Big Al and Sonny, solely because they were never involved in the family business and held down regular jobs. It was ironic that the one brother everyone always made fun of was doing just fine. Sonny's marriage was strong, he had a son who was doing well, he owned two cars and his own home. Big Al still lived in his palatial, well-appointed home with his upper-class wife. Joe was sure they missed the hunting cabin and the other trips the family took together. He was certain they continued to lay the blame for those losses on their brothers who had decided to live a life of crime. Joe hadn't seen much of either of them over the past year.

Of the four burglar brothers, Rizzo was the only one still around. Naz and Pete were serving out their sentences in prison and wouldn't be out for some time. Bugsy had left town after his trial and disappeared somewhere in southern Florida. Rumor was he got a job working for some deep-sea salvage company. Joe thought that maybe he was learning the skills he would need to go after that gold they lost in the river years ago.

One day, Rizzo asked Joe if he would like to visit Naz and Pete in prison the next time he went. Joe said sure, he would like to see them. He also was curious to see the inside of a maximum-security prison. Rizzo said he would ask his brothers to add Joe's name to the visitor list when he next spoke with them.

Sing Sing was one of the most notorious prisons in the country; it ranked right up there with Alcatraz. When Joe was traveling to and from college, the train he was took went right through the prison complex. Although he couldn't see anything but high stone walls on each side, it was still a thrill to be passing through the famous "Big House" Now he would have an opportunity to see the inside, but in a good way, as a visitor. He recalled his father-in-law once talking about witnessing the execution of Eddie Mays, the last prisoner to ride the lightning on Old Sparky at Sing Sing back in 1963. Joe had read about the executions of Julius and Ethel Rosenberg for passing on nuclear secrets to the Soviets back in the '50s. The prison had a lot of history, and being a history buff, Joe really wanted to see the place. He also really wanted to see Naz and Pete again. He couldn't remember the last time he saw them, but it was years ago.

Many things had changed over the past few years. Captain Marino had finally retired from the police force, but without ever fulfilling his dream of locking Rizzo away for good. However, he seemed busier and happier now than he ever had, with all the community functions he had time to enjoy. He even bought a small bar, which catered to all his cop buddies, both retired and those still on the force. Joe was relieved to no longer be pressed for information about Rizzo's crimes.

Joe also had had some major life changes. After his paintings started to sell regularly, he contemplated quitting his job to pursue a career as a full-time artist. It was a big step, one his wife was not too pleased about. She complained to her father about Joe wanting to quit his job, which led to Marino threatening to punch Joe in the mouth. But Joe had made his decision to live his dream, or at least give it a good try. As luck would have it, after he handed in his resignation at work, his art sales suddenly dried up. He sold nothing for the next six months, living off his retirement savings along with Janet's paycheck, which led her to become more embittered as the months went by. Joe was unsettled by this turn of events as well. He couldn't understand why his sales suddenly stopped. It was like some cruel joke was being played on him, one he did not find funny at all. He decided to give it one year. At the end of that time, if his sales hadn't improved, he would find a job and go back to work. Janet was not amused with that plan and gave Joe an ultimatum: Get a job now or she would leave him and file for divorce. They had found themselves drifting farther apart for years, so it wasn't much of a decision for Joe to make. Janet did not enjoy being part of the art world Joe was pursuing, and he knew she would never be happy.

The divorce was quick and easy, as no one contested it and there wasn't much property to divide between them. As irony would have it, Joe's sales soon picked up after their separation and he found himself suddenly doing quite well. He found a small apartment in the city and finally became the full-time artist he had always dreamed of becoming.

CHAPTER TWELVE—GOING UP THE RIVER

Rizzo picked up Joe about nine o'clock in the morning for their visit to see Naz and Pete. On the way there, Rizzo began telling Joe about some of the latest jobs he had pulled off with his new crew. He was still working with Snake Lips, which Joe was sorry to hear. It was obvious that Rizzo hadn't progressed at all over the years. He had learned nothing from his time in jail or his brothers' long incarceration. This was the only life he knew, in fact, the only life he truly wanted. Joe could understand that to a certain degree. After all, he, too, was finally living the life he had always wanted. He was thankful, though, that the constant threat of prison wasn't hanging over his head, and he was sorry that Rizzo didn't see the light and try to straighten out his life.

As they drove into the visitors' parking lot of the prison, Joe took notice of the manned guard towers, along with a score of patrolling correctional officers. Rizzo asked Joe to empty his pockets of everything except his wallet and any change he had on him. Joe asked about the change.

Rizzo answered, "That's for the vending machines in the visitors' room. The boys don't have no money. If they want something to eat or drink, we have to put the money in and pull the knob to get what they want, then step back so they can take it out of the machine. We can't pass them nothing or even touch them. The guards are always watching, so don't do nothing stupid."

Joe thought, no problem, I'm not touching anyone.

The large stone building loomed over them as they entered through a double door into the reception area. There was no mistaking the purpose of this place. It was cold, gray, and foreboding. As they patiently waited in line to begin the sign-in process, Joe looked around at the other visitors and noticed they were almost exclusively young women. Some had infants in their arms, while others dragged along older children who seemed incredibly bored and wanting to be anywhere but here. After handing over his driver's license and signing his name in the log book, Joe was allowed to line up with the other visitors in front of a locked door. A loud buzzer sounded as the door unlocked, and they proceeded down a long, bare, well-lit hallway.

Rizzo and the other visitors seemed to know the routine, so Joe just followed their lead. As they came to another door at the end of the hallway, they stopped and waited until another buzzer sounded. One of the women pulled the door open, allowing them to enter a large dining room with long rows of tables and chairs. The room was painted a pale green, and bright lights were shining down on the many visitors and inmates seated on opposite sides of the tables. A catwalk about eight feet above the floor surrounded the entire room, and more than a dozen prison guards stood there, intently watching the crowd below. The noise level was incredible, with everyone talking loudly to be heard over others who were crying along with the small children and infants. What a circus this is, Joe thought. This was a horrible way for people to visit their family members, even if they were criminals.

Rizzo and Joe walked to the end of one of the tables that had some empty chairs, then sat down waiting for Naz and Pete to join them. Joe noticed four other doors with small, mirrored glass windows, which he surmised were one-way mirrors that allowed officers to watch the room unnoticed. On the rear wall was a bank of vending machines containing a variety of candy and soft drinks.

After not seeing Naz and Pete for a few years, Joe was surprised at their appearance. They both looked like they had gained some weight, and none of it fat. They obviously had spent much of their time working out, lifting weights and building muscle. They were rather big guys to begin with, but now they looked truly menacing. Joe thought their new look was probably a mixture of having a lot of free time, as well as a defense mechanism for fending off any attacks from fellow inmates. Seeing their size and knowing their history, no one in their right mind would try to mess with these two, Joe thought. The fact that they were in here for murder made them untouchable.

As Naz and Pete walked over to the table, Naz said with a smile, "Hey, look who it is, it's Joe Shoes. You come back in to see the thieves."

Pete just silently nodded hello as they both sat down. Naz asked Rizzo about any news from the outside concerning his family or people they knew. Rizzo didn't have much to say, so the conversation turned to what Joe had been up to. Naz noticed the large silver and brass belt buckle Joe was wearing and asked where he got it. Joe said it was a gift from an art dealer in San Antonio, Texas, where he had an art show last year. Joe felt a little guilty talking about his travels to two guys who had been locked up for years. He played it down, then asked them both if they would like to have a couple of buckles like the one he had. He said he could get them each one if they wanted.

Pete said, "Naw, somebody would just steal 'em."

Joe tried to see if they held any resentment for Rizzo being free while they weren't. After all, Rizzo was just as guilty of that murder as they were, but he was a free man and they were going to stay locked up in here for a very long time. Naz seemed to have a positive attitude, but Pete looked depressed or maybe pissed off. Joe thought it was probably both, and that he had every reason to feel that way. If any of them truly regretted what they had done or the life choices they had made, it was Pete. He had been an unwilling accomplice in the murder scheme, but felt compelled to go along out of loyalty to his brothers. Joe wished he could do something to help him.

Rizzo asked if they wanted anything from the vending machines. They nodded yes, then stood up and walked toward the one containing soft drinks. Rizzo and Joe followed. Naz pointed to a Dr Pepper, Rizzo put in the correct change, pulled the lever, and then stood back as the soda can dropped into the bin. Joe glanced up at two guards watching them from above as Naz reached in to retrieve the can of soda. The procedure was repeated for Pete's selection, after which they all returned to their seats under the watchful gaze of the guards. The one-hour visit ended none too soon for Joe. He couldn't wait to get out of there. They said their goodbyes without shaking hands and promised to visit again soon, while Joe knew he would never come here again.

They stood by the exit door while Naz and Pete were escorted out of the room. The buzzer sounded, allowing Joe to push the door open and then walk briskly down the corridor to the door at the other end. He went to open it, but found it locked. Rizzo and the few other visitors in the hallway laughed at him as he pulled again on the door.

Rizzo said, "Where do you think you are, some hotel or something? They're not letting us out of here until they strip-search Naz and Pete and whoever else to see if we passed them anything. Sometimes it takes a while."

Joe felt like a caged animal. He had never been locked up against his will before. He couldn't imagine what it was like for Naz and Pete. All he could do was stand there and wait for the buzzer.

***

211

Joe was starting to make some real money for the first time in his life. He had signed a contract with a company that published limited-edition prints of his paintings and sold them nationally to hundreds of art dealers. Part of his obligation was to travel around the country for appearances with the various dealers who were selling his art. Sometimes he was gone for weeks at a time, leaving him worn out when he got home. According to his divorce settlement, he had Marie and Zachary every other weekend. He tried to make the visits fun, as a lot of divorced fathers do, by taking them to museums, parks, and zoos. He also spent time at his mother's house with Sandy and Rizzo and their two children. There was no longer a hunting cabin to go to, but Rizzo had just bought some acreage along with a mobile home in the same general area upstate with money he had acquired from a recent score.

Rizzo had received a tip from a friend of the owner of an exclusive fine dining restaurant. As Joe listened to Rizzo's latest success story, he continued to be amazed at how Rizzo often was informed about a lucrative score by a so-called friend of the victim. Perhaps it was jealousy of the man's wealth or maybe just a case of food poisoning from some bad shellfish. Whatever the reason, this was a way for the informer to seek a little revenge and also make some money for himself.

Rizzo said the informer told him that the restaurant owner kept large amounts of cash in his home, money he had not reported as income from his business. The man thought he was being very clever by keeping a large, exposed safe in his study. The safe contained little of value, but would serve as a decoy, occupying any potential thieves while a silent alarm sent a signal to the local police. His big mistake was foolishly bragging about his ingenious setup to the wrong person after having too many cocktails at a dinner party. He went on to reveal that he kept his valuables in another safe, this one built into the wall of a small hallway closet. He was sure that thieves could not discover its location. The informer, eager to get his hands on some of that money, got word to Rizzo and the countdown began.

When Rizzo met with the informer, they decided to let a little time go by before doing the job, to avoid raising suspicion on any of the dinner party guests. That is, if the restaurateur could remember saying anything at all, as drunk as he had been. Rizzo decided that he and Snake Lips could handle this job without any help. The informer had told them there could be a lot of money in that house and they wanted it all for themselves.

They were given the man's address and they found the house to be large and well secluded. The front entrance was secured by a large iron gate. The rear of the property was heavily wooded for about one hundred yards before ending alongside a subdivision. That neighborhood currently was a hive of activity. The residents were well known for competing with one another to see who could put up the most ghoulish displays for the Halloween season. The decorating contest happened every year and the neighborhood was a popular attraction, a place where strangers lurking about would not be noticed. It seemed perfect.

After hawking the premises for a few days, they learned the man's movements, when he left for work and when he returned. It was all too easy, as the demands of the restaurant business kept the man away from home most of the time. He was gone for long hours during the day and into the night. They also learned that he was divorced, so there would be no other family members coming and going at different times. The only other person they noticed entering the home was a cleaning lady who came by twice a week on a regular schedule, and they could easily avoid her. So, it was set. They decided to enter the house late in the afternoon on Halloween, when the streets would be full of people accompanying their kids trick-or-treating and enjoying the many displays. When the day came, Rizzo and Snake Lips casually walked the neighborhood, each carrying a bag of tools and dressed in black with masks covering their faces. Several times, children and adults who walked past them asked what they were supposed to be. They gleefully answered, "We're burglars," which led to laughter and compliments on their costumes.

They entered the wooded area unnoticed and made their way to the rear of the house. Already familiar with the simple alarm system from previous visits, Rizzo quickly disabled it, and then they both entered the house through a back door that was easily forced open.

Hearing Rizzo tell this story, Joe noticed that he had become a little less cautious than in the past by not having anyone on the outside keeping watch. Rizzo made it plain that he didn't want to share this score with anyone else. Joe thought his greed was making him careless.

Rizzo continued, telling how he and Snake Lips found most of the rooms in the house well lit. When they entered the study and saw the large safe sitting in the corner, they looked at each other, smirking. Rizzo did approach the safe and without touching it, examined it closely. He was sure he could crack it even if it was alarmed, but why waste his time? If the informant was right, it didn't contain what they came for. They left the study and came to a long hallway, where they saw several closed doors on each side. As Rizzo approached the first door, he noticed a keyhole in the doorknob. He slowly turned the knob and as he guessed, it was locked. He walked down the hall and saw that all the other doors had the same type of knob. Snake Lips carefully tried the other doors and found them all locked. They couldn't tell which one might be a closet.

"Now, you gotta think, why would that *stronzo* prick lock all the doors inside his house?" Rizzo said. "And from where I was, I can't tell if he has them alarmed on the other side with some kind of silent alarm he's supposed to have in there. So I'm thinkin' what he wants is to funnel everybody to that fuckin' safe he's got sittin' there, so they set off the alarm. Or maybe kick in one of these doors, which probably have alarms too. So now the guy really pissed me off."

Joe could tell that Rizzo was really enjoying telling this story.

He continued, "So I tell Vinny, 'Fuck the doors, let's go through the wall.' We started chopping a hole in the wall next to the first door. After we break through, we see it's a bedroom, so we move down to the next door and chop a hole in that wall, another bedroom. Next, we try the wall on the other side of the hall, another fuckin' bedroom. Now we're both pissed, so the holes got bigger as we went down the hall. We get almost to the end when we find the fuckin' closet.

"We chopped a hole big enough for us to get through and then threw all the clothes out on the floor. We started to check out the walls, which were made of wood that smelled like cedar. After starting to rip some of it down, we found a removable panel hiding the safe. I was surprised that the safe was so big, but it was a real cheap piece of shit. I was glad, because we spent more time in there than we wanted to already. I cracked it open and almost shit when I saw the stacks of money that were in there. I told Vinny to get our backpacks out of the bags and we started to fill them with hundred-dollar bills. That's all he had in there was hundreds. We took it all, cleaned him out.

"Then we packed up our tools and got the hell out of there. For a second, I thought, I don't know . . . maybe I should take a dump on the big dummy safe to leave him a message. But then I thought, nah, forget about it. As it is, that poor fuck will probably have a stroke when he gets home."

Rizzo continued with a wide grin, "You know what was the best part? When we were walking back through the woods, I was behind Vinny and reached under the flap of his backpack and took out fistfuls of cash. He never felt a thing. Later on when we divided it up, he had no idea I had thousands more in my pockets. Well, *ma va fanculo* to him and that other guy. You know he was wrong with what he was doin'—you shouldn't try to hide money from the government like that. It's not right."

"Yeah, I know how much that bothers you," Joe said as he smiled at the thought of Snake Lips getting ripped off.

"You know, anytime you want to come along with me, just say it. I'm still waiting for you to smarten up," Rizzo said.

Joe just shook his head and smiled.

Rizzo never told Joe how much money he made on that score, but it was enough for him to buy some really nice property, including a decent-sized mobile home. In a way, it took the place of the cabin they had lost. Rizzo was spending more time at his new country estate and even entertained the idea of moving there permanently.

Sandy was all for it. She was tired of living in the city and wanted a simpler, quiet life. They made the move when the weather turned warm, and for a while, with the change of scenery, they seemed very happy. Joe sometimes visited on weekends with the kids, but after a while, he noticed all was not well. The problem was Rizzo. He couldn't apply his trade up there in the sticks. He needed people around him, he needed places to rob. As far as he could tell, no one up there had any money or anything else of value worth taking. One weekend when Joe was visiting, he told him the only thing he had robbed lately was a toilet from some nearby house when his developed a crack. He laughed about what the homeowner would think when he went in to take a shit and found only a hole in the floor.

Rizzo even resorted to an old method of his to find out if somebody had money buried in a can or hidden away somewhere. He would approach some old farmer with something like a riding mower or a cache of tools or maybe even some guns to see if he was interested in buying anything. If the man agreed to buy some item, Rizzo would insist on cash. After the transaction was completed, Rizzo would smell the money for any traces of mildew or a musky scent, which would tell him the money had been hidden somewhere in the house and didn't come from a bank. He would then mark the location for a future hit. Rizzo even figured out a way to save on his electric bill by drilling a small hole through the side of the glass globe covering the meter. He would then periodically insert a small sliver of wood to stop the wheel from turning, thus interrupting the meter from logging the kilowatt hours used. After a few days when he removed the wood, he would plug the hole with a dab of clay to stop any condensation from building up inside the meter that would tip off the electric company something was amiss. Joe continued to marvel at the thinking process of the criminal mind. If all that creative ability was put toward a positive purpose, how the world would be a better place. But Rizzo would never see it that way.

It took only a few months for Rizzo to realize that he couldn't live away from all the action the city offered him. Sandy was content to stay put, but Rizzo was spending weekdays staying in his mother's house back in the city. He would drive up to visit on weekends, but only if he wasn't "working."

The beginning of the end came on one such weekend. Joe rode up with his kids for a visit, and they all decided to go to a local restaurant for supper. It was one of the better eateries in the area, offering a varied menu at reasonable prices in a classy setting. Sandy greatly enjoyed going there as often as possible to escape her rural everyday surroundings. She would go there for supper and sometimes for lunch during the week when Rizzo was in the city. She enjoyed making small talk with the waitresses and the restaurant became her only social outlet. They all enjoyed a great meal, complete with tea and dessert, and then Rizzo got up to go to the restroom and announced that he would pick up the check. Joe thanked him as they all prepared to leave. While waiting in the car, they saw Rizzo walk out the restaurant door and then break into a run toward them. He jumped into the driver's seat, started the car, and sped out of the parking lot. Surprised, Joe asked what was going on, to which Rizzo proudly replied that he had just skipped out of paying the bill.

Joe said, "Why did you do that? I had enough money to pay the bill."

Rizzo answered, "Save your money. This is better, no?"

The next sound they heard was Sandy screaming from the back seat, "What the fuck did you do? Why didn't you pay the bill? Turn around right now and go back and pay it. Do it now!"

"I'm not going back to that rathole. Fuck 'em," answered Rizzo loudly.

"That's it, that's it, you son of a bitch. I can't take this shit anymore. I've had it. You ruined it for me, I could never go in there again. It's the only fucking place I enjoyed in this fucking town and

218

now I can't ever go back. I'm so fucking embarrassed. I hate you!" Sandy screamed.

Joe had never seen his sister this angry. Even if he went back to pay the bill, it was too late. Sandy would never be able to face her friends in the restaurant again. He really felt sorry for her as she sobbed in the back seat.

Joe turned to Rizzo and said, "Man, you shouldn't have done that. You really screwed things up for her."

Rizzo smirked and said, "What's the big deal? So what? She can pay the fucking bill if she wants to. Tell them I forgot, that's all."

Joe looked at him and saw a man completely without remorse, without empathy, a total sociopath. He wondered why it had taken him so long to see the real Rizzo. All the people Rizzo had hurt in the past were just names to him. The stories Rizzo had told him were just that— stories. Joe didn't know any of the people who were victimized. It was never personal, not until now. Joe could not get past the incredible hurt this unfeeling asshole had just inflicted on his sister. This, indeed, was a watershed moment, he could feel it deep down inside. He knew Rizzo and his sister had been having problems in their marriage for years, but this may have been the final straw. He would be shocked if she didn't divorce him after this episode. When they arrived back at the trailer, Sandy put the kids to bed, went into her bedroom, and locked the door.

Rizzo sat at the kitchen table and started to laugh. "What the hell is she so pissed off about? She must be on the rag."

Joe stared at him in disbelief at the incredible stupidity he was witnessing. It was truly unbelievable. How could anybody be so dense, so out of touch with basic human feelings? The man truly had no soul.

They both went outside on the porch. Joe looked around at the countryside while Rizzo started telling him about some jobs he had lined up, some really good scores, he said. Joe wasn't listening; he really didn't care anymore. He was saying goodbye to the surroundings, knowing that this was all over and he would probably never come back here.

***

As Joe continued to advance his art career, he decided it was time to invest in some land. He was tired of living in the city in his small apartment and had accumulated enough money to make a change. He purchased two acres outside a small town upstate where he planned on building a log home in the quiet, pastoral setting. The property was heavily wooded and would take some effort to clear a spot where the house was to be built. He devoted much of his weekends when he didn't have his kids to cutting down large and small trees and clearing away piles of tangled underbrush. The smaller trees and brush could be burned on the site. The larger trees had to be cut up and split for future use as firewood or carted away.

That's when Rizzo entered the scene. He offered to help Joe by hauling the larger cut logs away in his truck. He said he could sell the wood in the city for a good price after it was split for firewood. When Joe asked if he was going to split the wood himself, Rizzo laughed and said, "Hell no! I know a guy who got a log splitter—he loves cutting up this shit."

Joe knew by now that Rizzo would not want to work that hard or get his hands dirty. Rizzo started to accompany Joe when he went to work on his property, but would only stay long enough to load up his truck. Once he had the wood loaded, he would drive off, leaving Joe to continue cutting down more trees and trimming the branches. Joe could have used his help, but had learned not to expect anything once Rizzo got what he wanted.

The one-time Rizzo decided to hang around and help with felling of one of the larger trees, Joe wished he hadn't. The tree was blocking the area where Joe wanted his driveway to begin. He would not attempt to cut it down by himself because it was near the county road, and if the tree fell in the wrong direction, it would take down the overhead power lines. If that happened, Joe would be responsible for replacing them, which would be very expensive. They both studied the tree to determine which way it would fall, but could not agree. Joe's reason for wanting someone with him was to get another opinion in case he was missing something. He had some experience from all the trees he had already cut down, but sometimes he had misjudged the way a tree would fall. Once, he looked on in helpless panic as a tree almost landed on his car. The tree twisted around as it fell, landing only a few feet from Joe's car. If his vehicle was crushed, he would find himself stranded there with no way of getting help, so he became very cautious when anticipating how a tree would fall.

He did not agree with Rizzo's opinion that the tree would fall away from the power lines. Joe studied the tree carefully and instinctively knew it would fall into the power lines no matter how they cut the base. The distribution of the branches, because of their weight, would determine how it fell. Rizzo was ready with his chainsaw to begin the cutting when Joe stopped him and asked if he had any heavy chain in his truck. He said he did, but laughed at Joe, adding that he was certain the tree would fall away from the lines. Joe could not afford to take the chance.

He drove his car directly next to the tree to be cut, then climbed on the roof, reached up as high as he could, and wrapped the heavy chain around the trunk. The end of the chain had a large hook that allowed him to secure it into one of the links. Then he moved his car to another large tree nearby and attached the other end of the chain around that tree in the same manner. Joe was grateful that Rizzo had enough chain on hand to do the job.

Joe moved his car far out of the way, and they cut a large notch in the side of the tree facing the direction they wanted it to fall. As they began to cut into the opposite side, the tree began to move. It moved slowly at first, then they could hear the wood cracking and squeaking as the huge tree began to fall. Joe looked on in horror as the tree leaned and started to fall in the direction of the power lines. They could only watch as it continued to fall, until the chain went taut, causing it to veer off and fall harmlessly to the side. Joe held his breath the whole time, while Rizzo just smiled.

If he hadn't secured the tree with that chain, Joe knew he would be in a world of hurt right now. He had the feeling that Rizzo would have enjoyed the chaos they would have created and he wouldn't care at all about the trouble Joe would have been in. The money he would have to pay to repair the lines, any possible lawsuits resulting from people losing power, along with probable fines, meant nothing to Rizzo. Joe knew he was taking a chance cutting down that tree, but it had to come down and he felt confident that he could do it. He was just glad he didn't listen to Rizzo's advice.

When Joe was ready to begin construction of his new home, he approached a local bank to secure a building loan. Confident he would have no trouble getting the funds, he was shocked and disappointed when he was flatly turned down. Besides the bank not willing to finance the construction of a log home, they also weren't happy with Joe's profession. When the bank agent asked Joe what he did for a living, of course he replied, "I'm an artist."

"Well, whom do you work for?

"I'm self-employed."

"How much do you make in a week?

Joe answered, "Well, that depends on if I sell a painting or not."

The bank agent asked, "Then you don't get a paycheck?

Joe answered, "No, I don't get a paycheck every week or every two weeks. I make money when I sell my art. Also, I receive quarterly royalties from a publishing company that sells my art prints nationally. It's all right here in my bank statements. I also own the property outright and that will be my collateral for the loan."

The bank agent again asked, "But you don't get a paycheck?"

Joe at this point just sat there and stared at him. The agent continued, saying that if Joe didn't have a steady source of income, the bank would be unable to loan him money. The agent then repeated that the bank's policy was opposed to lending money for the construction of log homes.

Joe left the bank feeling depressed and angry. He knew he made more in a year than that fucking *stugots* who just turned him down. He wondered if all banks would treat him the same way, keeping him from building his dream home. Maybe Rizzo was right after all, and playing by the rules was stupid and sometimes just didn't work. He thought for a brief moment of getting Rizzo to break into that crackerjack bank and clean them out. But then laughed at the thought and decided that he would have to find another way to build his house.

CHAPTER THIRTEEN—GO WEST, YOUNG MAN

One of the galleries in Colorado where Joe was exhibiting his work was planning a pre-Christmas show. New work for the exhibition had to be at the gallery by the first week of December, and Joe decided to drive there in his van instead of building crates and shipping his artwork. Although it wasn't necessary for him to attend the show, he had another reason for wanting to make the trip. After being rejected by the bank when seeking a loan to build his house, he had been thinking about leaving the area and heading west.

His many hiking trips and appearances visiting different galleries for art shows left him with a good idea of where he would like to settle. It would be a big decision. He would be leaving everything and everyone he knew, most importantly, his two children. That was the one thing that for now was holding him back, but it wouldn't hurt to investigate some locations for when the time was right.

He could make the trip to Colorado in three days of hard driving. With the center seats removed, his conversion van could easily accommodate the artwork, clothing and other items he would need while leaving room for the double bed to be left open. After the days' driving was done, he would pull into a rest stop when he got tired, then crawl into the bed to get a few hours' sleep. It was what he preferred to do instead of getting some overpriced room in some ratty motel chain. He was never concerned about his safety, as he always carried a Ruger .357-caliber revolver in his vehicle when he traveled. He knew he would probably never need it, but was glad on one occasion that he had it with him.

It happened at about two in the morning one day last spring when he was driving through Mississippi on his way to an art show in San

Antonio, Texas. After driving all day, he decided to pull into the next rest area he came to and get some sleep. Turning the radio volume up and opening his window all the way to fight off the drowsiness, he was relieved to see the sign stating the next rest area was one mile ahead. It didn't concern him the rest area was completely deserted and not very well lit, but he did find it odd that no other vehicles were parked there. It was late and he was extremely tired and knew he shouldn't drive any farther. He parked near the small comfort station under a dim light, locked the van, then went to sleep.

Not long after, he was awakened by the sound of approaching vehicles. He sat up in the bed, then parting the curtains to look outside, saw three cars that had stopped not more than a few yards away. Their headlights were shining right into Joe's van. He couldn't believe that someone could be that inconsiderate and began to curse the stupid assholes. Why would they park right next to his van when the whole area was empty unless they were up to no good?

Joe continued to watch as several young men exited the cars. He counted eight of them as he picked up the revolver that lay near him on the bed. He was planning his course of action in case they made a hostile move, but so far, they were completely ignoring him. Their focus was on one of the vehicles that seemed to have a mechanical issue. They opened the trunk of one of the cars and removed a length of chain, then hooked that car to the one that seemed to have a problem. With that done, they all returned to their cars and drove away with one vehicle in tow.

Joe was relieved, but still couldn't understand why they had parked so close to his van. It made no sense. It seemed to clearly be a hostile act, but then proved not to be. He was just glad he had restrained himself and waited for things to play out before taking any action. He also was glad he had a gun with him and vowed to never be without one whenever he traveled in the future.

***

As Joe was making his final preparations before leaving for his trip to Colorado, Rizzo stopped by and asked him where he was headed this time. Joe answered that he was going to drop off some artwork at a gallery and then spend a few days looking around Colorado. He knew Rizzo was aware of his many travels, but was not expecting what he heard next.

"Colorado, huh?" Rizzo said with a smile, then added, "You know, I got nothing to do right now. Maybe I should go with you. I could help with the gas, keep you company, and you know, keep you out of trouble."

Joe, taken aback by this unexpected request, stared at Rizzo, not saying anything for a few moments. Then he finally said, "You want to come with me? Why, don't you have things to do? I'm not really sure how long I'll be out there. What about Sandy and the kids?"

"Sandy's upstate with the kids and besides, I need to stay away from the bitch for a while. I know she's your sister and all, but sometimes she's a little *oobatz,*" Rizzo answered, not smiling.

Joe realized that Rizzo and his sister were still having major problems and the time apart would probably be a good thing, but wasn't sure his brother-in-law riding with him would be a good thing.

Looking into the van, Rizzo said, "See, you got plenty of room in there, and you got a good bed too. That's good, then one of us can drive while the other one gets to sleep. Just like we did in Canada."

226

Joe could tell Rizzo really wanted to go. Besides the trips to Canada and the cabin upstate, he knew Rizzo had never been anywhere beyond the metropolitan area. Going to Colorado would be a real adventure for him and Joe could remember that not too long ago, he himself craved such adventure. What would the harm be? His brothers wouldn't be going, Snake Lips sure as hell wouldn't be going. And it was true Rizzo could help with the gas, provided he didn't skip out of paying like he did in Canada. Joe would make certain to pump the gas to be sure he didn't. If they took turns driving, they could save a lot of time getting there and could avoid the unpleasant thought of both of them sleeping together in the bed, something Joe had no intention of doing.

"Well, if you really want to go, I guess there's enough room. I was going to leave tomorrow morning. Can you get your shit together, say, about ten o'clock?" Joe asked reluctantly.

Rizzo said he would have to see some people tonight, but he could be ready to leave in the morning. He then added, "Yeah, this will be good."

Joe wasn't so sure.

***

That night, all Joe could think about was what the hell did he just do? Why didn't he just have the balls to say no. Why did he feel sorry for him? He didn't think Rizzo would cause him any problems or start any trouble, but could he really trust him? He knew deep down inside the answer was no. He would just have to watch him closely, like he would a child.

The next morning, Joe drove to Rizzo's mother's house to pick him up, and seeing his father sitting on the front porch, decided to stay in the van and beep the horn. He still felt guilty about causing the old man to be arrested on that gun charge. Although he never really heard much about it, his sister once told him that the old man asked her why Joe brought those guns up to his place. She answered that he just made a mistake and was really sorry for the trouble it caused.

Rizzo came out, spoke with his father for a moment, then walked to the van and threw in his duffel bag. Joe asked him what his father had to say, wondering if the conversation was about him.

Rizzo laughed and said, "He asked me what day it was. I said, 'Why do you want to know the day? Why, you got an appointment?' He said, 'Ahh, she don't tell me nothing no more.' Then I said, 'So why do you care what day it is? Don't worry about it, the less you know the better.' The old man's losing his mind."

As they drove away, Joe said, "So he doesn't know what day it is, huh? So, then I guess he doesn't remember about being arrested on that gun charge. You know, I still feel bad about that whole thing. I don't even want to talk to him, afraid he might bring it up.

"You feel bad? Think how I feel. I lost all that money. Believe me, he don't remember nothing about it. I don't think he even remembers we had the cabin, so forget about it. After everything, losing that cabin was one of the worst things that happened. I did go up there one day just to take a look at the place. I don't know if that fuckin' lawyer still owns it or not. I mean, what the hell is he gonna do with it? He ain't goin' hunting up there, that's for sure. When I looked in the window and saw the way it was decorated inside, with all the fake flowers and fancy curtains on the windows, I figured he must have sold it to a couple of *fanooks*. There was nobody around, so I went to see if that gun you said you threw underneath was still there. The damn thing was there, alright. It was all rusty, but still in pretty good shape. I cleaned it up and sold it to a guy who collects 'em for eight hundred. So at least that's something."

"I can't believe it was still there. I should have thrown them all under the cabin," Joe said. "The truth is, I never should have brought them there in the first place. Man, that's one day I want to forget."

"You got that right," Rizzo said. "That was just more bad news piled on top of all the other shit that happened that week."

As they crossed the George Washington bridge, Joe thought about all the times he rode this route on his way to and from work at the Western Publishing Company. He wondered if his old boss Jim was still working there. He hoped not. He hoped that Jim had moved on and found something more meaningful. When he told Jim about his decision to quit and paint full time, his boss thought he was making the biggest mistake of his life, but Joe could detect a hint of envy. Jim would have loved to be able to follow Joe's lead and quit this job to pursue the life of an artist. But the truth was that his art didn't sell well if it sold at all, leaving Joe to feel uneasy whenever he sold a painting. After Joe left the company, Jim would call on occasion to see how he was doing. But after a while, the phone calls stopped and they lost contact. Joe smiled as they drove past the exit he used to take to work.

***

Their first stop would be a gallery in Fort Worth, Texas. At the last minute, Joe decided to alter his plans and drop in on the Texas gallery for two reasons. The first was that the gallery owed him money for prints they had purchased. They were now delinquent for over ninety days, so Joe thought he would pay them a visit and collect the money they owed him. The second reason was the weather. Being it was December, he thought it better to travel on a more southerly route as

229

much as possible to avoid any possible winter storms. It wouldn't be that much out of the way and Rizzo was agreeable, as he would get the chance to see some of Texas. Joe did try to warn him that the Dallas–Fort Worth area wasn't really what the west looks like. It was just another big city. Rizzo said he didn't care, he was just happy to get away for a while.

This was one of the few occasions that Joe had the opportunity to spend time with Rizzo one on one, without any outside distractions. He decided to pass the time by trying to understand what made this man tick. Was he really the unfeeling asshole he often displayed by his behavior toward others, including his family? Joe wondered if he ever had any feelings of guilt about the pain he caused by his criminal acts and his seemingly uncaring nature. He felt comfortable enough after knowing Rizzo for so long that he could ask him about these things. Of course, Joe wasn't sure he would get any truthful answers.

"So, I was thinking lately about Max Santoro's family. I don't know, but they must still be pissed about what happened. Did you ever hear anything from them?" Joe asked.

Rizzo looked over at Joe and said, "What the hell made you think about that? Why, did somebody contact you about it?"

"No, I was just wondering if you ever heard anything from his family, or his friends, or whatever. I mean they must all know you did it, even if you were acquitted."

"When I was leaving the courtroom after the trial on my way to jail for that bullshit gun charge, I saw some of his family in the hallway. I was getting on the elevator and they started yelling about how I was a murderer and blew that fuckhead's face off. That's the only thing I ever heard from them. I don't even think about it no more, it's in the past," Rizzo said as he shrugged his shoulders.

Joe sat there for a while then asked, "You ever feel a little guilty about how you and Bugsy beat the rap while your brothers got sent up? That's got to make you feel bad."

"What good does feelin' bad do? They got fucked, that's all. From what I heard, their useless lawyers sat there *mezzo morto* during the whole fuckin' trial. They should have used my guy, like Bugsy did. But those two stupid cunts were too cheap to use him, so they hired a couple of scumbags who didn't give a shit, just to save a little money."

Joe thought it wasn't just a "little money." His lawyer was pretty high-priced. But Joe could see that Rizzo didn't feel guilty about any of it, only anger at his brother's two wives for not hiring David Kaplin.

Then after a while Joe asked, "What about killing Max? You ever feel bad about that?"

"What, are you studying to be a priest? What's with all these bullshit questions? We killed that guy because he left us no choice, okay? It's that simple. He became a problem, and that was the only thing we could do. So, what are you looking for, a confession? You want to know if I feel bad about it? Well I don't. What I feel bad about is what happened after, all the fuckin' money I lost and then losing the cabin. I blame that *pezzo di merda* Santoro for all that."

Joe saw that Rizzo was getting defensive and was not going to ever admit feeling any guilt or sorrow for his past actions, so he decided not to ask any more questions for now.

***

231

After crossing the Mississippi River into Arkansas, they decided to stop for gas and something to eat at the next service area. So far, Rizzo was not impressed with the areas they had driven through, which he described as being one shithole after another. Joe told him that unfortunately, this was the way most of the country looked east of the Mississippi River. Things would get better the farther west they traveled. But again, he told him not to expect too much in Texas, explaining that the eastern part of the state was pretty much the same as what they had already seen.

Looking out the window as they drove on, Rizzo said, "Go west, go west, everybody always says, you got to go see the West. What the fuck for? This looks like the same as home, worse even. Does it all look like this? What about all the movies they make? You know, John Wayne, Clint Eastwood, all that shit. Where do they make those? Not around here, that's for sure."

Joe laughed, then said, "This is Arkansas, this is not the West. They don't film any movies here, not Westerns anyway. When we get to Colorado and you see the Rockies, you'll change your mind."

"I don't know, maybe I should have stayed home. I could have gone to the city dump and shot rats, even that's a whole lot better than this."

Now Joe really started to question the wisdom of taking Rizzo along on this trip. This was still the first day and he was already wanting to go home. Joe thought he would have to keep him busy, get him to talk about something he enjoyed.

"Hey, how much money did you say you got off of Snake Lips when you guys robbed that house on Halloween? You know, when you were walking through the woods and you started grabbing money out of his knapsack. Did he ever find out about that?"

232

Rizzo smiled then said, "Yeah, that was a pretty good score. I got a few thou off of him, he never knew."

Joe then decided to tell him about when Snake Lips stole that money from the government agent's cabin in Canada. He had never mentioned that to anyone before now.

"You know, I was really glad to hear that you stole money from that little bastard. That fuckhead almost got all of us arrested in Canada."

"Why, what did he do? I didn't see him do nothing," Rizzo said, sounding surprised.

Joe, smiling, then said, "You remember when we were all leaving and had to pay the agent for the fishing fees? We had to go in one at a time because the cabin was so small. Well, when I went in to pay, Snake Lips was still in there."

"Yeah, so?" Rizzo said.

"So, as I was paying the guy, Snake Lips walked behind him and saw this small metal box on the shelf. I stood there watching as he opened the box and took out all the money that was in there and shoved it in his pocket. Then he has the balls to wink at me as he went back outside."

"You're shittin' me, he did that?" asked Rizzo. "Why didn't you say something? *Madonn*, Al would have kicked his ass if he knew. Now, that was fuckin' stupid, even for him. You got to be careful when you rob. I mean, you got to be able to talk your way out of it if you get caught. If that guy found out the money was gone, he would know one of us took it. You know, that little *stronzo* fuck should have known better. He's not new to this, he could have got us all pinched. And Al was pissed about those guys walkin' off with a few axes? You saw him do it and didn't say nothin' all this time?"

"Hey, I didn't want to rat out the bastard, even if he did deserve it. I figured if the agent found out the money was gone, and came out confronting us, the truth would come out. I don't think anyone else would have covered for him. Still, you're the only one I ever told about this, so don't say anything, okay?" Joe said.

Rizzo answered, "You got no reason to feel any loyalty to him. Fuck him. I won't say nothing, but I can't believe he did that. I wonder how much he got?"

***

It grew dark as they drove through Little Rock. Joe was getting tired and asked Rizzo if he would like to drive for a while.

"Yeah, sure, as long as I know which way to go."

Joe told him to just stay on Route 30 heading toward Texarkana.

Rizzo said, "Tex ... who? What the fuck kind of a name is that?

"It's a city on the border between Arkansas and Texas," Joe laughed as he pulled off the road." Then he added, "But first you'll have to drive through Arkadelphia."

"Get the fuck out of here. What, you got me drivin' through all the wackadoo cities out here. Are you shittin' me? Who names these places?"

"I don't know, they are kinda weird. But there're small cities, so just drive through 'em. You won't see much from the interstate anyway," Joe said as he crawled into the bed.

Joe was awakened by Rizzo loudly saying they were in Texarkana, and now he was ready to take a break. Joe, still feeling tired, decided not to drive any farther that night. He said to Rizzo, "You know, I think we should just get a room and quit driving any more tonight. Besides, we'll be getting into the Dallas area tomorrow and I don't want to be tired driving through that mess."

Joe could see that this trip was going to cost him a lot more than it would have if he were alone. He didn't mind sleeping some nights in the van to save money. But if he and Rizzo were both too tired to drive, they would have to get a room or share the same bed in the van. That was not an option, so they got a room with two beds for the night. Joe paid.

They got up early the next morning, trying to beat the morning rush-hour traffic as they drove through Dallas. Rizzo was again not impressed with the surroundings. The confusing maze of roads and overhead ramps, along with the continuous buildup of traffic, made him glad he wasn't driving.

"So this is Texas, huh?" he said with a smirk. "Not for nothing, but why do you come out here so much? I mean, this really sucks."

"Yeah, I know, but there are art galleries here that sell my art, so I gotta come out here. The gallery I gotta see is in Fort Worth, it's not too far from here. I'll pick up my money, then we can head north out of this hellhole."

Arriving at the gallery, Joe saw right away that things were not going well. He spoke with one of the owners and got the bad news that they were declaring bankruptcy and would soon be closing for good. Joe calmly asked about the more than six hundred dollars still owed to him and received more bad news. They didn't have the money to pay him.

"Well, I don't like hearing that," Joe said as he stood staring at the owner. He had been dealing with Audrey and her husband, Tom, for a few years, but had never met them. Audrey went on to say how Tom was away right now and how sorry she was about not being able to pay Joe the money they owed him.

Rizzo smiled as he looked at Joe then said, "Well, now what are you gonna do?"

Joe looked around the gallery and noticed three of his prints that were framed and hanging on the wall. He knew well the cost of framing and figured the value of those frames would equal or surpass what the gallery owed him. Without asking, Joe walked over and removed the prints from the wall, saying that he would take these as payment for what they owed him. Rizzo seemed to like that idea and walked over to help Joe carry the artwork. As Joe started to leave, he turned to Audrey and said that he was sorry about them losing their business, but at least now they were square.

Out in the van, Rizzo asked, "Why did you take only these? You should go back and get more. What the fuck, they're goin' out of business anyway, no?"

"These three were my prints, the ones they weren't gonna pay me for. So now I got my prints back along with three frames that are worth over three hundred bucks each. I came out of this okay. It's just damn lucky I was here before they locked the doors. They sure as hell weren't gonna pay me anything, so fuck 'em."

Joe carefully placed his recovered artwork in the van, and then they left Fort Worth, heading northwest toward Amarillo.

Joe knew that it wasn't uncommon to see dead animals on the side of an interstate. Many are struck by vehicles as they try to cross the highway, mainly during the overnight hours. But nothing prepared him for the sight of the dozens of dead, broken bodies of animals and birds littering both sides of the highway. Besides deer, armadillos, and other small animals, there were scores of dead owls. Joe had never seen anything like it before. He knew from his research into Indian culture, along with conversations with some Indians he had met, that owls were considered a bad omen. Some believed owls were harbingers of death, and wouldn't even want to look at them. Joe, for a brief moment, thought of stopping to gather up some of the feathers, which were beautiful and would be good reference for his paintings. But he knew the owls were a protected species and having any feathers was a federal offense accompanied by a stiff fine. So, he passed up the temptation.

"Did you ever see anything like this? Joe asked Rizzo. "I mean, I've seen dead animals on the road before, but this is unbelievable."

"Why don't you stop so we can get a couple of 'em. I'd like to have one stuffed, that would be pretty cool."

"Yeah, I thought about that, but you're not allowed to have them. There're protected," answered Joe.

"Protected! They don't look protected to me. Who's protecting them? There's hundreds of 'em laying dead all over the place, whoever's protecting them ain't doin' a good job," Rizzo said, laughing.

"I know, It's pretty crazy. There're protected by the federal government. You're not allowed to hunt them or even have them in your possession. Even just the feathers. If the feds catch you with them, you'll get a big fine and maybe jail time," Joe said.

"That's a lot of bullshit. We're not hunting 'em. We're just pickin' up feathers off the road. They can't prove we killed any of 'em. They're already dead, for Christ's sake. What are you supposed to do, just leave 'em there so they rot? That don't make no sense. But the more I think about it, I know the reason why all these owls died here," said Rizzo with a smile.

"Yeah, why? Joe asked.

"They all died tryin' to get the hell out of Texas," laughed Rizzo.

They drove on along the highway of death, with Joe starting to get the uneasy feeling that maybe all this really would prove to be a bad omen.

***

They decided to stop for the night in Amarillo. The weather was turning colder and the thought of driving on through the night and fearing a midnight collision with some wild animal made for an easy decision. Joe knew that Rizzo didn't have any credit cards, so it was up to him to again pay for the room. He didn't mind so much, but was hoping Rizzo would at least pay for his own meals. He never thought to ask if Rizzo had any money with him. He just assumed he did.

They found a small motel, got a room, and then went to a nearby restaurant for supper. As they were seated, Joe had to ask, "So, did you bring enough money with you?"

Rizzo, looking surprised said, "Yeah, I got enough. Why, are you running short already?"

"No, I'm fine. I was just wondering if you brought enough. But, okay, good," answered Joe, a little embarrassed.

"You know what? Since you paid for the room, I'll pick up the tab for supper. How's that?"

Immediately, Joe remembered how Rizzo skipped out of paying the bill when his sister blew up at him, so he asked in a half-joking manner, "You're not going to skip out of paying like that other time, are you? You know we're staying right next door."

"Hey, come on. What do you think I am? I want to pay the bill, that's all. You got a suspicious mind," Rizzo answered with a broad grin.

Joe knew he was up to something.

When they finished eating, Joe got up to go to the restroom. As he was walking away, he looked at Rizzo who laughed and said, "Christ almighty, I told you I was gonna pay. I'll wait here until you get back."

Coming out of the restroom, Joe saw Rizzo standing in line before the cashier, preparing to pay their bill. At first, he felt relieved that Rizzo wasn't going to try and leave without paying, but soon noticed that something was wrong. When the cashier rang up their bill, the amount of the check seemed much too low to cover what they had ordered.

Rizzo quickly received his change, turned to Joe and said, "Okay, let's go."

Outside the restaurant, Joe asked, "That bill didn't seem right. It looked like it was too low."

Rizzo laughed, then said, "You noticed that, huh? It's a little trick I learned a long time ago. As I'm walking toward the cashier, I look at the tables where the people already left. Sometimes they leave the money for the bill on the table. If I can read the bill and the amount is less than mine, I switch 'em."

"Is that what you did? What if somebody sees you doing it?" asked Joe as he looked over his shoulder back at the restaurant.

"You gotta do it like you own the place. You can't act suspicious, and you gotta be fast. No one ever notices. The waitress will just think those people stiffed her, that's all."

"Yeah, but the waitress will remember who ordered what and know somebody switched the bill."

"Did you see how often she came around? She probably still didn't pick up that bill. And the other thing is, you gotta get out of there fast," Rizzo said as he picked his teeth with a toothpick.

Shaking his head, Joe said, "Well I guess we're not having breakfast in there tomorrow."

As they entered their room, Joe hoped this trip wouldn't turn into a cross-country crime spree. He was going to have to watch Rizzo more closely.

***

The weather made a turn for the worse the next morning. The TV news reported the drop-in temperature, along with a cold front bringing snow showers and icy conditions over a wide area. This was what Joe was hoping to avoid. He knew he was taking a chance driving out here in winter, but sometimes in the past the weather wasn't that bad. From

240

this point, they would be heading straight north on Route 287 toward the Oklahoma border. Their route would take them across the Oklahoma panhandle and into Colorado. They would continue north until they hooked up with I-70 west, then on to Denver. It all looked pretty easy on the map, and if they pushed, they could make Denver without having to stop again. That is, if the weather cooperated.

After eating a quick breakfast at a different restaurant, they gassed up the van and headed out. The road condition seemed fine at this stage, although traffic was a bit heavy. They were still treated to the spectacle of dozens of dead animals and birds on each side of the road.

Rizzo, noticing the bleak, flat, empty landscape said, "I guess nobody around here gives a shit about all these dead bodies laying around. It must smell like hell during the summer. And where's all the fuckin' trees? There's no trees around here. No wonder these birds kill themselves tryin' to get the hell out."

Joe, keeping a careful watch on the road, didn't answer.

Rizzo said, "Look, anytime you want me to take over, just say it. I drive in this kind of shit all the time."

Joe knew Rizzo was more than capable of driving in this kind of weather, but this was his van, and he wanted to drive as much as possible. They continued on as the weather grew worse. Snow was now blowing sideways across the road, making visibility difficult. The conditions didn't seem to bother the truckers, though. They passed Joe in the left lane, speeding along like it was the middle of summer. As they passed, they kicked up clouds of blowing snow, which reduced Joe's visibility to almost whiteout conditions. Joe cursed them as he slowed down, trying to keep the van in his lane. Again, Rizzo offered to drive, seeing that Joe was getting on edge. Joe told him he could take over in a little while. It was still early and they had a long way to go.

The snow let up a little as they crossed the border. Joe made the announcement, saying they were now in Oklahoma.

All Rizzo could say was, "Oklahoma, hell, this just looks like more Texas, and that ain't sayin' much."

They were both getting hungry, so Joe said they could stop up ahead in Boise City for lunch. He added that Rizzo could take the wheel afterward if he wanted.

The bridge was barely visible from Joe's vantage point. He had no idea it was there as he began to cross it doing about fifty miles an hour. The road so far had been clear of ice, so he wasn't driving as carefully as he should have been. Besides, they were both tired and hungry, wanting nothing more right now than to stop for a break. At first, Joe didn't notice the sideways motion the van was taking. He let off the gas when he realized they were sliding toward the opposite side of the road. Now aware that they were on a bridge, he saw that the approaching lanes dipped low enough to block the view of any traffic heading toward them. Not knowing if any vehicles were about to crest the hill on the bridge and slam into him, he very slowly turned the wheel, trying to get the van back on his side of the road. He knew to always turn into the direction of a skid to avoid spinning out, but fearing they might be involved in a head-on collision at any moment, he slowly turned the other way.

It didn't work. The van began to spin violently. All Joe could do was hold on. He looked over at Rizzo and saw him staring straight ahead with both hands on the dashboard. As the van spun around, Joe could see that it was heading for the concrete barrier on the opposite

242

side of the bridge. It's going to be bad, Joe thought as he prepared for the impact. The front of the van hit the concrete first, shearing off the front grill and sending the hood flying through the air. Still spinning, the rear of the van hit next. The force of the impact was so great that all the windows except the windshield shattered, as the van again slammed into the concrete on the driver's side. It slowly came to a stop, facing the way they had come only moments ago.

Joe sat there unable to accept what had just happened. All he could think to say was, "We're fucked."

He looked over to Rizzo and asked him if he was all right. Luckily, they both were wearing their seat belts, which undoubtedly saved them from any serious injury. As the initial shock started to wear off, Joe realized that the steering wheel was bent down on both sides, indicating that his chest must have violently hit the steering column. He didn't feel any pain yet, but knew he eventually would. The next thing they noticed was the temperature. With all the windows gone, snow and frigid air was circulating around them. Rizzo reached for his coat as he opened his door to get out. Joe's door was jammed and would not open, so he had to climb out on Rizzo's side.

Other motorists who saw what happened started to come over to see if they were all right. Some were surprised that they were unhurt after witnessing the violent crash. They all walked around the twisted vehicle, commenting on the amount of damage it had sustained. Pieces of the van were strewn on both sides of the highway as well as over the embankment. When Joe and Rizzo looked over the concrete barrier and down the embankment, they realized how lucky they were. If that barrier wasn't strong enough to stop them, the van would have careened off the bridge and landed forty feet below, surely killing them both. Still, they weren't feeling very lucky right now.

The reality of their situation began to sink in. They were stuck out there in the middle of nowhere without a vehicle. This van wasn't going anywhere but the junkyard. The other motorists walked back to their warm cars and began to leave, making them feel even more alone. The landscape was flat and bleak, without any signs of civilization.

Rizzo zipped up his coat, looked at Joe, and said, "Okay, college boy, what do we do now?"

Joe thought that was a good question. "I wonder if any of those good citizens were able to contact anybody and send help. We're gonna freeze to death out here," he said.

Just then, they heard in the distance the wailing of a police siren. As the police car approached, they felt both relieved and somewhat uneasy. Joe ran through a checklist in his mind of the documents the cop would surely ask for. His driver's license, registration, and insurance card were all current, as was as the inspection sticker on the van's windshield, which by some miracle was still intact. They both stood there hunched over in the cold as the officer pulled up alongside. They watched as he put on his hat and stepped out of his car. Joe could see that he was middle-aged and overweight as he zipped up his heavy parka.

The officer looked them both over and asked, "Who is the owner of this vehicle?"

"I'm the owner," Joe answered.

"So, what happened here?" the officer asked.

"The van started to spin out on the bridge, then I lost control as it hit the concrete barrier," Joe explained.

The officer took out a small pad from his pocket and began writing. "How fast were you going?" he asked.

"About fifty."

"Well, you were going too fast," the officer said, then continued writing on his pad. "Were you both wearing your seat belts?"

"Yes, we were," Joe replied. He was surprised that the trooper didn't seem concerned or even ask if either of them was hurt. He just kept writing on his little pad.

Lowering the pad, the cop looked at Joe and asked, "Which way were you heading when you lost control?"

Joe pointed to the west. The officer again lowered his pad, stared at Joe, and then said, "Well, let me ask you this: If you were heading west, then why is the van facing the other way?"

Joe's mouth fell open as he stared back at the officer. Was he joking? He had to be joking. Was he trying to lighten up a serious situation with a little humor? Seeing that there was no humor in the cop's eyes or demeanor, Joe finally said, "That was the direction the van was facing when it stopped spinning."

Rizzo, trying to stifle a laugh, turned and walked to the front of the van.

The officer nodded as he wrote on his pad, then said, "Well, it looks like you boys will be back on the road soon."

Again, Joe stared at him in disbelief. How could he say something like that? Couldn't he see that the windows were blown out, and along with that, the entire front end was gone. Joe exclaimed, "We can't drive this thing—half the motor's gone!"

Then for the first time, the cop started to carefully look over the wrecked vehicle. He slowly walked around to the front while still writing down notes. When he reached the back of the van, he stopped and asked Joe, "Where is your license plate?"

Joe answered that he didn't have any idea where it went. The back of the van was crushed and the plate must have flown off somewhere.

The cop again looked Joe in the eye, and in a serious tone said, "You know, if somebody picks up that plate then robs a bank, they're gonna come after you."

"Yeah well, I'll worry about that when it happens. I got enough to worry about right now," Joe said in a mocking tone.

The cop then told Joe to follow him back to his car. He asked if he had any weapons on him, to which Joe said no. He told Joe to get in the front seat. Rizzo came over and asked if he could get in the back seat to get warm. The cop said no. Rizzo had to stand there shivering while Joe handed over his paperwork.

The officer looked over Joe's license and insurance card, then checked to see if Joe had any outstanding warrants or traffic violations. When everything came back negative, he told Joe to step outside. Joe got out of the car and walked over to Rizzo, who did not look happy.

"Why didn't that *facha di gots* let me in the car?" Rizzo said. "I'm freezing my nuts off out here. So, is he done with us, or what? What did he say? How do we get the fuck out of here?"

The cop walked over to them and said, "Well, what do you boys want to do?"

"Is there a motel around here? Somewhere we can go to?" asked Joe, as he coughed and spit into his hand. He saw a small amount of blood in his hand, then showed it to Rizzo.

"That ain't good, buddy," Rizzo said.

The cop told them about a motel a few miles up the road as he radioed in for a tow truck.

Joe, concerned about the blood he had just coughed up, asked the cop, "Say that I start coughing up blood later on, do I call 911 or what?"

The cop laughed and said, "There's no 911 around here. I guess you'll have to go to the front desk of the motel."

Joe couldn't believe the surreal situation they found themselves in. One minute they were doing fine just driving along, and an instant later they were in this alternate universe of Okla-fuckin-homa. When the tow truck arrived, the cop talked with the driver for a minute, then walked over to Joe.

"The driver will take you to the motel and allow you to empty the vehicle before he pulls it away," the officer said. "One more thing—here's a citation for driving too fast in unsafe conditions." He then turned and got back into his car.

Joe got really pissed and was about to protest when Rizzo stopped him.

With a smile, Rizzo said, "You better not say nothin' or that *stronzo* fuck will write you up for littering too. There's pieces of the van all over the road."

They both watched as the porky, dimwitted public servant drove off in a cloud of blowing snow. The tow truck driver hooked up the van, then began to pick up the broken pieces that were scattered all over the road. Joe and Rizzo lent a hand to speed things up. They never did find the license plate. With the van in tow, Joe told the driver to take them to the nearest motel.

***

The tow truck pulled up to a small, single-story motel that looked like something out of a horror movie. There was nothing else around it except for a restaurant sharing the same parking lot, and together they looked as if they were built at the same time by the same builder decades ago. It was the only sign of civilization Joe and Rizzo could see in any direction, and they were both grateful to get out of the cold.

Joe walked through a door marked "Office" to see about a room.

A middle-aged woman walked in and asked, "Can I help you?" She then noticed the tow truck outside her window and said, "Oh, is that your van? Were you involved in an accident? I hope no one was hurt."

Joe answered, "Yeah, that's my van, alright. At least what's left of it. We spun out on that bridge down the road. It was covered in black ice that I didn't see until it was too late."

She said, "Well, I can tell you that you're not the first one to do that. It happens a lot around here. They should really spread salt on it when it gets icy, but they never do. How many nights do you plan to stay?"

"I'm not sure yet. We'll have to rent a vehicle somewhere," he said as Rizzo entered the office.

"The driver out there wants to go, so we need to unload the van. You got a key yet?" Rizzo asked.

The woman handed Joe the key for Room 3 as he filled out the registration form. He gave the key to Rizzo, who went out to open the room door so they could begin emptying the van.

The only door on the van that would open was on the front passenger side. All the others were jammed shut from the collision. The tow truck driver produced a crowbar, and Rizzo used it to pry open the side and back doors. Joe reached in to retrieve his keys, but the ignition key was jammed. He had to remove it from his keyring to free his other keys.

For the first time since the accident, they saw the amount of damage the van sustained. The entire body of the vehicle was twisted from the impact, which had caused the windows to shatter. All their belongings were piled up and thrown about. To Joe's relief, the original art pieces for the exhibition in Denver seemed to be undamaged. But the same could not be said for the framed prints he picked up at the gallery in Fort Worth. They were completely destroyed. The frames were broken, as was the glass, which in turn tore the art prints. They were a total loss. Joe laughed to himself at the thought that sometimes, you just can't win.

They quickly piled their belongings inside the room, checked the van one last time to be sure they got everything, then quietly watched as the van was pulled away. Joe thought this is how a pioneer family must have felt if their horses died, leaving them stranded in the middle of nowhere. All of a sudden, he felt very alone.

Joe and Rizzo decided to walk over to the restaurant to get something to eat and plan their next move. Right away, Joe noticed the sign over the door and motioned to Rizzo to look up. Even with Rizzo's limited reading ability, he laughed and said, "Yeah, they sure got that right." The white sign said "No Man's Land" in bold red letters. Wow, Joe thought, was that ever an appropriate name.

When they entered the dining room, the other people seated there all stopped talking and stared at them. They heard whispers saying, "Those are the boys who wrecked." It was very creepy.

Joe leaned over to Rizzo and said, "I know what's going on here. All these people wrecked on that bridge and now they can never leave. It's like *The Twilight Zone*."

Rizzo said, "Don't fuck around. I'm getting the hell out of here if I have to crawl."

They sat at an empty table as the waitress came over to drop off two menus and ask if they wanted a cup of coffee. Joe answered yes, while Rizzo asked for tea. The waitress gave him a quick smile, then went off to get their drinks. When she returned, she asked them if they just had a wreck.

Joe answered, "Yeah, we did. They just towed our van away, so we're stuck here for now. Don't they ever spread salt down on these roads around here?"

She laughed, then asked, "Did you get the ticket?"

Joe looked surprised, and asked, "What ticket?"

"The one he always gives out for driving too fast on icy roads. He gave the mailman one the other day for the same reason when his mail truck flipped over. He gives that ticket to everybody. He even gives them out during the summer, if it's raining or just windy. We all laugh about him around here."

Joe, not amused, said, "Yeah, well, I got one too."

"Anyway, it looks like you guys didn't get hurt, so that's a blessing," she said smiling.

Then Joe remembered coughing up some blood a while ago and asked, "Is there a hospital anywhere nearby in case we start coughing up blood or something?"

Looking concerned, she asked, "Why? Are you coughing up blood?"

"Naw, just in case, you know."

She answered that there wasn't a hospital nearby, but there was a clinic in town, about six miles away. Joe wondered if they would come and get him, or if he would have to walk there if he developed a problem. He and Rizzo each ordered a hamburger and while eating, noticed that the shock of the accident must be wearing off, as they both began to tremble.

***

The town of Boise, Oklahoma, was not a big place. As he and Rizzo sat in their gloomy motel room, Joe looked through the telephone book, hoping against all odds that there would be an agent from his insurance company nearby. He was pleasantly surprised to find one. He called and left a message, giving his name, room, and phone number. For now, that's all they could do. Joe was waiting for Rizzo to break his silence about the accident. He was sure Rizzo would at any minute start to rant about what a fucked-up trip this turned out to be, and Joe would have to agree with him. It didn't turn out too well, that's for sure. As they both lay on their beds, Rizzo finally found his voice.

"Not for nothin', but you know you fucked up on that bridge. You turned the wrong way in that skid. They didn't teach you in college about what to do when your car starts to skid? I thought you knew about that. If I was drivin' we'd be far away from this shithole."

"Yeah, I know why we skidded and then spun out. I was tryin' to get the van back on our side of the road before we got hit from anybody coming the other way, but it didn't work," Joe said quietly.

"Thing is, what the fuck do we do now? I can't call nobody to come get us. Nobody's gonna come all the way out here, and I don't fuckin' blame 'em," Rizzo said.

"I'll talk with the insurance agent tomorrow and see if we can rent a car someplace. They've got to have cars to rent if people keep skidding off the roads," Joe said as he spit into his hand, this time without seeing any blood.

Joe was still shaking from the accident, but tried to get some sleep. He was awakened during the night by Rizzo bending over him, just inches from his face.

Startled, Joe yelled, "Whoa, what's going on?"

Rizzo smiled and said, "I just wanted to see if you were still breathing. You sounded like you were choking there for a while. I don't want you dying and leaving me out here, *capeesh*? Let's get back first—then you could die if you want to."

"Thanks for caring so much, you scared the shit out of me. Don't do that again," Joe said as he turned over and faced the wall.

The next morning as they walked to the restaurant, Rizzo noticed how the icicles hanging from the buildings were all sideways and not pointing straight down.

"Look at that shit," he said. "Even the fuckin' icicles in this place are all wacked. We gotta get out of here."

"If that insurance agent doesn't call soon, I'll call him back. I got to report the accident and maybe he can help us get out of here," Joe said as they entered the restaurant.

When they returned to their room, the telephone was blinking, indicating that there was a phone message. Joe was relieved to hear the insurance agent ask him to call back. Joe called and the agent told him he would come right over to pick them up.

Arriving at the insurance office, the agent asked them to explain the accident and let him know if either of them was hurt in any way. They both said they were fine, but a little shaken up.

"That's no wonder," said the agent, whose name was Roy. "According to the manager of the salvage yard, the van was completely totaled. So, let's file the claim. I need a list of any of your personal items that were damaged or destroyed."

Joe told him about the framed artwork that was broken to bits, thinking maybe he could recoup the loss. At least that would be something positive to come out of this.

The agent asked where they were from and what they did for a living. Joe said he was an artist. Rizzo said he just worked odd jobs, whatever might come up. Roy then started talking about the history of the surrounding countryside, mentioning how the Comanche Indians used to camp here in the summer months, but left the area in winter because it was so brutal.

Rizzo laughed and said, "Then why do you live here? Not for nothin', but I think the Indians had the right idea and got the hell out of here. This place looks good for nothin, and speakin' of getting out of here, we gotta rent a car or something so we could leave. I don't want to wait around till spring if I got to walk out of here."

Roy sat back in his chair and with a slight smile, said, "Well, I'm sorry to have to tell you this, but there aren't any rental agents around here. The nearest place you can rent a car is Amarillo."

"Amarillo! Are you serious? How would we even get there?" asked Joe.

"There's a bus that comes through here on Thursday," Roy said. "You can take it to Amarillo and then rent a vehicle. But you'd better call first and make a reservation to be sure they have any available."

Joe could not believe what he had just heard, along with the situation they were in. Here they were, stranded with no place to rent a car, no 911 service if they were hurt, sideways icicles, and nothing to be seen in any direction except blowing snow. He felt like they were somewhere in the middle of the Gobi Desert instead of the United States. He never thought the country had places that were so desolate like this. Not expecting any more help from Roy, Joe asked him to drive them back to the motel.

Once back in their motel room, Joe looked up rental agencies in Amarillo to see about reserving a car. He really didn't want to wait here for four days and catch a bus back to where they had just come from,

254

but right now, that was their only option. Even that choice quickly vanished when after calling three rental agencies, they all said they wouldn't have anything available until the following week. With the bus coming through only on Thursdays, that meant they would have to hole up here for almost two weeks. Rizzo was about to lose it. He threatened to go out and steal a car if Joe didn't think of some way to get them out of there.

Joe sat on the edge of the bed, racking his brain to come up with the name of someone nearby he could call on for help. Then it came to him. The gallery in Denver. He knew the owner, Jack, had a good sense of humor and might even think this whole mess was hilarious. It was the only thing Joe had left to try. If it failed, he was out of ideas.

Joe was right about Jack. At first, he thought Joe was kidding around about being stranded, but then became serious, asking if they were all right. Joe assured him they were fine, only stuck here without any way of getting out. He explained the whole story, which Jack did find humorous.

"So, where are you again?" Jack asked.

Joe answered, "We're at a motel just outside Boise City, Oklahoma, on Route 287."

"Boise City, where the hell is that?" Jack asked as he started to laugh.

"It's like the last town in the panhandle of Oklahoma in the middle of nowhere, and I mean nowhere. It's just south of the Colorado border. You can check it on the map. We really need someone to pick us up. I wouldn't ask you if there was another way."

"Do you have the paintings for the show with you?" Jack asked.

255

Joe answered, "Why, is that all you care about?"

"I need to know if I can write off this trip as a business expense—you know, picking up artwork for the show. If you guys want to come along too, we'll try and make room," Jack said with a laugh.

"Hey, you want to write it off, that's fine. So, when do you think you'll be here?"

Pausing for a moment, Jack said, "I'll send my delivery guy to get you. He's pretty good at finding his way around, even in Oklahoma. Sit tight. He'll be there as soon as he can."

When Joe hung up the phone, Rizzo peppered him with questions. "What did he say? Is he gonna get us? When is he coming?"

Joe told him what he knew, then they both put on their coats and crossed the parking lot through the howling wind and snow toward the "No Man's Land" restaurant.

***

It was almost 11:00 p.m. when they saw headlights suddenly shine through the windows of their room. Joe opened the door and saw a white cargo van pull up in front of him. The driver cut the engine, then doused the lights. The young man stepped out into the swirling snow as Joe motioned him inside. He introduced himself as Steve and he shook hands with Joe and Rizzo.

Steve said that Jack told him to get back to the gallery as soon as possible, and asked, "Are you guys ready to load up?"

Rizzo stood by the open door looking out at the storm and said, "I don't think it's a good idea to drive in this shit. It's snowing like a Comanche out there."

Joe thought, "snowing like a Comanche?" What the hell did that mean? Then he guessed Rizzo was just using the new word he had learned from the insurance agent about the fierce Indians who used to live here.

"Yeah, Rizzo's right." Joe said. "We're not goin' anywhere tonight. We already wrecked one van and don't want to get into another accident. Besides, look out there—it *is* snowing like a Comanche. We'll leave in the morning."

Steve shrugged his shoulders and agreed, so they settled in for the night. With Rizzo and Joe taking the beds, Steve found a place to sleep on the floor.

The storm had passed in the night, leaving the morning sky bright and clear, but still bitterly cold. Joe gladly checked out of their "oasis," paying for the three-night stay.

Rizzo didn't even want to eat breakfast at the restaurant, saying, "Let's just get the fuck outta here while we can."

Joe thought Rizzo really believed they might be stuck there forever. Joe sat in the front seat alongside Steve, while Rizzo bundled up in the back sitting on their two duffel bags full of clothes.

As they left Boise City and continued on through the frozen landscape, Joe turned and asked Rizzo, "So, how do you like your trip out west so far?"

"What, are you fuckin' shittin' me? When I get home, I'm gonna tear out every page of my atlas west of New York. You'll never catch my ass out here again. So where are we goin' now, and how long is it going to take? I'm freezing my nuts off back here."

Steve answered, "I got the heater turned up all the way, but they're not so good in cargo vans like this. It took me about six hours to get down here. We might make better time going back now that it's daylight and the weather cleared up."

They drove on, passing a few semis that were jackknifed on the side of the road and one that was flipped over on its side. Joe was glad they had decided to wait until morning before leaving.

The Gallery of the West was a hive of activity, with the staff getting ready for the upcoming exhibition. Jack was happy Joe made it before the deadline and that his artwork wasn't damaged in the wreck. He was sorry, though, that he wouldn't be able to spend much time visiting with Joe, as he was extremely busy. Joe told him not to worry, and that all they wanted to do now was rent a vehicle so they could get back home. It had been a stressful trip. Joe thanked him for sending Steve down to Boise City to get them, otherwise they would still be there.

Calling for a rental car, Joe faced unexpected disappointment when he was told that any car rented had to be returned to where it originated. It seemed renting a car wasn't going to get them home. They would have to secure a moving truck to be able to drop it off back in New York. Jack told them of a Ryder truck lot a few blocks from the gallery. Joe rented the smallest truck they had available, but it was still much larger than they needed. The truck was capable of hauling three rooms of furniture, while all they had were some broken art prints and two duffel bags of clothes. With no other choice available, they drove the truck back to the gallery, loaded up their meager belongings, and bid farewell to Denver. Rizzo was able to catch a glimpse of the Rockies through the low-lying clouds, but didn't care one bit.

***

While planning this trip, Joe had set aside some time to do a little exploring of the area, but now he forgot about that and headed east as fast as he could. He wanted this trip to end, and he wanted to be free of Rizzo. Not that he was a problem, it was just that Joe knew he was miserable and really had no purpose in being here. Joe thought how this trip had been a near-total disaster. They were both almost killed, his van was totaled, and they were stranded for days, which could have easily turned into weeks. The artwork he collected toward a bad debt was destroyed and this trip was costing him a fortune. In hindsight, he realized that he should have shipped his paintings to the gallery and stayed home.

As they headed east on Route 70, they decided to call it a day and spend the night in Limon. Rizzo's spirits were lifted just by the fact that they were heading home. They arose early the next morning, ate breakfast, then hit the road. Joe estimated that if they pushed hard, they would be home by the end of the week. Rizzo became very talkative for the first time in days, asking Joe many questions about all kinds of things. Joe was surprised when Rizzo inquired about Dominic Marino, his former father-in-law.

Joe laughed, then asked, "Why do you want to know about him?"

"I don't know, sometimes I miss the old days, you know? He was trying to nail us for so many years, it became sort of a game. I know he was happy about us goin' up for that murder, and it really pissed him off when me and Bugsy got off. Do you still see him anymore?"

"Not really. Whenever I pick up the kids, he's always gone somewhere—one of his clubs or he's at his bar. I don't go there, it's full of cops. Boy, he had a real hard-on for you. Remember, he wanted to set you up to rob his house so he could kill you."

"You know, I still wonder if he really does have any money down there. I mean, enough time has gone by. I don't think he still would be waitin' for me," Rizzo said with a smile.

Joe was about to answer when he noticed in his side mirror a state trooper following them with his lights flashing. He turned to Rizzo and calmly said, "There's a cop behind us, we're being pulled over."

Rizzo turned to check if he could see anything, but he couldn't because of the truck blocking his view. "Are you sure? I can't see back there," he said, still trying to see something.

"Yeah, I'm sure. It's a state trooper. What the hell does he want? I wasn't speeding. I guess he has nothing else to do," Joe said, beginning to feel nervous.

He then thought to ask Rizzo if he had brought anything with him that might pose a problem if they were searched. He never thought to ask him before now. The stress of the accident and being stranded for days had left Joe unable to think of anything but how to get home. He knew Rizzo wouldn't have any drugs with him, but what about a gun? He had one in his duffel bag. Did Rizzo have one as well?

As he pulled onto the shoulder and stopped the truck, he turned to Rizzo and asked, "Did you by any chance bring a gun with you?"

Rizzo laughed and said, "You know I ain't supposed to have a gun. I already served time for having an unlicensed gun, remember? Why do you think I got a gun with me?"

"Because I know you, that's why. You always had one when you went upstate. I can't believe I didn't ask you before now."

"Well, I guess you do know me, Yeah, I got one. It's in my duffel bag in the back. Why? Didn't you bring yours?"

"Yes, I did, mine's in my duffel bag too. I hope this *facha di gots* doesn't want to search us," Joe said as he cut the engine.

The next thing they heard was the state trooper yelling for Joe to exit the vehicle with his hands visible. Joe stepped out of the truck, saying to Rizzo, "What the hell is this guy's problem?"

The officer told Joe to walk slowly toward him with his arms outstretched and then to stop in front of his patrol car. The trooper was a short, pudgy young man with red cheeks who looked like this was his first day on the job. Joe thought he had a snappy uniform, though. Unsmiling, the cop stared into Joe's eyes and asked, almost yelling, "Have you been drinking?"

Joe, surprised at the accusation, answered, "It's ten o'clock in the morning."

The officer yelled back slowly, "Have … you … been … drinking?"

In a loud voice, Joe answered, "No."

The officer whipped a pen from his pocket, and holding it in front of Joe's face, told him to follow it with only his eyes. He then moved the pen back and forth from side to side. Joe wanted to bust out laughing as he followed the pen, but thought he'd better not.

Visibly annoyed, the trooper returned the pen to his pocket, then asked Joe in a hostile manner, "Why didn't you stop when I first flashed my lights at you? You kept driving for miles."

Joe told him that he pulled over as soon as he saw him behind the truck. The officer said that Joe was weaving all over the road as if he were drunk, and then when he refused to stop, he was about to call for backup. Joe just shrugged his shoulders and smiled. The trooper asked Joe where was he from and where was he going. Joe explained about the accident and having to rent this truck so they could return home.

After taking Joe's driver's license, the trooper told him to stand there as he walked toward the front of the truck to speak with Rizzo. Joe, without thinking, started to follow the officer, who then turned and screamed, "I told you to stand there!" Joe froze on the spot and threw both hands into the air.

Joe could see people in passing cars staring at him as they drove by, probably thinking a major drug bust must be going down. He heard the trooper asking Rizzo the same basic questions, then he walked back over to Joe, who lowered his arms. He asked Joe if he could look inside the truck. Joe knew he could refuse permission, but that would only add to this *stronzo's* suspicions, and then he probably would call for backup. The only thing Joe was worried about was if this guy would find the guns they had in their duffel bags. He didn't know what the gun laws were in this state, but he was sure their discovery would not be overlooked.

Seemingly uncaring, he said, "Yeah, you can look if you want to." As he opened the lock, he noticed the officer was watching him intently, probably to see if Joe was nervous, causing his hands to shake. For a brief moment, he thought of joking that all they had in there were about fifty Mexicans, but probably half of them are dead by now, but he thought better of it. He could tell this prick had no sense of humor.

As Joe lifted the back door of the truck, he saw the officer actually jump back with his hand on his gun. Joe had to wonder what was this guy expecting to come out of there. The trooper slowly looked over the few items, describing each one to himself as if taking inventory. He then started to feel Joe's duffel bag, squeezing it in his hands. Joe made the comment that all the bag contained was clothing, saying nothing about the .357 Magnum he had in there.

The officer told Joe to shut the door and step over to his car. He asked Joe if he had any weapons on him, to which Joe answered no. He asked Joe to get in the front seat as the officer entered the driver's side. He called in and checked if Joe had any outstanding warrants or criminal history. Joe felt the cop was certain that something would come up, that these guys had to be dirty. It was the second time in the past week that some cop had checked on Joe's possible criminal history. He was just thankful that Rizzo wasn't driving and his history wasn't being checked, which might have led to a further search. When the results came back negative, the officer asked for it to be repeated. It turned out that his big bust was just that, a bust. He looked annoyed as he handed back Joe's license and told him from now on to slow down and keep the truck from weaving out of his lane. Joe said it was hard to drive that truck in all this wind, but he would do his best.

***

They crossed the border into Kansas without Rizzo being the least bit impressed. Looking out at the bleak landscape, he said, "How can anybody live out here? These people got to be *oobatz*. Look at that house out there. There's nothing around it for miles, not even trees."

263

Joe agreed that it was strange where some people decide to live, and this wasn't anyplace he would want to spend his life.

All Rizzo said was, "You got that right."

Joe mentioned that since the truck was rented in his name and he was the only authorized driver, it would be better if he drove from now on, in case they were stopped again. Also, it would be better if the police out here didn't go digging into Rizzo's arrest records, which might lead to problems.

Rizzo gladly agreed. "If you want to drive, that's fine with me, just get us the fuck home," he said.

Hours later, after stopping for gas and something to eat, they continued east on Route 70. Rizzo laughed and said, "You know, you could stop for gas and drive until the tank is empty, then stop again and it will look like you were in the same place. I never seen so much nothing in my whole life."

He then noticed something as he looked down the embankment off the side of the road. "What's all those bundles blowing around down there? They look like what you see in Western movies blowin' across the streets."

Joe looked, then answered, "You mean the tumbleweeds?"

"Yeah, that's it, tumbleweeds. Look at 'em, there must be hundreds of 'em down there. Pull over, let's stop and get some."

Joe thought, what the hell, he would like to get a few for himself. He pulled off the road onto the shoulder and cut the engine. They both descended the embankment, kicking tumbleweeds as they went. As they kicked them, the ever-present wind carried them through the air for quite a distance. It then became a game to see who could kick one the farthest. They continued enjoying kicking the tumbleweeds until Joe glanced back at the truck and said, "We got company."

Rizzo turned to see a state trooper leaning against the front of the truck with his arms folded over his chest, staring at them. He said, "Christ, don't these cops out here got nothin' better to do than crawl up our ass? What, is it illegal to kick tumbleweeds?"

Joe answered, "I guess we're gonna find out," as they both slowly walked up the hill.

"So, are you boys enjoying yourselves?" the trooper asked them with a slight smile on his face.

"Well, yeah, we kinda were," Joe answered, smiling back. "We thought we'd pick up a few and take them home. The only place we ever saw them was on TV Westerns. We're not breaking any laws, are we?"

"No, you're not breaking any laws. In fact, the ranchers around here would like to see them all gone. They keep tearing up their fences. But I never saw anyone stop to kick tumbleweeds, until now. So where are you boys from?" the trooper asked.

Joe answered, "We're from New York. I was delivering some artwork to a gallery in Denver when I wrecked my van in Oklahoma." Joe then went on, describing about the accident and having to rent this truck to be able to drive home.

Still smiling, the trooper said, "I can see that being from New York, tumbleweeds would be a novelty." Then losing his smile, he added, "Mind if I take a look inside your truck?"

Surprised at the sudden change in the trooper's demeanor, Joe shrugged his shoulders and for the second time that day, said, "Yeah, sure, I don't mind."

As Joe slid open the back door, the officer took a quick glance inside and said, "This is a major route for smugglers coming from Mexico, bringing drugs and illegals to the eastern states. I didn't really think you boys were smugglers, but we're always on the lookout for any suspicious or odd behavior involving large vehicles. Watching you two down there fit the bill of odd behavior, so I had to check it out." He then added, "Seeing all the room you have back here, you can take as many tumbleweeds as you like."

After the trooper drove off, Rizzo, who was looking over the tumbleweeds as the trooper talked with Joe, walked up and asked, "Didn't he even check your license?"

Joe answered, "No, he just wanted to see if we were smuggling Mexicans or drugs. You believe that? They don't seem to give a damn about tumbleweeds around here—he said we could take as many as we want."

They both threw in about a dozen, then continued on their journey, wondering how long it would be before the police stopped them again.

***

Still in Kansas, they made a brief stop at Old Fort Hays, which again failed to impress Rizzo. He didn't understand how this collection of small buildings could be considered a fort. There was no wooden stockade surrounding the area like in all the Western movies he ever saw. It was just another disappointment he suffered through on this trip. They decided to stop for the night in Abilene, which Joe said was a major cattle town during the Old West cattle drive days. Rizzo just looked around, shaking his head at the endless number of motels and fast food restaurants.

They got a room in one of the motels, and being tired of eating fast food, found a steak house nearby to have a well-deserved good meal. The small, privately owned restaurant was lavishly decorated and looked more like a whorehouse, which made them both a little uneasy. After they were seated, a well-dressed middle-aged man came over and introduced himself as the owner. He asked them where they were from and if they had a room for the night. He said if they didn't, he owned a rooming house nearby that had a vacancy and would gladly accommodate them. Joe quickly said that they already had a room, but thanks anyway. The owner smiled and told them to enjoy their meal, then hurried off. As the young waitresses passed by their table, they would glance over at them and giggle.

"That guy's a fuckin' *fanook*,"Rizzo said.

Joe said with a laugh, "Do you think he is? Don't you want to stay at his rooming house?"

"Get the fuck outta here. Do you think it's even safe to eat here?" Rizzo asked.

"Yeah, I think so. The place looks clean and I'm sure the food is good. Just don't say we're goin' home with the guy."

"Let's just eat and get the fuck outta here, okay?"

Early the next morning, they got up and continued the drive east as fast as they could. After two more full days of driving, thankfully without any more incidents, they arrived back home, much to Rizzo's delight.

As he walked to his mother's house carrying his duffel bag, Rizzo turned to Joe and said, "Now remember, the next time you go out west, don't call me."

CHAPTER FOURTEEN—MOVING ON

The rift between Rizzo and Sandy had widened to the point where she finally filed for divorce. It was a long time in coming, and there were no regrets from either party. After the split, Rizzo was spending all his time in the city and living at his mother's house. Sandy was content to live up in the country, away from the embarrassments she had suffered because of her criminal husband. She was starting a new life with her children away from Rizzo. Joe wished her well, but didn't see much of his sister now that she remained upstate most of the time.

He occasionally saw his former brother-in-law in the coffee shop they both frequented. Joe found it humorous that Rizzo relished talking to his circle of friends about their trip out west. He enjoyed talking about it more than he had enjoyed actually doing it. He even tied one of the tumbleweeds they brought back to the hood of his Jeep, driving around like it was some kind of trophy. Joe finally settled with his insurance company, while refusing to follow Rizzo's urging to pad the claim with thousands of dollars in personal belongings. He was not interested in insurance fraud just to fill Rizzo's pockets. He didn't expect any reimbursement from Rizzo for his share of the expenses, and was not disappointed.

Whenever Joe ran into Rizzo at the coffee shop or on the street, it was always the same thing. Rizzo would say something like, "Hey, Joe Shoes, *che ne dici*? You still painting pictures?" Joe would answer yes, he was. Then Rizzo would ask him how much money he was making, and Joe would always play it down by saying, "Not too much, it's been a little slow lately." Then Rizzo would say, "Yeah, I know, you're the kind of guy who keeps his money in the bank, right?"

Joe always answered that yes, he did. He knew when Rizzo was fishing for information and he didn't trust him one bit. If Rizzo knew Joe had any money lying around, he wouldn't be able to stop himself from taking it, no matter how long they had known each other. A thief was a thief, always, and Joe had learned that the old saying was right. There was truly no honor among thieves.

***

A thief is always a thief. That fact really hit home after Joe's father died suddenly from lung cancer. Joe didn't have any idea his father was so ill until his mother called him one night asking to see him right away. His parents had just gotten back from the hospital with the bad news that his father's cancer was so far advanced it would be only a matter of weeks before he succumbed. After his father's death, Joe was saddled with the job of cleaning out his welding garage and disposing of all the welding equipment, along with the piles of tools and scrap metal that had built up over the years. After over thirty years in business, the garage needed a lot of cleaning up and clearing out. The job of deciding what was worth trying to sell and what was just scrap wasn't easy for Joe, who had a limited understanding of the welding business. He decided to run some ads in the local paper, along with calling other repair shops in the area to hopefully find buyers.

Over the next few weeks, Joe spent part of his days meeting with people interested in buying the welding machines, as well as anything and everything else connected with his father's business. After no one expressed any interest in them, the racks full of iron bars and pipes would be sold to a scrap dealer. All the pipes except three, that is. Before his death, Joe's father told him that three of the pipes on one of the racks contained large amounts of cash he had stashed away. He had kept that knowledge hidden from everyone, including Joe's mother.

Now he had to disclose his secret to Joe so the money would not be lost to the family. He told Joe to turn it all over to his mother without anyone else knowing about it, including other family members—especially other family members. Joe understood and agreed.

After the funeral, as Joe began his task of liquidating his father's business, he was visited by Rizzo, along with the one person he never wanted to see again, Snake Lips. Rizzo said he came down there to see if he could help in any way, but Joe knew the real reason they were there. As Rizzo spoke to Joe, his eyes were darting back and forth, scanning the garage for anything of value. Snake Lips was even more brazen, looking under tables and in corners, and even boldly entering the small office. With a knowing smile, Rizzo asked Joe if there was anything really heavy in there that he had to move out and said he would be glad to help.

After a moment, Joe answered, "Nah, I don't think there's anything that heavy in here that I'm going to take. I'll probably take some tools, but that's about it. The stuff I can't sell will go to the scrapyard."

Joe knew exactly what Rizzo was referring to. Somehow, he had heard about a large steel cylinder containing hundreds of silver coins that Joe's father had hidden away somewhere in the garage. The cylinder was over three feet high and over a foot wide. A three-inch pipe was inserted and welded to the center on one end, which allowed access inside the cylinder. Joe's father had placed the cylinder behind one of the many work benches in his garage, with the open end of the pipe extending about a foot above the tabletop. He had placed some steel rods and other pipes next to it, making it completely inconspicuous. Over the years, Joe's father would empty his pockets of silver quarters and half-dollars and drop them down the pipe at the end of each day. Only silver coins went down that pipe, and that continued over the years until the government stopped issuing them.

How Rizzo found out about it was a mystery. It seemed he had a sixth sense about these things. Regardless of how he heard, he obviously was unaware of its current whereabouts. Years ago, Joe's father had removed the cylinder from the garage and buried it one night in the backyard of his home. Joe watched as he then planted a small pine tree directly over it in case any nosy neighbors were watching and then would think he was just planting a tree.

The three pipes with the hidden money were still in the garage, however, and he couldn't risk Rizzo finding them.

Joe smiled then said, "You know, I'm a little worried about someone breaking in here while there's still some of this welding equipment around. I've got some people coming in a few days to pick up the portable welding machine and the rest of the welding rods, and those oxygen and acetylene tanks have to go back to the distributor because they were leased."

Rizzo stared at Joe, wondering where he was going with this.

Joe continued, "I think I'm going to stay here for the next couple of nights just to watch over the place. This is a really bad neighborhood. There's an alarm, but it's old and it would be easy enough for someone who knew what they were doing to get through. I'm thinking I'll pull my car in here and sleep in the back seat with a shotgun, and I swear, if anyone tries to break in, I'm not going to say a word, and I'm not going to look to see who it is. I'll have my shotgun with me, and I'm just going to shoot."

Rizzo didn't react in any way to what Joe was saying. He looked around the garage once more, then said, "Well, good luck with all this fucking mess. What I think you should do is light a match and burn it all down. Let me know if you need any help with that," he added with a smile.

After Rizzo and Snake Lips left, Joe locked the doors and decided it was time to cut into the pipes that contained the hidden cash. He really didn't want to spend the next few nights sleeping in his car, so he knew he'd better get the money out of there as soon as possible. He searched the large racks containing an assortment of iron rods and pipes until he found what he was looking for. His father had told him that three of the eight-foot-long pipes had a bend on each end, indicating they were the ones containing the money. He pulled them down to the floor and dragged them over to a work bench.

He tightened the first one in a vise, then picked up one of the many hacksaws lying around and began to saw through the pipe near one of the bent ends. He did the same on the other side, thinking it would be easy to push the rolled cash through the pipe using a long iron rod. He was wrong. The rolled-up money wouldn't move an inch, and he feared if he pushed too hard he might tear it up. He had no choice but to carefully cut the pipe closer to where the money was stuck. He cut slowly as he rotated the pipe in the vise until he was able to bend it and break it off. He could see the rolled cash wrapped in plastic at each end and was thankful he had decided against cutting straight through, as he would have cut one of the rolls almost in half. He repeated this technique four more times on the first pipe, until it was empty. Joe had two more to go, and now more than ever, he wished Rizzo was someone to be trusted, because he could use the help. But he knew Rizzo would stuff as much of the money as he could in his pockets without being seen. That's just the way it was. It was his nature.

It was nearly midnight when Joe cut free the last roll of bills. He then searched around the garage until he spotted some canvas bags on the floor in the small office. As he put the plastic-covered rolls in one of

273

the bags, he noticed that all the bills seemed to be hundreds. He counted thirty-eight rolls in all and knew there must be many thousands of dollars there. Obviously, his father didn't have much trust in banks, or anyone else for that matter. Joe laughed to himself, thinking that if his father had been killed suddenly in an accident, no one would ever know about his hidden treasure. Some scrapyard flunky might have found it, or it might have been burned up if the pipes were recycled. Anyway, he had it now, and his only concern was how to keep it hidden away from prying eyes and sticky fingers.

He exited the garage through a small side door, then he scanned the surrounding area to be sure no one was lurking around, and got into his car. He pulled the car up to the side door, then got out to unlock the trunk, leaving it unopened. He reentered the garage, shut off the lights, picked up the canvas bag and his shotgun, and locked the door behind him. Placing the bag in the trunk, he laughed at how his little Volvo was again carrying an interesting cargo. He drove home, thankful that he wouldn't have to make good on his threat to sleep in the garage in case the place was burglarized. If Rizzo and Snake Lips wanted to break in now, let them. There was not much left in there worth taking.

***

After turning the found money over to his mother, they both decided to dig up the cylinder buried in the backyard. There was no telling how many coins were in there, and with the price of silver currently at an all-time high, it was a good time to find out. The little pine tree his father had planted had grown and the ground beneath it was as hard as concrete. Joe decided to wait for a rainstorm to loosen up the dirt and make it easier to dig. When the right day came, Joe started digging around the base of the tree. He noticed right away that the roots had become thick and strong, making it difficult to dig beneath them. This was not going to be an easy job.

Just then, Joe looked up and got a sinking feeling when he saw Rizzo walking over to him with a smile on his face.

Still smiling, Rizzo asked, "So what are you doing, digging for buried treasure?"

Joe was amazed at the man's timing, and he couldn't believe his luck. Rizzo was the one person he didn't want to see right now, and Joe knew very well he wouldn't leave now that his suspicion was raised. There was evidence of Rizzo digging around the property lately, mainly under the covered front porch. He knew there had to be money buried around there somewhere and he was hell-bent on finding it. And if he ever did find anything, Joe knew with certainty he wouldn't tell anyone what he found.

Joe had to think fast. Nothing would make Rizzo want to leave now, except maybe if Joe asked for his help. Knowing Rizzo's distaste for getting his hands dirty, he knew Rizzo would refuse if Joe asked him to help with the digging. That would not be enough to cause him to leave, though. But then Joe came up with a plan that just might work. He said his mother wanted this tree removed because it was blocking the sunlight to her flower garden and the roots were really strong, making it hard to dig up.

"Do you have your Jeep parked out front?" Joe asked.

Rizzo nodded as he looked down into the hole Joe was digging.

Joe asked, "Do you think you could pull this thing out with your Jeep? It would sure save me a lot of work."

Joe knew this was just the kind of thing Rizzo would love to do. He would get to drive into the yard and tug on a tree until he ripped it out of the ground. That just might satisfy him that Joe wasn't digging for any other reason than pulling out the tree.

As expected, Rizzo jumped at the chance to have a little fun. He drove his Jeep into the yard, backed up near the tree, and fastened a length of chain around the tree trunk. He hopped into the Jeep and then proceeded to spin the tires, throwing up clods of dirt and grass, wrestling with the tree until he pulled it free. Joe stood near the empty hole with his shovel, ready to throw in dirt in case the cylinder became visible. He needn't have worried. As soon as the tree broke free, Rizzo beeped the horn and drove out of the yard and down the street. Joe knew he would drive around the city for some time, dragging that tree behind him and enjoying the spectacle he was making.

Joe's hasty plan was working better than he had hoped. He now had time to finish digging up the cylinder and get it hidden in his mother's basement before Rizzo had any idea what had transpired. He wouldn't cut it open until he felt it was safe to do so without any interruptions. When he finally did open it a few days later, with the price of silver being what it was, he estimated the contents to be worth well over seventy thousand dollars. If Rizzo had any clue how close he came to finding it, he would be sick. Now it was all tucked away in a safe-deposit box. Joe rejoiced in knowing that he dodged another bullet by keeping Rizzo from finding the buried coins he knew existed somewhere and had been actively searching for.

The façade of friendship between Joe and Rizzo was getting ever thinner. After all the years of their association, Joe knew that Rizzo would take advantage of anyone if it benefited him, and Joe knew he was not immune. It was disappointing that this man who had been a member of Joe's family and together shared many adventures had to be constantly watched, and it was proving tiresome.

***

Joe had long ago abandoned hope that Rizzo would wise up and give up his life of crime. Then one day as he was leaving the neighborhood coffee shop, he looked up to see Rizzo speeding around the corner of the street in a large yellow backhoe. Joe had never seen Rizzo operate anything like that, but he wasn't surprised when he saw him quickly drive past and wave. Rizzo could just step in and drive anything; it was one of his few talents. The truth came out later that day when Joe saw him again and asked him about his new job.

Rizzo laughed and said, "Nah, me and Vinny boosted that thing last night, that's all. We were drivin' back from upstate last week and passed a construction site. We spotted this backhoe sitting there. It looked pretty new, so we went back that night to hawk the place. We saw the night watchman leave at about twelve-thirty and stay away for a few hours. We went back the next night and he did the same thing, so we knew we would have enough time to get it away before he got back."

Joe asked, "How did you drive that thing all the way back here?"

Rizzo laughed again and said, "We drove it onto a flatbed truck, then took that too. You know what the gauges alone are worth on that thing? We got it sold to a guy who's going to chop it and sell the parts. He's taking the truck too. It'll be a good score."

For a minute there, Joe thought Rizzo had gone straight and took a construction job, but then realized what a naive assumption that was.

After more than twelve years of palling around with Rizzo and his family, Joe now felt he needed to keep his distance. Everything had changed. The fun times had been over for quite a while, but left behind were some humorous memories, along with some others that were not so good. He was still thankful that he was not arrested by that state trooper years ago when he had all those guns in his car. That one episode could have ruined his life, and it was so close to happening. To this day, he still felt his heart jump whenever he was driving and looked up to see a police car behind him. Even though he now had nothing to fear, he knew that feeling may never leave him. His art career was doing well, so he no longer felt bored or dissatisfied with his life. His craving for adventure was being fulfilled by his frequent hiking trips out west to gather reference material for his paintings. He truly loved his new career and didn't want anything or anyone to screw it up.

Even after all the troubles and dangerous circumstances that came with associating with Rizzo, and although he didn't see him nearly as much as he used to, in spite of all that, Joe had to admit that in some small way, he still liked the guy. He couldn't help it. The man's personality was engaging, and perhaps that was his best asset, and what made him so dangerous.

As he was sitting at home one evening, working on a painting for an upcoming gallery exhibition, Joe paused, then put down his brush and took a sip of tea. He sat there looking at the unfinished work, feeling satisfied on how everything was going, when the telephone rang. Not giving it a second thought and having no idea of the impact it would have on his life, he answered it.

"What are you doin'? Mind if I come over?" he heard Rizzo say. "I got something to show you, and believe me, you're really gonna like it."

The End

47150032R00170

Made in the USA
Lexington, KY
05 August 2019